HER SECRET

As Allegra came around the corner of the hall-way, her brows drew together. The door to her room was slightly ajar. She was always very careful to shut it firmly, but perhaps one of the maids had been in to dust or change the linens and had not closed it properly.

It swung open at her touch.

"Max!" Her surprise was so great she nearly let the sketchbook slip from her fingers. The initial feeling of shock quickly changed to one of wariness, especially on noting his ashen face and the set of his jaw. "What are you doing in my bedcham-ber?" she demanded in a voice barely above a whisper, though she feared she already knew the answer.

He rose from the edge of the bed. "Close the door, Mrs. Proctor. I believe we had better talk." His hand gestured toward her open trunk, where a pistol, a length of rope, and an assortment of men's clothing lay in full view. "Perhaps you would care to explain what is going on here?"

Coming in February

The Beleagured Earl by Allison Lane

Hope Ashburton was dismayed to learn that her family home had been gambled away to a disreputable earl. But the new owner, the notorious Maxwell Longford, seemed genuinely interested in restoring her ruined estate—and stealing her heart, as well....

0-451-19972-3/$4.99

A Worthy Wife by Barbara Metzger

Aurora's fiance was dashing, well-bred—and already married! Fortunately, the scoundrel's brother-in-law was determined to save Aurora from disgrace—even if he had to marry her himself....

0-451-19961-8/$4.99

The Rebellious Twin by Shirley Kennedy

Clarinda and Clarissa Capelle are identical twins—but when it comes to the social graces, they're complete opposites. Especially when they both fall in love...with the same handsome Lord!

0-451-19899-9/$4.99

To order call: 1-800-788-6262

SECOND CHANCES

ANDREA PICKENS

A SIGNET BOOK

SIGNET
Published by New American Library, a division of
Penguin Putnam Inc., 375 Hudson Street,
New York, New York 10014, U.S.A.
Penguin Books Ltd, 27 Wrights Lane,
London W8 5TZ, England
Penguin Books Australia Ltd, Ringwood,
Victoria, Australia
Penguin Books Canada Ltd, 10 Alcorn Avenue,
Toronto, Ontario, Canada M4V 3B2
Penguin Books (N.Z.) Ltd, 182–190 Wairau Road,
Auckland 10, New Zealand

Penguin Books Ltd, Registered Offices:
Harmondsworth, Middlesex, England

First published by Signet, an imprint of New American Library,
a division of Penguin Putnam Inc.

First Printing, January 2000
10 9 8 7 6 5 4 3 2 1

 REGISTERED TRADEMARK—MARCA REGISTRADA

Printed in the United States of America

PUBLISHER'S NOTE
This is a work of fiction. Names, characters, places, and incidents either are
the product of the author's imagination or are used fictitiously, and any resem-
blance to actual persons, living or dead, events, or locales is entirely
coincidental.

Chapter One

"You *what*?"

The young man shifted uncomfortably in his seat. "You said I might inquire as to a suitable person." A note of defiance had crept into his tone.

The Earl of Wrexham regarded his son over steepled fingers. It was not the challenge to his authority that disturbed him, rather the pinched, confused look that pulled at the lad's sensitive mouth. Not for the first time in the past few months did he wonder whether he had been fair in keeping Max isolated up in the wilds of Yorkshire for so much of his life. It hadn't really been a concern until recently, for the two of them had gotten on splendidly together. But now it seemed that everything he said rubbed the lad in the wrong way. Lord knew, it was difficult enough to pass from adolescence into manhood, but perhaps the transition was made even more awkward with only a father for company and no other young men the same age to cut a caper with. Not that Max showed any inclinations toward wildness—that, in fact, was another cause for concern. The lad was perhaps a trifle too studious. . . .

"The applicant is most qualified, I assure you," continued his son.

"You might have consulted me in the matter before making such a decision," replied the earl dryly. "I do have a modicum of experience in this sort of thing."

"You are always . . . busy," muttered Max, struggling manfully to keep his lower lip from jutting out as if he were six instead of nearly sixteen.

Wrexham's brows came together. Was he really such a neglectful parent? It was true that he spent a goodly amount of time in the library, but the lad had never voiced a complaint before. Why, his own nose was usually buried in a book as well. A sigh escaped the earl's lips. At least in another year or two, Max would finally be able to enter Oxford and study to his heart's content.

Until that time, however, there was this matter to attend to.

"But was it truly necessary to appeal all the way to London? Surely—"

"You know as well as I that I've exhausted the store of knowledge of any of the vicars within a few day's journey of the Hall," interrupted Max. "So why not advertise in London, if one advertises at all? You have always told me to eschew bargains and purchase the very best quality one can."

The earl's mouth crooked ruefully at having his own pompous advice thrown back at him, but he had to admit his son was right—on both accounts.

"Very well. I shall meet with the man, and if he is as qualified as you say, there is no reason why he shouldn't be hired as your tutor." He smiled pleasantly. "After all, it is an abominably long journey he has endured to reach us."

The young man swallowed hard. "I . . . I should warn you of one little thing, sir."

Wrexham folded his long hands on the tooled blotter of his desk. An eyebrow arched up in query.

"Ah . . ."

"Go on, Max." The earl's lips twitched in amusement. "Do you wish to warn me that he has a harelip or a squint?

"Actually, it's not a he."

Allegra Proctor stiffened in her chair. The roar of the oath was audible even through the heavy oak of the library door. The young viscount, obviously unaware of the usual social graces, had bade her take a seat in one of the formal gilt chairs flanking a long console in the hallway rather than in the drawing room, so she was more privy to the discussion between father and son than the earl realized.

Things did not seem to be going well.

Drat it, she thought as she shoved an unruly lock of hair back into the prim bun wound tightly at the nape of her neck. It would be most annoying to have to turn around and make the arduous trek back to London now that she was so close to her goal—not to speak of 'the expense that she could ill afford. Her hands tightened round the worn fabric of her reticle and her chin rose a fraction.

A deal was a deal, she reminded herself. The ad had asked for a *person* of certain qualifications, and upon examination of her credentials, she had been hired. So the earl could bloo . . . blooming well live up to the bargain. Surely, the little matter that neither of the parties was legally entitled to enter into such an agreement was a mere technicality.

A fleeting smile came to her lips at the thought of the meeting earlier that morning. She wasn't sure who had been more shocked—the young viscount on learning the scholar he had hired was a female, or herself on learning that her employer didn't as yet shave. Given the initial misgivings, the long carriage ride back to Stormaway Hall had proceeded amazingly well. The young man had quizzed her rigorously—and quite knowledgeably, she had to admit—until finally his expression had relaxed and a boyish grin had split his face.

The pronouncement that, as far as he was concerned, she was bang up to the mark and could start that afternoon had gone a long way to relieving her first fears. And she, too, was well pleased with the situation. The young man was undeniably bright, which was infinitely more appealing than dealing with a sluggard. But on top of that, he was refreshingly direct, with none of the haughty airs and graces she had come to expect from those possessing a title. His emotions were as readable as an open book, ranging from childish enthusiasm to coming-of-age awkwardness in the span of a few minutes. She found herself wondering if it was his father whom he was unconsciously imitating when he drew his dark brows together in an attempt to look forbidding.

She shrugged. She had no doubt she would learn that soon enough. Again, she thought back to part of the conversation that had taken place as the carriage drew closer to the Hall.

"Not exactly," had been the young man's reply when asked if his family was aware of the new addition to their household.

"Since we are going to be studying the nuances of language, sir, that answer will not fadge. In this instance there can be no equivocation. It is either yes or no," she had said.

His eyes had slid to the floor of the carriage. "My father is actually very broad-minded. He has studied a vast range of cultures and history, and with his scientific bent, he does not jump to conclusions—"

"I take it that is a no."

He had nodded.

Hah! In her experience, there were precious few men broad-minded enough to . . .

The door flung open, and the young viscount stalked out with as much dignity as his wounded pride would allow. "The earl will meet with you now," he said, casting a last, withering look over his shoulder. A few other unintelligible words followed, but Allegra imagined they weren't meant for her ears in any case.

She rose and smoothed the travel-worn gown over her slim hips. "Thank you, sir. I hope we may start this afternoon, as you suggested."

His mouth twitched as if he were going to speak again, but then he merely made a quick nod and walked quickly down the hall, his long, coltish legs beating an angry tattoo on the polished parquet.

The eyes facing her from across the massive desk were equally disturbed, though by his languid posture and impassive countenance it would be impossible to guess anything was amiss with the man seated in front of her.

"Take a seat, " said the earl curtly, dispensing with all pretenses of civility.

She did, noting that she needn't wonder anymore as

to where the young viscount had learned to look intimidating.

A long silence stretched out before them. Logs hissed and crackled. The large Scottish deerhound stretched on the Oriental rug in front of the fire whined softly in his sleep.

Allegra repressed a smile as she calmly ignored the earl's scrutiny. No doubt it was a highly effective technique in most cases—people found the lack of words more unnerving than being shouted at. But he was wasting his time trying to scare her. She didn't scare easily.

Perhaps sensing just such a thing, Wrexham finally spoke again. "Perhaps you would care to explain to me this absurd situation."

Her eyes came up to meet his. "Absurd? The only thing that seems absurd, sir, is that I have traveled for days to take up a position for which I have been deemed qualified, only to be threatened with dismissal before I even have a chance to begin. It seems hardly fair." When she was angry, the emerald color of her eyes would fleck with gold. At this instant, the sparks were flying. "In fact, it seems *more* than absurd," she went on. "It seems completely cork-brained."

Wrexham stared at her in disbelief.

"You won't find many people of my ability willing to come to the wilds of this place. How long has your son waited before he found me? How long will he wait if you send me away?"

The earl's black brows came together once again.

"He is a very intelligent young man. He needs some intellectual challenge, else he is apt to become bored—and bored young men get into trouble."

"He needs a tutor! A young man does not have a . . . a governess."

"What is the difference?" she shot back. "If I can do a good job, why should anything else matter?"

He looked nonplussed for a moment. "I . . ." Then his look became even darker. "I warn you, miss, if you are one of that sort of female who thinks to cozen up to an impressionable youth and encourage a certain attachment—well, he does not come into his majority, or his money, for quite some time. And I shall have something to say about it in the meantime."

"I have no idea what you mean, sir," she answered coldly. Of course she knew exactly what he meant.

The earl had the grace to color slightly. "How old are you?" he demanded in an effort to conceal his discomfiture.

"Old enough to be of no interest to a fifteen-year-old," she countered. Observing the few threads of silver at his temples she added, "And you needn't worry that I shall attempt to sink my hooks into you either, my lord. I have no interest in gentlemen nearly in their dotage."

"Dotage! I'll have you know I'm not yet forty," he managed to sputter, before he realized the utter indignity of gracing her words with a reply. His jaw snapped shut.

"In fact, I have no interest in men for that sort of reason at all," she went on. "Believe me, the parson's mousetrap has no more appeal to me than it evidently has for you. But as my employer, you have a right to ask the question. I am twenty-nine."

He made a show of studying the sheaf of papers in front of him. "Miss, ah, Proctor," he began.

"Mrs.," she corrected.

His head shot up.

"Widow."

"My condolences," he muttered.

"The same to you. I understand from Max that you have also lost a spouse."

"It was a long time ago," he replied in a low voice as he fell back to perusing the sheet on top of the pile. Suddenly, he looked up again and spoke to her in Greek.

She answered without hesitation. For the next twenty minutes they were like two prizefighters in the ring—he hurling arcane questions at her in Latin, Greek, French and Italian, she punching back the correct answers with equal aplomb. Finally, he left off and his fingers began to drum on the desk.

At the sound, the deerhound stretched, then padded over toward the desk.

"Well, boy, aren't you a lovely animal," murmured Allegra.

The dog changed directions.

"Have a care, Mrs. Proctor. Sasha does not suffer strangers to touch. . . ."

The huge shaggy head plopped in her lap. "Animals seem to like me," she said softly as she scratched behind its ears.

Wrexham muttered something under his breath.

She cocked her head to one side. "Excuse me, sir."

"I said I shall inform you of my decision later today."

"Then if you don't object, I shall work in the meantime with your son on the first canto of Dante. He seemed particularly anxious to consult with someone on the translation of a certain passage." She paused. "That is, if I may first be allowed to freshen up and perhaps request a cup of tea and some toast."

The earl started. "Do you mean to say Max brought you to see me before making sure that you were settled and served refreshments after such a long journey?" He shook his head as he rang for the butler. "Good Lord."

"He can hardly be blamed, sir. I doubt he has much practice in that sort of thing," she pointed out. "Perhaps it is another reason why a different sort of tutor would do him good. Since he has his heart set on Oxford, he shall no doubt spend time in London and should learn proper manners and the proper courtesies toward the opposite sex." She paused. "It seems he has precious little example to follow at present," she added in a low voice.

Wrexham made a strangled sound at the back of his throat.

There was a discreet knock on the door, and the butler entered. "Yes, your lordship?"

"Rusher, see that Mrs. Proctor is shown to a chamber where she may freshen up, and have Cook prepare a tray of . . . whatever she would like."

The man bowed. "Madam, if you will follow me."

The earl turned back to Allegra. "Do not think that this means your position is by any means secured. I have not finished with you on this matter," he growled.

"I'm sure you have not," she muttered to herself as she rose and followed the butler out the door.

*   *   *

The earl stared into the fire, arms crossed disgruntledly over his broad chest. Just how in the devil had his orderly and comfortable world been turned on its ear in the space of a morning? He had a good mind to seek out Max and give him a good boxing about the ears. But a prick of conscience made him admit that it was perhaps his own head that needed the set-down. How was it that a stranger had immediately sensed that his son was bored and restless when he had been blithely oblivious to the young man's turmoil.

Damnation. Was he failing with Max, too?

He rubbed at his temples, trying to assuage the beginnings of a splitting headache. The notion that a female could be a proper teacher for a young man was outside of enough, though he had to grant that she certainly knew her subjects. Try as he might, he hadn't been able to catch her out on a single point, and that was not something he could say about any of the so-called learned men of his acquaintance.

She had spirit as well. The trip must have been exhausting, and yet, without even a splash of water or a cup of tea, she had faced his patent disapproval with both courage and grit. His mouth twitched in grudging respect. And she'd given as good as she had taken. His fingers paused as they brushed over his hair. There wasn't so very much grey there—how dare the chit imply he was in his dotage!

He rose stiffly and began to pace before the fire. Sasha rolled to one side and regarded his master with one eye.

"Mutt," growled Wrexham. "I expected more loyalty from you."

With a wounded expression, the animal levered himself up and shambled over to bury his nose in the earl's hand.

"Oh, very well." He gave a reluctant sigh and began to scratch Sasha's muzzle. "Us old dogs have to stick together, I suppose. You're forgiven." The animal gave a whuff of contentment before flopping back down on the rug.

The earl turned his attention back to the matter at

hand. It simply wouldn't do. He'd not make a fool of himself by engaging someone so unsuitable. . . . Then he recalled the wounded look in his son's eyes, the need there to be allowed to make some decisions, to begin being treated as an adult instead of a child. Max rarely asked for anything, but this morning he had asked for the right to choose his own tutor.

Wrexham sighed again. It wasn't as if Mrs. Proctor wasn't eminently qualified. And she was from a respectable family. The glowing letters of recommendation had mentioned she was the daughter of a scholarly vicar, now deceased, though they had made no mention of Mr. Proctor. Perhaps just until a more suitable candidate could be found. . . .

He moved from the fire, and in his haste his knee caught the edge of the desk. An involuntary grunt of pain came to his lips. Damn the leg. It was acting up again, and just the slightest misstep or jarring made any sort of movement an ordeal. He waited a few minutes for the worst of it to pass. Clenching his teeth, he left the library and climbed the curved center stairs, forcing himself to walk normally. He absolutely refused to limp. Old men limped.

Max had turned the schoolroom into a study more befitting his age. An oaken bookcase had been built along one wall, its carved acanthus leaf moldings and heavy shelves stained to a rich honey color that fairly glowed in the afternoon sun. Books were stacked, a trifle haphazardly, from floor to ceiling. A large, ornate desk hauled down from the attics had replaced the scarred and ink-stained ones that had served previous generations of budding Sloane scholars.

His son's tastes were beginning to veer toward the melodramatic, noted the earl with a rueful grimace as he took in the pair of matched brass lion's head lamps flanking a statue of a voluptuous Greek goddess. It was another thing he had failed to notice. His eyes strayed to a large, rather ghastly painting of a stag being pulled down by a pack of hounds, which hung on the opposite wall. Why, it was as if the lad were becoming an utter stranger right before his eyes. Another stab of guilt knifed through him.

The two of them had pulled their chairs up to the desk. A tray holding the remains of a squab pie, crumbling Stilton and a pot of tea had been pushed aside to make room for a large, leather-bound book, and both heads were bent over it in rapt attention. Max was voicing his opinion. In his unguarded enthusiasm, his voice was warbling over a full octave, from boy to man in one sentence. Wrexham suddenly felt a wrenching poignancy as he listened to the familiar tones. In another few years the boy would be grown and gone.

Allegra smiled. "An interesting point of view, to be sure," she said, careful not to appear to ridicule the young man's opinion. "But perhaps you might consider that Dante was speaking of something else." She launched into a patient and well thought out explanation of the passage in question. Despite his resolve to the contrary, the earl found his assessment of her rose more than a notch.

Max suddenly turned, as if sensing the earl's presence. Wrexham was jolted to see his expression harden.

"Father," he said, the lack of enthusiasm evident in his tone.

The earl stiffened to his full, considerable height. "I trust you have been properly looked after, Mrs. Proctor. If there is anything else you require, you have only to inform Rusher or the housekeeper, Mrs. Gooding."

Allegra looked up. "Everything is quite fine. I thank you for your gracious hospitality, my lord."

The earl could swear he denoted a twinkle in her eye. Was the chit mocking him? He frowned slightly, but continued. "I have decided that for the time being, you may remain—while I take charge of finding a suitable replacement. Under the circumstances, having compelled you to travel such a distance from your home, we owe you that much."

She inclined her head a fraction. "Again, how gracious of you, sir. I am in your debt."

His eyes narrowed. This time the sarcasm was not as

veiled, but he let it pass for the moment. More important was the flush of relief on his son's face.

"You see, I told you, Mrs. Proctor. He is quite reasonable when presented with the facts. I had no doubt that he would make the right decision." Max's tone, though striving to sound self-assured, made it evident that he had thought no such thing.

"I have instructed Mrs. Gooding to make up a chamber for you. You will take your meals with the other hired help or in your room, as you choose. You may set the hours of study. Other than that, your time is your own, but I expect you will not distract others from their tasks. Is that clear?" The earl's voice sounded cold and stilted, even to his own ears.

"Father!" Max's face twisted in embarrassment at the earl's overbearing manner.

"Quite, my lord," answered Allegra calmly. "I shall endeavor to be as . . . unobtrusive as possible."

Wrexham had no choice but to be satisfied with that. He turned on his heel and returned to the sanctuary of his library.

It was his own conduct he was less than satisfied with.

The earl eyed his son over the rim of his wineglass, then took a long swallow of the rich claret. The lad hadn't uttered a word since sitting down at the table. The footmen removed the soup and served the next course.

"How did the first lesson go?"

Max looked up. "Very well, sir," he answered, an edge to his voice, as if daring the earl to challenge him.

"I'm glad to hear it."

A look of surprise crossed Max's face, then he returned to pushing the slice of rare sirloin around on his plate. After a few minutes he spoke up again. "Why did you have to be so rude?"

Wrexham laid down his fork. "I beg your pardon?"

"You were! You needn't have spoken to her like that."

"It had nothing to do with rudeness. She is an employee, hired help. I was merely spelling out the rules," explained the earl. "You must remember she is not a guest here."

The lad glowered.

Wrexham cleared his throat. "I'm sorry if I haven't been as attentive as I should have been. I hadn't realized . . . that is, I shall endeavor to spend more time with you." He gave a slight chuckle. "Perhaps we could embark on a study of art. It might help to improve your taste in—"

"What's wrong with my taste?" cried Max hotly.

The earl stopped, perplexed. He hadn't meant it that way.

Max crumpled his napkin and threw it on the table. "May I be excused, please." Without waiting for an answer, he shoved back his chair and left the room, letting the door fall closed with a resounding bang.

"Bloody hell," muttered Wrexham. He stared down at his own plate, but found that he, too, had lost his appetite. With an exasperated sigh, his hand went for the bottle of claret instead. Taking up his glass, he rose and limped off to the library.

Allegra pulled the bedcovers up to her chin. It was a most pleasant room, flooded with sunlight in the afternoon from the two tall mullioned windows opposite her bed and warmed by a generous fire in the neat little hearth. Though not large, the space was tastefully appointed, with a large dresser and armoire of pleasing proportion arranged on one wall, and a small desk and chair of excellent quality near the comfortable bed, its coverings of muted blue and pale rose echoed in the chintz curtains and patterned rug. The painting that hung over the desk proved, on closer inspection, to be a rather nice Dutch seascape from the hand of a well-known artist. Someone had a discerning eye for both art and design. All in all, it was an accommodation more befitting a guest than a servant. Despite appearances to the contrary, it appeared that the Earl of Wrexham could be a civil host when he chose to be.

Civil, perhaps, but odious in the extreme, as well as arrogant, high-handed and opinionated. But what else should she have expected? He was a lord, a member of the *ton*—and a male. Her mouth curled slightly in disgust. At least he was not an ignoramus, like most of them.

Nor was he a preening peacock with garish waistcoats and ridiculously high points to his collars. In fact, he had been dressed quite sensibly. His simple linen shirt and modest cravat were appropriate for the country, as were his buckskin breeches and plain polished Hessians, devoid of pretentious tassels or other annoying geegaws. And it was evident he didn't resort to padding in order to fill out the broad shoulders of his impeccably tailored black serge coat. It was nearly as black as his thick, raven locks, worn rather longer than was fashionable.

She couldn't repress a grin. She had scored a hit there. Yes, the Earl of Wrexham had proved to be as vain about his personal appearance as the rest of the bloody swells. The look of outrage on his face when she had referred obliquely to the flecks of grey at his temples had been worth the risk of being sacked on the spot. Not that it was true—the implication that he was well into his dotage, that is. She recalled his lean, strong hands, the breadth of his chest and the long, muscled legs that she hadn't been aware of until later that afternoon. No, he was not quite over the hill. . . .

She gave a shake of her head. But there was no reason to dwell overlong on the earl. He was of no concern now that she had managed to overcome his objections to her presence. Thank goodness for Max. It was lucky that he seemed to have taken a liking to her right off. That had been the key, she was sure. No amount of knowledge or skill with languages would have overcome the earl's natural prejudices. But something in his eyes that afternoon had told her his decision had been swayed by his son.

Her grin softened into a smile. He was a nice lad, not at all like other young men of title she had been acquainted with. He was remarkably bright as well, which she hadn't expected. That part of her job was going to prove much more stimulating than she had imagined.

Already they were engaged in a course of study that promised to keep her on her toes.

But enough of Wrexham *père* and *fils*. That was not why she was here.

She noted with great satisfaction how far her plans had progressed in the last few months. It had been an extraordinary piece of luck that Lucy had spotted the ad for *a person of consummate education, expert in both modern and ancient classical languages, to take up a position in northern Yorkshire*. . . . She had been racking her brains on how to contrive an extended stay in such a distant place, given her lack of funds and, more important, lack of a plausible reason to be there. Now she had solved both those problems in one fell swoop.

It was time to plan the next move. She chewed thoughtfully on her lower lip. The earl had played right into her hands by admonishing her to make herself scarce once lessons were over for the day. He could have no complaint if she chose to take long walks through the countryside. Even better, perhaps he wouldn't begrudge her the use of a horse. But she would have to be careful. Regardless of what else she thought of him, he was no slowtop. Those piercing, slate blue eyes didn't miss much, she imagined. It wouldn't do to arouse his suspicions.

Her eyes strayed to the battered trunk with her possessions. She had brought just about everything she needed—a goodly length of rope, a long black cloak, a pair of men's breeches and a shirt, a small lantern and a set of picklocks.

And a pistol.

But first things first. Tomorrow, she would start by becoming familiar with the surrounding area and learning just how close Westwood Manor was.

Though the earl was not unusually partial to spirits, this evening he felt like draining the bottle. In fact, he already had. He stared glumly into the fire, then poured himself a stiff brandy to wash down the claret. Settling back into his comfortable leather wing chair, he stretched his long legs out to ease the ache in his bad knee. As if sensing his master's depressed spirits, Sasha padded over and settled his grizzled muzzle on Wrexham's thigh. The earl gave a reluctant smile as his fingers scruffed through the grizzled whiskers.

"Well, old boy, at least *you* do not seem inclined to bite my head off tonight."

The big dog licked his hand, then thumped down by the side of the chair, his shaggy tail giving a wag or two before his eyes closed in sleep.

Wrexham swirled the amber liquid in his glass. It was enough to drive a man to drink, he groused. First some unknown, sharp-tongued, bluestocking *female* had arrived on his doorstep with the intention of taking up residence. Then his heretofore amiable son had behaved in a manner that, had he been a daughter, would have been termed throwing a fit of vapors. He shook his head as his eyes strayed longingly to the open book on botany experiments sitting on his desk. Somehow he had a feeling it would some time before he could turn his undivided attention back to its pages.

Something else was nagging at him. How could she say Max was bored? Why, the lad like to study as much as he did. Granted, there was little excitement or turmoil at Stormaway Hall, but that had suited both of them quite nicely.

It wasn't boring here, merely . . . quiet.

His brows came together in a menacing line. A mere chit wasn't going to upset their ordered existence. Max was simply going through some growing pains. Wrexham decided he would make an effort to take him out for a bit of riding and grouse shooting—or perhaps a regular game of chess after supper. The lad would come around in short order.

As for Mrs. Proctor—well, he couldn't deny that she would bring a spark of new ideas to the schoolroom, and that was for the better. After all, he wasn't so crusty as not to realize that the same old books could become a trifle . . . dull. But if she thought for a moment that his generosity of this morning could be interpreted as a sign of weakness, she would learn who was boss here in very short order.

He brought himself up with an audible chuckle. The wine and brandy were addling his head, causing him to exaggerate the entire situation out of all proportion.

Really, now—how much trouble could the daughter of a scholarly vicar cause?

Chapter Two

Max put his pen down. "I'm famished. I think I shall ring for some of Cook's scones and a pot of tea. Would you care for some as well?"

- Allegra smiled as she surveyed the gangly limbs hunched over the leather-bound copy of Dante's *Inferno*. The lad seemed to have sprouted another few inches since her arrival. Why, pretty soon he would be equaling his father's not inconsiderable height. "Tea would be lovely," she said. "But as for scones, well, breakfast was only two hours ago."

He grinned. "I can always find room. Especially for scones or gooseberry tarts."

His unruly mane of dark hair fell across his brow as he returned to studying the pages, nearly obscuring his eyes from view. They were a shade lighter than the earl's, and usually filled with a great deal more good humor. The few times she had crossed paths with Lord Wrexham during the past two weeks, his had positively glinted with disapproval. But he seemed to be as good as his word—as long as she did not upset the routine of the household, it appeared he was content to . . . ignore her. That suited her just fine, especially as it didn't look as if he had made any progress in arranging for her replacement.

Max had certainly not ignored her presence. The lad was as hungry to expand the horizons of his knowledge as he was to consume the cook's excellent pastries. Unlike other young men of the nobility with whom she had had acquaintance, he showed none of the studied boredom or petulance that so pervaded their manner. Neither was he spoiled nor haughty—she had to credit the earl with that. Max came to his studies each morning with an unflagging enthusiasm and inquisitiveness that couldn't help but win her approval, and even her respect.

More than that, she liked him. She hadn't expected to, but she did. As well as being intelligent beyond his years, he was unassuming and open, rather like a big puppy who hadn't yet learned his strength. There was something endearing about the way he looked when voicing his opinion, how his features revealed the battle of manly self-confidence seeking ascendancy over child-like timidity. It reminded her so much of another young man. . . .

She was suddenly aware that Max was speaking to her. "I'm sorry. I'm afraid I was woolgathering."

He grinned again. "I do that all the time. Father is forever teasing me about having my head in the clouds."

A maid brought in the tea tray, and Allegra poured both of them a cup.

"What I asked was, have you lived for a long time in London?"

"Actually just for the past four months," she replied. "I went to live with my cousin and tutor her son after my father died. I have spent most of my life in Kent, where my father was a vicar."

"What about when you were married—" He stopped abruptly, and blush spread over his face. "I'm sorry," he stammered. "I fear that's bad manners, isn't it, to ask you such a personal question."

She smiled reassuringly. "You may ask me what you please, Max. I'm afraid I'm frightfully hard to put out." A glint of humor crept into her eyes. "Though I don't promise to answer everything."

He looked very relieved he hadn't offended her.

"As for my husband, he was my father's curate. And my matrimonial state did not last long. He was carried off by a bout of influenza six months after we were married."

Max bit his lip. "My mother died of that as well."

It was Allegra's turn to feel awkward. "I'm sorry. That

must have been very difficult for you. How old were you at the time?''

"Eight."

Something about his manner told her he wanted to talk about it. "Do you miss her terribly?"

To her surprise, he didn't answer her right away. His fingers tightened around the china cup as he stared at the pattern of tea leaves on its bottom. "She was very beautiful and very lively—everyone said she was the toast of the *ton*. She loved the balls and the dinners and the concerts in Town. I . . . didn't see her very much." His breath caught in his throat, then the rest of his words came out in a rush. "But I understand. She was so very . . . busy."

Allegra felt a welling of sympathy for him, as well as a touch of anger for the lady who obviously had little care for her child. "I'm sure she would have been very proud of what a fine young man you have turned into," she said softly.

Max looked at her eagerly. "You think so?"

"Without a doubt." She paused. "It must have been difficult for your father, too."

Max's eyes dropped once more, and he crumbled what was left of his scone between his fingers. "He doesn't discuss it with me."

"Sometimes it is very difficult for a person to talk about . . . a great loss. No doubt he misses her as much as you do." Perhaps that explained why the earl had never remarried, despite the fact that, with his title and fortune, he must have had more than his share of caps thrown at him by scheming mamas.

He pushed away the plate of scones and propped his chin on his hand. "You don't like him, do you?"

Allegra was startled by his question and took her time in answering. "I don't know your father," she replied carefully. That much was true, at least.

Max eyed her with a penetrating gaze that was unnervingly like his father's. "He hasn't exactly shown you his best side. He's a decent sort, for fathers." He hesitated, as if mulling over his own words, and his eyes dropped to the desktop. "Actually, he's more than decent. He's a great gun, though you wouldn't know it from his behavior toward you."

She smiled at the lad's naivete. "Max, an earl does not go out of his way to be charming to the hired help. Furthermore, he does not believe my presence here is in your best interest. It is to his credit that he cares enough about your feelings to allow me to stay until he can find another tutor."

"I suppose," admitted Max. "But I don't want you to leave. You are . . . nice."

It was a long time since anyone had said anything as touching as that. "Why, thank you, Max. I should be sorry to leave you as well. We shall just have to wait and see."

The lad gave a reluctant sigh and bent back over his book.

Things were proceeding slowly, thought Allegra as she walked along the narrow path. She hadn't realized how isolated the area was and how great the distances were. It had taken her all this time just to get her bearings and figure out the shortest routes. She would need a horse, however. That much had become clear.

That shouldn't prove an insurmountable obstacle. She had been out riding with Max several times and was beginning to know her way around the stables. The earl's grooms kept the place in perfect order, but she had noticed that there was little attention to keeping things under lock and key. It wouldn't be difficult to slip in one night after everyone had retired. Their sleeping quarters were far enough away from the stalls that if she was very quiet . . .

But she wasn't nearly at that stage of her plans yet. She glanced down at the sketchbook under her arm. It was only today that she had managed to get her first glimpse of Westwood Manor, and even that was from afar. She would need to have a much closer look.

At least her charcoal and paper gave her a perfect excuse. Few people would pay any notice to an insignificant female engaged in filling her pad with ordinary landscapes and views of the stately houses. She didn't draw overly well, but that wasn't the point. At night she could study which approach was best and where the windows and doors were located.

She tugged at the strings of the large, ugly bonnet that nearly obscured her features. It was deucedly uncomfortable during her long walks, but it made it unlikely that anyone would recognize her face.

Yes, she thought with grim satisfaction, she had thought of everything.

Her mind was so occupied she failed to notice that the earl had reined his mount to a halt and was watching as she scrambled over a tall stile. Smoothing her skirts down over her sturdy half boots, she suddenly became aware of his presence. Though the unbecoming bonnet shaded most of her face, a hint of a frown peeked out from beneath the broad brim.

Drat the man. She really preferred to avoid him as much as possible.

"Oh—good afternoon, my lord." Her tone was as chilly as her expression.

He inclined his head a fraction. "It appears you are partial to taking the country air."

"Lessons are over for the day. I am following your wishes to make myself scarce."

"I did not mean it literally, Mrs. Proctor," he replied dryly. "Do not feel that you must . . . wear yourself to the bone."

Her lips repressed a smile. So the earl actually had a sense of humor. "I enjoy doing a bit of sketching," she said.

Wrexham raised an eyebrow. "I wouldn't have expected you to indulge in such a frivolous pursuit."

"It does not met with your approval? Perhaps you consider it a pastime fit only for *young* females."

The earl dismounted with an easy grace and fell in step beside her. A flash of amusement shone in his eyes at her last comment, though he chose to ignore her challenge.

"What you choose to do with your own time is your concern, Mrs. Proctor," he answered as he casually wrapped the reins of his dappled grey stallion around the long fingers of one hand. "My concern is with Max."

Her eyes shot up to meet his. "Is something wrong?"

"Not at all," he admitted. "Max has made great progress in his studies. He has responded well to your teaching."

She looked at him warily. "I trust you do not mean to imply . . ."

"No. I do not believe you are throwing your cap at my son."

"I should hope not," she muttered. "Why, I'm almost old enough to be his·mother."

The earl regarded her creamy complexion and the errant wisps of honey-colored hair that curled around her ears. A smile tugged at the corner of his lips.

"Max is a highly intelligent young man," she continued. "It has been a pleasure to work with such a good student." She hesitated for a moment. "He is also unfailingly polite, cheerful and courteous."

"Unlike his father," murmured Wrexham.

She opened her mouth as if to speak.

"It does seem that his moods have improved considerably," he went on, without waiting for a reply from her. "At least he is no longer flying into the boughs every time I speak to him." He shook his head. "I know this is an awkward age for him, but I was beginning to think he couldn't abide my very presence."

"You needn't worry on that account, my lord. Max thinks you are—how did he put it—a great gun."

"He said that?" The earl's features softened perceptibly.

"Indeed he did."

"Thank you, Mrs. Proctor," he said after a moment. "You did not have to tell me that."

She decided to change the subject. "I was wondering, sir, have you made any progress in finding a new tutor for Max?"

Wrexham walked on for a few paces before answering. "No. I have not." His eyes strayed to the scudding grey clouds moving in over the craggy hills. "It seems we are in for some rain shortly. I fear you had best come up with me if you are to avoid getting drenched."

"That is not at all necessary. I don't mind a spot of rain."

"Max would no doubt ring a peal over my head if you took a chill and were unable to preside over the schoolroom." Before she could argue any further, his hands came around her waist and lifted her effortlessly up across the saddle.

He mounted as well and steadied her until she was settled into a more comfortable position in front of him. Her skirts fell in folds over his left knee and she was disconcertingly aware of the warmth radiating from his muscled thigh. To her further dismay, his arm circled her waist as he took up the reins in one hand.

"Really, my lord! There is no need for you to trouble yourself . . ."

His face was quite close to hers. The spicy, slightly exotic scent of bay rum and leather filled her senses as he replied, "Ulysses can carry both of us with ease."

"Well, as long as he can find his way home," she murmured.

He threw back his head and laughed. "I shall have a care that the sirens do not lure us off course."

In spite of herself, she smiled, too. She had forgotten how refreshing it could be to have a lively conversation with someone whose sharp wits and obvious erudition matched her own. Most people didn't understand her pithy observations, or simply missed her meaning altogether. She had a feeling the Earl of Wrexham was a man who missed very little.

She would definitely have to be on guard.

But at present, all she could think about was the disturbing closeness of his arm circling her waist. The chiseled strength was evident, even through the fabric of his impeccably tailored riding coat. It wasn't as if she had never been this close to a man before. But somehow Harry hadn't been quite like this. . . .

"Do you ride?" inquired Wrexham as he spurred the stallion into an easy canter.

"Yes," she replied, thankful for the prospect of a conversation to take her mind off other thoughts. "I grew up in the country."

"And where was that?"

She bit her lip, ruing her hasty words. The earl was quick enough that he might put two and two together later on. "Not far from London," she said, hoping it would do, then quickly went on. "Max has kindly taken me out several times and showed me some of the local sights. I should like to explore more, that is, if it meets with your approval."

He made no attempt to press her on her origins. "Please feel free to make use of the stables."

Well, at least she had accomplished something useful.

"You would be well advised to listen to my son's advice on what areas to avoid," he added. "There are some spots where the trail can be dangerous if one is not familiar with the terrain. Max knows them all—he is bang up to the mark as a rider."

But not as bang up to the mark as his father, she couldn't help thinking. The earl displayed natural grace in the saddle, his seat firm, his touch on the reins controlling the spirited stallion without any perceptible effort.

A stretch of rocky ground caused the horse to change gait, throwing Allegra back against his broad chest.

"Oh!" Her entire body stiffened as she tried to maintain some space between them.

His arm tightened, drawing her even closer. "Don't worry, I shall not let you fall, Mrs. Proctor." His voice took on a touch of amusement. "You might try to relax a bit—despite what you might think, I don't actually bite."

She was glad he could not see her face, for she reddened at the idea that her thoughts were so transparent.

"I . . . I have no idea what you mean, sir," she countered.

He merely gave a soft chuckle and urged his mount into a faster pace.

As they rode into the stable yard, a groom came out, and Wrexham handed Allegra down. She made a show of smoothing out her gown and readjusting her bonnet in order to cover her unsettled emotions. The earl landed lightly beside her and brushed a bit of dust from his fitted buckskins. A drop of rain fell on the brim of his beaver hat.

"Ah, you see, you have been spared an unpleasant walk." He gave a slight bow. "Good afternoon, Mrs. Proctor."

Clutching her sketchbook to her chest, Allegra mumbled a suitable thanks and hurried toward the manor house.

A glimmer of a smile played on Wrexham's lips as he tossed the reins to the groom. So, she wasn't made of iron. It was gratifying to know the woman's composure could be affected. He had felt that in their first meeting she had kept him off balance and had come out decidedly ahead.

The second round he gave to himself.

But he had to grant she had spirit, as well as intelligence. Most people in her position would be falling all over themselves to gain his good graces, while Mrs. Proctor made no attempt to curry his favor—in fact, she made no attempt to conceal her distaste for his presence. He supposed he had given her good reason to form such an opinion. His manners and his words had been less than civil, and yet he couldn't help feeling the reasons ran deeper than that. There was something about the new tutor he had yet to decipher.

In any case, he found himself almost looking forward to the next bit of verbal sparring. She was certainly up to his weight in terms of quick wits, and there was no denying she had a dry sense of humor he wouldn't have expected in a female. In fact, it had been rather stimulating to trade jabs with a person his equal. Not that he was bored with only Max for company, but things promised to become rather interesting at the Hall.

Wrexham settled into a wing chair by the fire and opened the newly arrived book from London on the latest agricultural methods of increasing crop yields. The rain pounding against the mullioned windows of the library showed no sign of abating. It was going to remain nasty for the rest of the day, he thought with some smugness. The chit would have been half drowned before she made it back to the Hall.

Hardly a chit, he reminded himself. Just because her slender form and creamy complexion made her look as though she were barely out of the schoolroom—his mouth quirked as he recalled her own words about being old enough to be Max's mother. What fustian! That was certainly a gross exaggeration. After all, she was not quite of an age to wear a turban. . . .

His brows came together. Why the devil was he thinking about her? It was not as if she was a diamond of the first water. Her nose was a little too strong, her cheekbones a little too sharp, her mouth a little too wide to be called beautiful. But it was a face of rare character. Something in the depths of her smoky green eyes was intriguing. Or maybe it was just that he hadn't been around a female—any sort of female—for longer than he cared to remember. With a rueful grimace he forced his attention to the opening page of his book.

Damnation. It had to be about sowing seeds.

Allegra slid from the saddle and followed Max to the top of the ridge. A deep gorge lay before them, and water cascaded down the rocky falls, a blaze of white against the weathered stones. On the other side, rolling green hills dotted with grazing sheep climbed up toward the craggy, windblown moors, somber in their bleak hues of slate and granite.

Max slanted a guarded glance toward her.

"It's quite magnificent," said Allegra softly, drinking in the wild splendor of the vista.

He seemed to let out his breath. "I thought you'd understand," he said, allowing himself a slight smile. "Lots of people find it forbidding, but I think it's quite beautiful."

She nodded in agreement.

"I sometimes come here alone with . . . a book of poetry." He dropped his head and kicked at a loose stone, as if suddenly aware that the admission might sink him in her esteem. "I daresay you think that's rather silly of me." It was worded more as a question.

"Not at all, Max. I think it's rather wonderful."

He gave a shy grin. "Actually, I picked it up from Father. He's the one who first showed me this spot and told me how he enjoyed the rhythms of verse matched with the rhythms of nature—the sound of the rivers, the rustling of the leaves—"

"Your father sits in the wilds and reads poetry!" She couldn't keep the disbelief out of her voice.

Max's head tilted to one side. "I thought you approved."

"I do, it's just that . . . I hadn't quite expected it of him, of all people."

"You still think him a real dragon, don't you?"

Allegra turned to gaze out toward the moor. A certain trust had developed between them, and she did not want to jeopardize it by telling an untruth. "Max, it really is not important what I think of your father." After a fraction of a pause, a faint smile stole to her lips. "I assure you, it makes not a whit of difference to him what my opinion is."

Max looked as if to say something further, then shrugged and let the subject drop. "Would you care to see the ruins of the old abbey? It's not far from here."

"That sounds lovely."

They walked back to the horses and retraced their way down the winding trail. As her mare followed behind Max's chestnut stallion, Allegra couldn't help but think on how the young viscount continued to surprise her. He had a sensitivity that was rare in any young person, but especially one brought up in a world of privilege and pampering. That he appreciated the raw magic of words and of untrammeled nature showed a real depth of perception, a maturity beyond his years. And despite having every need catered to, he was also remarkably unspoiled. Rather than take advantage of his position, he treated everyone on the vast estate—servants, grooms, tenants—as real people, not mere lackeys to do his bidding.

She shook her head slightly. Perhaps the earl deserved

more credit than she had been wont to accord him. There must be another side to him other than the ill-tempered, toplofty demeanor he displayed in her presence. After all, any man who read poetry. . . .

Max called out to her and pointed toward a cluster of weathered stone walls perched on a knoll overlooking the roaring river. Creeping vines and masses of ivy had twined themselves among much of the tumbled blocks and crumbled mortar, but parts of the nave still poked heavenward, taller than the majestic oak spreading its gnarled limbs over the mossy granite of the outer walls. It was a beautiful, if desolate sight, one to attract the imagination of a lad given to romantic notions. She made a mental note to add Byron to their list of poetry and scientific works.

Their mounts splashed through a shallow crossing, and Max led the way up to the ruins. Leaving the horses to graze along the grassy perimeter, they climbed through the fallen slabs of granite until reaching the top of the west chapel, where a section of stone still stood high enough to afford a breathtaking vista of the countryside to the east. Max sat down, legs dangling over the mossy parapet and leaned back on his elbows, head thrown back to welcome the sudden appearance of the sun. Allegra joined him, and there was a companionable silence as they both seemed occupied with their own thoughts.

"Thank you, Max," she said simply, after some time.

He gave her an inquiring glance.

"For sharing your special places with me," she explained. "And your confidences. I'm very honored."

A faint blush began to color his face, and she looked away quickly, pretending not to notice. Max recovered his tongue after a moment. "When you like someone, you want to share the things that you find special," he replied in a hesitant voice.

"I know exactly what you mean." She shaded her eyes as she looked off into the distance. "I daresay there aren't many people for you to be friends with here."

He shook his head. "When I was younger, I played with some of the children on the estate, but now they are busy with work, and, well, things change." His face screwed into a wry expression. "Besides, they aren't really interested in talking about the same things as I am."

"What of the other estates in the area? Are there no people your own age?"

"Most families are in residence only during the grouse season. And only Westwood Manor and Hillington are close by."

Allegra squinted at a distant building framed by a large tract of beech and oak woods, its light stone gleaming in the scudding afternoon light against the canopy of dappled greens. "Which is that one there?" she asked, knowing full well the answer.

"Westwood Manor."

She felt a slight stab of guilt at turning the conversation to her own purpose, but she could not afford to pass up the chance to learn what she could. "Ah, I believe that is the place I saw on one of my walks. An impressive house, is it not. I attempted a few sketches, but my skill doesn't do it justice." She let a slight pause steal in. "I nearly lost my way back to the Hall, though. Is it really as far as it seems?"

"There's a shortcut through the woods. You go down past the lake, and you'll see a trail running off to the right, past the gamekeeper's cottage. It's quite easy to follow."

That was a very valuable piece of information, she realized. "Such a magnificent home must belong to an important man."

"The Marquess of Sandhill owns Westwood, though he is not here often."

"Surely your father enjoys seeing kindred souls—your families must dine with one another?" It would be a stroke of rare luck to discover so easily a night Sandhill was to be absent from Westwood.

"Father may visit occasionally when they are up from London, but on the whole, he tries to avoid it, even though the marquess is said to have an extensive library."

Allegra sucked in her breath, but Max didn't seem to notice as he chuckled over some private remembrance.

"Actually, Father finds the fellow a prosy bore. Says he is unforgivably ignorant, considering what treasures he has. Pearls before swine is the term he used, I think."

"Some people acquire priceless things simply out of greed," she said softly.

Max looked at her quizzically. "Are you acquainted with Lord Sandhill?"

Her lips compressed in regret of her rash words. It was apparent she would have to be as careful around the son as around the father. She forced herself to laugh, hoping her voice didn't sound as strained as it did to her own ears. "I am hardly in the habit of keeping company with such prominent members of the *ton*."

He grinned. "You aren't missing anything. Lady Sandhill is an insufferable bore as well, puffed up with the sense of her own importance."

Allegra fiddled with the strings of her bonnet, somehow relieved to learn that neither Max nor the earl cared overly much for their neighbors. Why it should matter, she wasn't sure. After all, her plans were none of their business. Picking up the folds of her skirts, she rose. "I suppose we had better return, lest you be late for supper." A mischievous tone crept into her voice. "I wouldn't want to give your father any cause to think me a bad influence on you."

Max scrambled to his feet. "You? A bad influence?" he scoffed. "How could he possibly think that!"

Clouds the color of slate hung low over the moor. But despite the threat of rain, Allegra took up her sketchbook after a light nuncheon and headed with resolute strides toward the lake Max had spoken of. If there was a shortcut to Westwood Manor, she meant to explore it thoroughly and learn every twist and turn, so that she could find her way without misstep, when the time came.

A glance at the ominous weather had convinced Max to remain indoors after the lessons were done for the day. Though she enjoyed his company, Allegra was not sorry he had decided to wrestle with a particularly difficult passage of Virgil rather than ask if he might accompany her. It certainly wouldn't do for the lad to notice her taking any further interest in the neighboring estate. He was too sharp by half not to put things together later on if she didn't keep a closer rein on herself. Still, the information she had gleaned had been worth the risk.

A few drops splashed onto her sketchbook. Max was also too sharp by half to be wandering around like a goose in the rain, she thought ruefully as she hurried her steps along the path.

Wrexham turned his attention from the library window—and the lone figure striding toward the copse of elms—back to the pages of his treatise on the productivity of different soil types. It appeared that Mrs. Proctor was one of those stubborn types who insisted on taking a constitutional, no matter what the weather. Well, it served her right if she got thoroughly soaked this time. He shifted in his comfortable chair and moved his long legs closer to the warmth of the fire, the slightest touch of smugness stealing into his expression. She should have better sense than to venture out on a day like this.

Several hours later, Allegra returned through one of the back entrances and shrugged out of her rain-spattered cloak, her spirits nonetheless undampened. She had been lucky in all respects. Although a light mizzle had fallen intermittently, the leaden skies had not opened up on her. And as her chilled fingers fumbled with the strings of her bonnet, she noted with grim satisfaction that even if they had, the drenching would have been well worth it. Max's casual comment had proved to be invaluable. The new route was perfect.

It was almost time to put her plans in motion.

She scraped the mud from her half boots and quickly made her way up the stairs, looking forward to changing into dry clothing and fetching a hot cup of tea. After supper there would be ample time to sit down to study her sketch pads. There were still some final decisions to be made.

As she came around the corner of the hallway, her brows drew together. The door to her room was slightly ajar. She was always very careful to shut it firmly, but perhaps one of the maids had been in to dust or change the linens and had not closed it properly.

It swung open at her touch.

"Max!" Her surprise was so great she nearly let the sketchbook slip from her fingers. The initial feeling of shock quickly changed to one of wariness, especially on noting his ashen face and the set of his jaw. "What are you doing in my bedchamber?" she demanded in a voice barely above a whisper, though she feared she already knew the answer.

He rose from the edge of her bed. "Close the door, Mrs. Proctor. I believe we had better talk." His hand gestured toward her open trunk, where a pistol, a length of rope and an assortment of men's clothing lay in full view. "Perhaps you would care to explain what is going on here?"

Chapter Three

~

"And perhaps you would care to explain what you were doing snooping through my belongings," replied Allegra calmly, though she was gripping her book so tightly that her knuckles were nearly white.

Max had the grace to look discomfited. "I did not exactly mean to be snooping through your trunk. I was having difficulty with a Latin word and remembered you had mentioned that you had a special dictionary. I knocked, then thought you would not mind if I borrowed it for the afternoon. When it wasn't on your desk, I opened you trunk without ever thinking . . ." There was a catch in his voice. "I cannot believe that you are nought but a charlatan! I prevailed upon my father—much against his wishes, as you well know—to allow you to take up your position. I thought you were my friend, but is this how you mean to repay us—by . . . by planning to murder us in our beds and rob . . ."

"No!" she cried. "I promise you, Max, this has nothing to do with you or your family."

His eyes betrayed how much he wanted to believe her, despite his grim countenance. "Well? I am listening."

Allegra let out a sigh as she sat down the bed. "Would that you would simply take my word." Her voice rose in question, but a dogged shake of his head made it clear he would not be fobbed off so easily. "No, I didn't really imagine you would," she murmured. A long silence ensued as she found herself wondering whether the earl would haul her before the local magistrate or show a semblance of mercy and merely cast her from the house with the warning to be gone from the area by nightfall. She gave an involuntary shudder. Could one be transported for simply the intention of committing a serious crime?

Then she chided herself for cowardice. It was no use lamenting the consequences of her actions. She had known full well the risks involved. . . .

"Please, Mrs. Proctor. Tell me the truth."

There was something so eloquent about his simple appeal that she found herself wavering in her resolve to keep her secret.

"Oh, Max." Still she hesitated. Then she looked at his anxious face, raw with doubt, and made up her mind.

The tale took much longer than necessary, since he insisted on interrupting every few sentences.

"The bloody bastard," he exclaimed, when she had finally come to the end.

"Max!"

"Sorry. Father says it—but only when he's really, really angry," he admitted.

She gave a tight smile as she wondered what epithet the earl would use in her case if he knew what Max now knew. "I'm still your tutor, and as such, I must ask that you moderate your language, young man."

He grinned. "Very well. I shall keep a more careful rein on my tongue. But when are we going to begin—"

"*We?*" she interrupted.

Max looked puzzled.

"*We?*" she repeated. "*We* are not going to begin anything. You must have windmills in your head if you think for a moment that I am going to let you get involved."

"Of course I'm going to help you!" His eyes had a dangerous light to them. "Do you think I'd stand by and see such an injustice go unpunished if I could help it?"

Allegra bit her lip. "Max," she began patiently, "I told you the story to show I trusted you. Now, you must trust me when I say there is no way I can allow you to get mixed up in this affair. Why, only think of how your father would react if he knew . . ."

"I'll tell him. I'll tell him everything if you don't let me help you."

She stared at him, aghast. "Why, that's blackmail, Max!"

He crossed his arms and stood firm.

"It's . . . ungentlemanly!" she continued.

That, at least, brought a touch of color to his face. "Well, it's for the higher good," he countered.

Her mouth opened, then closed again.

"Besides," he went on before she could speak. "You are going to need help if you really mean to carry this off. For instance, how will you ever learn when Lord Sandhill is to be out for the evening? Or how do you think you will manage the wall surrounding the gardens without assistance?"

Dead silence ensued. Those were just the sorts of questions she had been asking herself.

"You see!" he cried triumphantly when she didn't answer.

"Max, this isn't a game. It's dangerous, and if you are caught . . ." She blanched. "I don't even want to think about it."

"Then we must see that we don't get caught."

She started to argue, but he cut her off. "I'm not a child anymore, Mrs. Proctor. I can make up my own mind on what is right and wrong. Please. Let me help you."

"Do I have a choice?"

He shook his head. "Actually, you do not."

She closed her eyes. "Why do I have the feeling that somehow I'm going to regret letting you talk me into this."

Max couldn't repress the gleam of adventure in his eyes. "You won't, I promise you. Now, let's see that drawing of the west wing."

Allegra reluctantly opened her sketchbook. "Heaven help me if your father ever learns of this."

Max gave a wan smile. "Heaven help us both."

The day was one for curling up by a roaring fire. A cold, intermittent drizzle had been falling since first light, and the sharp gusts blowing in off the moor seemed early harbingers of the coming autumn. Allegra set aside a bit of mending she was doing and decided to visit the kitchen for a cup of tea. There had been no lessons that morning, as Max had engaged to go shooting with his father, so she was accorded the rare pleasure of an entire day to herself. But already most of it was gone, taken up with the little tasks she had been putting off for an age. After a comfortable coze with Cook, there might still be time to browse through the earl's splendid selection of books for a volume to borrow before the owner returned.

Allegra finished her steaming cup while listening to the litany of ailments that could plague a female of indeterminate years if certain draughts and powders were not consumed each day. Excusing herself with a smile and a promise to pay heed to such sage advice, she slipped through the pantry, relieved to have escaped without having to actually sample the noxious brews. A narrow corridor led back to the main wing, and she was just turning the corner when a small back door opened and the earl and Max came in.

Mud encrusted their boots, and drops of water clung to the thick wool of their hunting coats. A brace of grouse dangled over Max's shoulder, eyed with a hungry intensity by the shaggy hound at his side. The raw weather had brought an edge of color to the cheeks of both father and son, and with his windblown locks tousled in boyish disarray, the earl hardly appeared a gentleman in his dotage. In truth, Allegra had to admit, he looked more an older sibling than aging parent. His lean form radiated the same youthful energy as Max's, but there was also a vibrant masculinity about him not yet evident in his son.

They were unaware of her presence and a friendly bantering continued as the door fell closed.

"You young pup," exclaimed Wrexham. He threw a playful cuff at Max's head. "You think you could plant me a facer, do you? Not very likely!"

Max dodged the blow. "If I could spar with Gentleman Jackson for a bit, I bet I could put you on your tail!"

he retorted. Then his voice turned wistful. "Couldn't we visit London soon? You promised that when I was no longer a child—and look! I'm nearly as tall as you!"

The top of Max's head almost touched the earl's nose. "A veritable giant," he drawled, drawing a yelp of outrage from his son.

"You're mocking me!" Max jabbed a punch at Wrexham's shoulder, and the two of them fell into a mock scuffle. Feathers began to fly as Sasha took advantage of the lad's lapse of attention and began to snap wildly at the swinging birds.

Allegra stifled the urge to giggle.

The earl's head came up abruptly, and he caught sight of her. He straightened slowly, running his long fingers through his damp locks and tugging his coat into some semblance of order.

"Good afternoon, Mrs. Proctor," he said with a slight inclination of his head.

Before she could answer, Max gave his father one last push from behind, ruining the earl's efforts at formality. He stumbled forward, nearly catching his chin on a rack set up for drying wet outer garments. "Jackanape! Have a care or the old dog shall box your ears yet," he exclaimed, but there was a twinkle in his eye.

"Father is being a bear! He won't agree to take me to London," complained Max. "Tell him it would be . . . educational!"

Allegra couldn't repress a smile. "Family discussions are best entered into by family members only. So I am well out of this one."

The twinkle in Wrexham's eyes was even more pronounced. "A wise decision, Mrs. Proctor."

"I could only come out in someone's bad graces, no matter which side I should champion," she pointed out.

"And whose good graces would you wish to keep?"

She regarded him cooly. "Really, my lord, on that I think we both know there is very little choice."

His lips twitched, but before he could make a reply, Max spoke up again. "Well, there is another matter you might help us settle. Father and I have been arguing over a passage of *The Aeneid* for the entire walk home and I should like to know your opinion. We were just going to have tea in the library—perhaps you would care to join us?" A flash of challenge sparked in his eyes on glancing at his father, as if daring him to contradict the invitation.

"Max," replied Allegra, "I hardly think your father wishes . . ."

"By all means, Mrs. Proctor, please join us."

She could hardly refuse. Aside from being unspeakably rude to refuse a direct invitation from the earl, no matter how grudgingly extended, it would hurt the lad's feelings. "I should be delighted, then," she murmured.

The glint in Wrexham's eyes told her he knew she would be anything but. "Excellent. We shall be down as soon as we have made ourselves presentable for company. Shall we say in twenty minutes?"

Max broke into a satisfied smile. "I'll tell Cook, since I must drop our trophies in the kitchen." He hoisted the birds for Allegra's benefit, drawing a baleful look of reproach from the hound. "Oh, come along, Sasha," he added. "You shall have a special treat for your day's work."

Exactly twenty minutes later, the earl appeared in the library, looking, once again, every inch the titled gentleman. Not a hair was out of place, not a wrinkle sullied the expensive navy merino wool of his perfectly tailored coat or buff pantaloons. But neither did he have the look of having fussed over his dress either, noted Allegra with reluctant approval. His cravat was knotted with a casual elegance, and his shirt points were unfashionably low, bespeaking of comfort rather than foppishness. His waistcoat was an understated stripe with nary a fob or chain adorning its front. The only glint of gold came from the heavy signet ring on his right hand. She couldn't help but think that perhaps the earl's natural grace had something to do with an athletic form that needed little help from a tailor to show to advantage.

Her hands brushed her own rather worn gown, and she was suddenly aware of its outdated design and less than flattering styling. Then her chin rose a fraction. As if it mattered how she appeared to the earl, she reminded herself!

Max clattered to a halt outside the door, made one last effort at smoothing his unruly locks, then entered with a studied air of nonchalance that drew a ghost of a smile from his father. Allegra noted with further approval that he had the sense to refrain from commenting on the lad's attempt to appear quite the adult. A maid entered with a large tray bearing tea and an assortment of cakes. The sight of piping hot apple tartlets quickly melted Max's resolve to act like a lord. With a boyish grin, his hand shot out to filch one of the morsels before the tray was on the table.

Wrexham gave his son a pointed look as the lad polished off the last bite.

"Sorry," said Max with a sheepish look. "It's been a devilishly long time since breakfast."

"You had a successful hunt, then?" asked Allegra quickly, changing the subject before the earl could begin any lecture on manners.

"Oh, excellent!" he replied. "And I brought down more of the birds than Father."

"I must have forgotten to wear my spectacles," murmured Wrexham.

That brought a peal of laughter from Max. "Hah!"

The earl glanced at Allegra. "You are lucky not to have children, Mrs. Proctor, as they inevitably grow up to mock one's old age—" He cut off his words abruptly. "Max, perhaps you would pour a glass of sherry for Mrs. Proctor." As his son crossed the room to where the decanter sat on side table near the earl's desk, Wrexham turned back to her. "That was unforgivably clumsy of me," he said quietly. "Please accept my apologies."

Allegra had gone ashen at his first words, but she was surprised he seemed to have noticed. She was even more surprised when, on meeting his gaze, she saw only genuine concern in his eyes. Confused, her head jerked toward the fire.

"Think nothing of it, my lord. After all, one's servants are not expected to have feelings, are they?" The sharpness of her tone sought to mask the realization that for the briefest of moments she was mortally afraid she might disgrace herself with a tear.

Wrexham's mouth compressed in an expression of consternation rather than anger.

Allegra took a deep breath, immediately regretting having revealed any hint of emotion to the earl. "Now it is my turn to say I'm sorry," she added quickly. "That was a churlish reply to you. Please, let us forget the entire matter."

Any further words were forestalled by the arrival of Max with the sherry.

"Thank you, Max." She accepted the glass, grateful that her hands betrayed no sign of her inner agitation.

The earl continued to regard her thoughtfully throughout the brief exchange with his son. Then he gestured for them to be seated. "Perhaps you would be kind enough to pour, Mrs. Proctor?" he asked politely.

By the time she had finished the mundane task of handing around the cups, Allegra had recovered her composure. And as Max lost no time in steering the conversation toward the disputed passage of Virgil, there was little opportunity to dwell on the incident. She gladly entered into an animated discussion involving the nuances of ancient Latin. She had little trepidation about exposing her intellect to scrutiny—it was her feelings she preferred to keep hidden away.

A short while later, as she refilled their cups and passed the plate of pastries, she found herself more perplexed than ever. It had nothing to do with the subject matter, though no definitive opinion had been reached as of yet. Rather, it concerned the earl himself. It didn't seem possible that a man who had shown himself to be ill-tempered, arrogant and high in the instep could also be so amusing, perceptive and quick-witted.

His relationship with Max also went against all that she knew of the *ton*. In her experience, they spent precious little time with their children. Why, most fathers were barely aware of any progeny, the mere existence of an heir being satisfaction enough that duty had been done. But the interplay she had witnessed that afternoon between the earl and his son made it clear that Lord

Wrexham had spent a considerable portion of his life raising his son. Beneath the gruff discipline and dry sense of humor was a bond of real affection she had never expected.

Drat the man. She wanted to dislike him. It made things that much easier. . . .

". . . Mrs. Proctor?"

Her head snapped up.

Max grinned. "Mrs. Proctor wool-gathers, too."

"So I see," drawled the earl.

To her dismay, Allegra felt her cheeks redden. She was certainly managing to make a complete cake of herself.

"I was asking whether you had enjoyed seeing a bit of the wilds of Yorkshire."

"Very much so," she answered. "Max has been an excellent guide."

"It is not to everyone's taste," observed the earl.

"I find great beauty in its ruggedness—"

"She especially likes the ridge," interrupted Max. "You know, where you like to go to read poetry."

To Allegra's secret delight, she thought she detected a spot of color on the earl's cheeks. He cleared his throat and took another swallow of tea.

"I also showed her some of the neighboring manors," continued Max.

She shot him a warning glance.

"Speaking of neighbors, was that Lord Sandhill I saw riding out toward Hingham the other day? He usually arrives to take up residence for a few weeks about now, doesn't he?"

Allegra restrained the urge to kick him.

Wrexham shrugged. "No doubt it was. I believe Squire Trenney mentioned he had invited the entire family for dinner next Tuesday. We are asked as well."

Max made a face. "Not me! Wild horses couldn't drag me to that," he muttered as he cast a triumphant look Allegra's way.

The earl chuckled. "No? I have to admit, I cried off. Can't imagine a more boring evening myself, what with Trenney prosing on about his various ailments and Sandhill exaggerating his consequence in London." He drained the last of his tea and stood up. "Now if you will excuse me, I have some estate matters to attend to before supper."

Allegra rose hastily.

"No, please, Mrs. Proctor. I'm sure Max would be happy to enjoy your company for a while longer." He bowed slightly. "Perhaps we might continue our debate on Virgil at a later time—I don't believe we have come to any sort of agreement, have we?"

Noting the twinkle in his eye, she could hardly keep from smiling in return. *Good Lord,* the man *did* have a sly sense of humor.

"No, sir, we have not."

"Ah, well, as I said, perhaps later."

As soon as he had left the room, Allegra turned to Max with a stern countenance. "That was foolhardy. You must promise me that you will abide by my judgment and not take matters into your own hands again, else I will be forced to abandon the whole thing."

"But we learned when Sandhill is to be absent from home!" he protested. "And Father didn't suspect a thing."

She shook her head doggedly. "If you think that much escapes your father's notice, you are sadly mistaken. Believe me, we cannot be too careful around him. Do I have your promise?"

His boot scuffed at the Aubusson carpet, and it was only with great reluctance that he finally answered her. "Oh, very well." Then his face brightened considerably. "Shall we ride near Westwood Manor tomorrow? I have a capital idea—Father bought me a brass spyglass on his last trip to London, so that I might observe the birds up on the moor. We can use it for studying the west wing of the manor house and the approach to the library window."

She had to admit it was an excellent idea, one that would certainly help minimize the risks involved. Still, she could not shake the uneasy feeling that allowing Max to participate in such a dangerous venture was wrong on her part. She sighed as the lad waxed on about the par-

ticulars of the next day's reconnaissance. Short of truss-
ing him in his bed on the appointed night, or throwing
herself on the mercy of the earl, she had little choice
but to proceed as planned.

Her jaw set as she reminded herself that the plan did
not include getting caught.

Wrexham laid aside his copy of Virgil with a bark of
laughter. The deerhound lifted one lazy lid in inquiry,
but his master merely shook his head and continued
grinning into the fire. On rereading the passage in question, he could only marvel at the cleverness of her inter-
pretation. It took both a keen mind and equally keen
sense of the absurd to suggest such a shade of meaning.
And to think that it came from a female—he wasn't sure
whether he felt shock or admiration.

His head continued to wag. There was no question
Mrs. Proctor was an intriguing individual. Her intellect
was undeniable, but she also displayed a spirit and back-
bone he wouldn't have expected from one in her position. She was quite unlike any other female of his
acquaintance. Now, if she dressed her hair in a less severe style, one that drew attention to those flashing
green eyes, and dressed to accentuate that willowy form,
she would be passably attractive. . . .

He caught himself with a start. Well, at least it seemed
she was true to her word and had no intention of luring
his son into anything improper. He had been most careful to observe the interaction between the two of them,
and he had to admit that any changes in Max were all
for the better. The lad was expanding the boundaries of
his knowledge and powers of reasoning by leaps and bounds.
And more than that, he seemed happier, less inclined
to snap at the slightest provocation. A friendship had
developed between them, and given Max's isolated up-
bringing, he realized how important the relationship was
to the lad, no matter that the person was a female. Thus
far, his son's feelings had not developed into anything
more dangerous, so there appeared little reason to
interfere.

Still, he was not convinced that the arrangement was

the wisest decision he had made. Perhaps it was time to contemplate a trip to London. It had been an age since his last visit, and there were any number of reasons to consult with his man of affairs. Then he could also take charge of interviewing a proper candidate for his son's tutor. Max would not be happy with the idea, but maybe the prospect of a sojourn to Town would help assuage any anger. He would make a point of letting the lad help decide on Mrs. Proctor's replacement.

A twinge of guilt ran through him on recalling her words on the unfairness of being dismissed without having a chance to prove herself. He supposed this was even more unfair since she had shown herself to be an outstanding teacher. The truth was, she was going to be sacked merely because she was a female. It was an injustice, but life wasn't fair, was it? He was sorry to cause her hardship or pain—

His dark brows came together. How in the devil had he uttered such a callous remark at tea? Usually he never behaved in such a cow-handed manner, but the words had slipped out before he realized the import of what he was saying. He hadn't missed the spasm of pain that had flickered momentarily in her eyes or the draining of color from her face. He had hurt her with his casual comment.

Surely, she couldn't think that he had meant to be cruel? As he mused over the question, his mouth twisted into a wry grimace. Why wouldn't she think he had set out to deliberately wound her? He had made his displeasure with her presence clear upon her arrival, and since then he had not exactly treated her with a good deal of courtesy.

He shifted uncomfortably in his chair. Somehow it bothered him more than he cared to admit that she would think him capable of such shabby behavior. His fingers came up to rub at his temples, and he found himself wondering where she had acquired the notion that anyone with a title was a lout. Well, there was nothing to do for it, except endeavor to be more civil for the rest of her short tenure. And of course he would see that she had excellent references and a generous severance.

Yet somehow, despite all the careful logic and undeniable reasons he was right, Wrexham couldn't shake the feeling that what he was contemplating was less than admirable.

Max coiled the rope with a look of grim satisfaction. "You see, it really needs two people. I'm not sure you would be able to manage by yourself."

Allegra dusted off her hands on the seat of her breeches. "I don't deny that your help makes it easier. But I should have found a way. Now put the things back in the bag and let me change before anyone catches sight of us."

Max choked down a laugh as they walked away from the abbey ruins back toward where their horses were grazing. "Can you imagine Father's face if he saw you now?"

"That's not funny, Max," she muttered, but a smile did creep to her lips. "Good Lord, he'd have a fit of apoplexy. He already accused me of trying to seduce . . ."

"He did *what*?"

"Oh, never mind," she replied, regretting her hasty words. "I think I've convinced him that I'm not trying to cast my lures at you. But he'd hardly approve of this—" She gestured down at her long legs. She stepped behind a cluster of thick bushes and began changing back into her gown.

"How dare he interfere in my affairs," fumed Max as he waited, arms crossed, brows drawn together in unconscious imitation of the earl.

Allegra had to struggle to keep from laughing at the unwitting double entendre. "Well, he *is* your father," she pointed out. "He's only trying to look out for your welfare."

"Hmmph. You sound like you are defending him."

She fastened the last of the buttons and tucked the errant wisps of hair back into the bun at the nape of her neck. Then after straightening the tucks of her bodice, she reappeared with the breeches and linen shirt neatly folded and tucked under one arm. "It is not a matter of defending him—it's that I cannot fault him for caring about what is best for you."

Max pulled a face and said something unintelligible under his breath. But his thoughts quickly came back to the matter at hand. "How is it that you know how to climb a tree or scale a wall? All of the young ladies of my acquaintance would fall into a fit of vapors if required to perform anything more arduous than lifting a teacup. I mean, Miss Cranbrook and her younger sister nearly fainted when I suggested they join me in a raid on Farmer Wilmot's orchard."

"I am not a lady," Allegra reminded him. "A fact for which I am eternally grateful," she added in a low voice. "Ladies have a great many rules and constraints on their behavior. They are not encouraged, or even allowed, to indulge in such hoydenish ways. My childhood allowed a good deal more freedom, despite being the daughter of a vicar." She smiled at the recollection. "The neighboring children of my age were mostly boys, so I learned to keep up if I wanted to be part of the adventures. I assure you, I filched my share of apples."

Max grinned in answer, but then his expression turned serious as he mulled over her words. "I hadn't thought about it overly, but it doesn't sound as if things are quite as fair for females."

"Ah, welcome to the ways of the polite world," she said with a touch of asperity.

The lad looked slightly abashed.

"I'm sorry, I didn't mean to snap at you." Allegra let out a heavy sigh. "That's actually very perceptive of you. No, many things are not fair, as you will soon see when you make your first forays into Society. But you will be shielded from most of them because you are a male and have both title and wealth."

Max's brows knitted together. "I suppose it is understandable that you dislike anyone with wealth and privilege, but surely not all of the *ton* are unprincipled. I mean, Father is not like Lord Sandhill in the least."

"No, but even your father is well used to getting what he wants. He brooks no opposition to his will."

"He is not so unreasonable as you imagine," said Max. "When I disagree, he is always willing to listen to me."

Allegra regretted her earlier cynicism. The lad would learn of the real world soon enough. "Well, perhaps your father is different," she conceded in order to put a period to the conversation. But she doubted it, she added to herself.

Chapter Four

Wrexham shifted restlessly in the oversize leather chair. His eyes fell away from the printed page and watched the flames flicker toward embers. It was late, but somehow he didn't feel ready to retire. His leg ached from a long day spent in the saddle, and the nagging discomfort would no doubt keep sleep at bay, at least for a time. Something else was bothering him, something he couldn't quite lay a finger on. Normally he was more than content to spend the evening engrossed in his books, but of late the words lay cold and meaningless on the stark white paper. He laid the volume aside with a sigh of exasperation, then rose. The notion of a trip to London was becoming more and more appealing. Perhaps a change of scene would alter his flat mood. Not that he was unhappy, he reminded himself, but perhaps too much of the same thing was making him a trifle . . . bored.

He opened the inlaid box on his desk and took out a thin cheroot. The night was still pleasant, and it was evident by the soft wash of silvery light over the gardens that the stars and moon were clearer than usual in the northern sky. The earl walked to the drawing room and threw open the French doors. A stroll in evening air would be just the thing for improving his frame of mind.

A puff of smoke wraithed around the furled buds of a climbing rose as he lit up and gazed out over the carefully tended plantings to the rolling lawns and then distant moors looming up behind the manor house. His feet left the graveled path, and his boots moved noiselessly over the thick grass as a chorus of crickets broke the stillness, and the low boxwood hedge rustled in the light breeze. It was inordinately peaceful, he thought as he turned the corner to the east wing of the house. He enjoyed the sounds of the country over the clatter of wheels on cobblestones and the shouts and curses of the crowded city streets. Still, it would only be for a short time, and Max would be ecstatic to visit London.

His eyes strayed up to his son's window as a fond smile ghosted over his lips. It was dark tonight, though many times he had noted the faint glow of a candle that revealed he was not the only one who spent half the night with his nose buried in a book. At least now the lad seemed to be getting the intellectual challenge that he craved.

Wrexham's gaze drifted over the long expanse of stone to Mrs. Proctor's room. It, too, showed no sign of life. He felt a twinge of conscience at the thought of turning her out despite the excellent job she had been doing. It was for the best, he assured himself. Max would be better suited with a male tutor, and the young widow would be more comfortable in a different situation. He would make sure that his man of affairs gave her sterling references. . . .

The cheroot nearly slipped from his lips as he saw a booted leg swing over the sill of her window. A figure clad in a thick jacket and breeches scrambled out onto the ledge, took hold of the thick vines growing up the side of the carved limestone and began to climb down. If he hadn't been so nonplussed, he might have chuckled. Was the prim, proper Mrs. Proctor engaged in a liaison with one of his grooms or gardeners? She was, after all, a widow and allowed a good deal more leeway than an innocent girl. And by the way her green eyes could flash with fire, he had sensed there was more than ice lurking beneath her steely reserve. Still, he could not tolerate such illicit behavior from his employees. He would have to deal firmly with her in the morning. At least now he had an adequate reason for terminating—

The earl's jaw dropped even lower as he caught movement at Max's window. Another dark form began to descend to the ground. His initial shock turned to seething anger as he looked once again at the figure climbing down from Mrs. Proctor's window and realized it was no man.

How could he have been blind to the fact that the worthless baggage was indeed bent on seducing his son? Her acting ability certainly rivaled that of Mrs. Siddons, for he wouldn't have believed it possible if he hadn't seen it with his very eyes!

He stood absolutely still as the two of them dropped to the ground and met for a hurried conference beneath a bower of ivy. As they began to move off, keeping to the shadows of the tall privet hedge, the earl ground out his cheroot beneath his heel and, with a string of silent oaths, started after them. As he fumed, he couldn't help but wonder what they were up to—surely a tryst could have been arranged without going to the trouble of sneaking out into the wilds of Yorkshire, especially since he had played the fool and been blithely ignorant of what was going on beneath his very nose.

It gave him some little gratification that perhaps Max felt a reluctance to betray the trust shown in him within the Hall itself. The direction turned toward the stables. So that was it, thought the earl with a curl of his lip— an empty stall, a roll in the hay. He could hardly blame the lad, he supposed. He was reaching an age when it was only natural to feel . . . certain urges, even more so if urged on. It was the widow he wanted to shake until her teeth rattled.

The two figures up ahead swung one of the doors of the stable open just a crack and disappeared inside. Wrexham stopped for a moment as he debated what to do next. He wasn't sure he wanted to humiliate his son by catching him with his breeches down around his knees in his first attempts at being a man. He wasn't so far into his dotage that he couldn't imagine what that would be like. But on the other hand . . . His breath came out in a sigh.

Good Lord, it was deucedly difficult to be a father at times.

As Wrexham pondered his predicament, the door

opened again, and his son and his companion came out
leading two horses. The Earl's brows came together in
puzzlement as he noticed the heavy bag tied to the back
of one of the saddles. They came close enough to where
he was standing hidden in the shadows that he could
catch their whispered words.

"I think it better that we lead the horses some distance down toward the lake before mounting," said Max.
"That way, we won't risk waking the grooms."

The other figure merely nodded assent.

With his curiosity as well as his anger piqued, the earl
slid into the stable as soon as they had moved away. It
would take him only a few minutes to have Ulysses
ready, and he knew in which direction they were going.

So much for a simple stroll in his gardens.

Allegra and Max tethered their mounts in a copse of
trees they had picked out the previous week. She took
the small lantern out of the bag, while he slung the thick
coil of rope over his shoulder. In his youthful eagerness,
he was nearly sprinting toward their destination, and Allegra had to place a hand on his shoulder to temper
his energy.

"Have a care," she cautioned. "We cannot afford a
mistake."

He nodded and immediately slowed his steps. As they
approached the garden wall of Westwood Manor, he
gently tested the iron gate. As they suspected, it was
locked. Allegra removed a thin oilskin packet from the
pocket of her jacket and drew out a thin length of metal.
She inserted it into the rusted lock, and after a few jig-
gles the deadbolt slid loose with a satisfying snick.

"How did you learn to do that?" whispered Max in
amazement.

She grinned. "I shall explain it to you later." She
pushed at the gate very slowly, and it opened with little
noise. "We could have used the rope here as well, but
we may welcome a faster means of exit."

After surveying the gardens for any sign of activity,
she motioned for Max to follow her inside. They reached
the wall below the library window without incident. Al-

legra gazed up at the smooth expanse of stone, while Max shook out the length of coils. From their observations, they knew there were no vines or a tree to provide an aid to their ascent. There was, however, a ridge of slate tiles set above one of the upper bay windows that could provide an anchor for the iron prong at the end of their rope.

Max weighed the heft of his line for a moment, then made the first toss. The prong failed to catch and clattered back to earth with what seemed like an inordinate amount of noise.

Allegra winced.

"Sorry," muttered Max as he gathered the rope for the next try.

They waited a moment to make sure no outcry was forthcoming, then she signaled for him to go ahead. "I doubt we shall get many trys," she whispered aloud, though she knew from his grim expression he was as aware of that possibility as she was.

This time, the claws lodged in between the pieces of slate. With an audible sigh of relief, Max tested its hold. The prong didn't budge, even under the full pull of his weight. He yielded the rope to Allegra with obvious reluctance.

"I still say I could help you search faster," he said in a low voice.

"We agreed that you would stay here and keep watch."

"I know, but think on it. Even if I do see someone, precious little good that will do. You would never have time to get out. I could be of much more assistance if I come with you."

Allegra hesitated. She forbore to reply that he, at least, would have ample time to make his escape if he stayed on the ground. But what he said made good sense. "You promise to do exactly as I say?"

He nodded vigorously.

"Very well. But I go up first, and when I say we must leave, you will do so without argument."

"I promise."

With one last tug on the rope, Allegra started up the wall.

An incredulous expression spread over Wrexham's face as he watched his son scale the wall of his neighbor's manor and disappear into the second-story window. He had left his horse near the others and followed their steps through the unlocked gate into the formal gardens behind Westwood Manor.

Who the devil was she, to add housebreaking to his son's curriculum? More to the point, what the devil were they up to? He couldn't imagine that Max would be tempted into such transgressions by mere money. The lad received a generous allowance, which he seemed to use only for books. No, the little hussy must have lured him into this with the promise of something other than material gain.

With a wry grimace, he thought back to only a short while ago when he feared that Max was in danger of becoming too staid. Then he edged his way nearer to where the rope dangled from the open window. A glance up had shown that clouds were beginning to scud across the sky. The darkness would help obscure any movements and elude any pursuit.

Well, there was nothing else for it but to attempt to extricate Max before he really ended up in the suds.

"Help me lift this painting off the wall," whispered Allegra. They had already checked every volume on the shelves, and she had made short work of the locks on Sandhill's desk. "The safe is here. I'll start on it while you go through the drawers."

Max gave her a hand in lowering the heavy gilt frame to the floor, then carefully lit the small lantern they had brought with them so that he might better examine the contents of the desk.

"Draw the curtain," she reminded him. "And hurry."

They both set to their appointed tasks with a sense of urgency. Allegra had decided that they should not remain in the library over a quarter of an hour. Already nearly half the allotted time was gone. Her fingers fumbled with the slender picks. This type of lock was proving more difficult than the others.

A low exclamation from Max nearly caused her to drop the implements to the floor.

"Ssshhh!"

"Sorry. I thought I had found something important," he whispered as he put the papers back. Making sure nothing else was disturbed, he shut the drawer and jiggled one of Allegra's picks so that the lock clicked back into place.

Both of them were so engrossed in what they were doing that the sound of approaching footsteps went unnoticed. It was only the faintest scratch of metal against metal as the knob of the door was turned that caused Allegra's head to come up.

She cried out a warning, just as a burly shape lunged at the lad. He managed to twist aside as the thick cudgel came down toward his head so that the blow was only a glancing one. Still, the force of it dropped him half senseless to the carpet.

The footman raised the stick again.

A heavy ash walking stick topped with a silver stag's head leaned up against the hearth. She snatched it and swung wildly at the fellow before he could hit Max again. The shaft caught him flush on the temple. With a low groan, he staggered a few steps, then collapsed in a heap. Allegra rushed to where Max lay.

"Good Lord, Max, are you all right?" she said, taking his head between her hands.

His eyes fluttered open and he essayed a weak smile. "Yes, yes. I'm thick-skulled enough, as you know. I imagine we had better take our leave." His attempt at humor didn't disguise his groggy voice, and he didn't seem to be able to move his limbs.

She bit her lip. Already there were sounds of movement downstairs. They had only a few minutes in which to make their escape.

"Max," she whispered urgently. "You have to get up!"

A noise at the window caught her attention. Had the rope been discovered as well? Sure enough, a large figure pulled himself over the sill. Allegra grabbed up an oversize book that had fallen from the shelves, determined not to go down without a fight. As soon as the man turned, she hurled it straight at his midriff. There was a whoof of air as the heavy tome knocked him off balance, followed by a string of curses.

"Lord Wrexham!" gasped Allegra.

"Father!" cried Max weakly as he struggled to a sitting position. "I can explain—"

The earl was at his son's side in two strides. "Later," he snapped. "Can you stand?"

"I . . . I think so."

Wrexham's arm was already around Max's waist, lifting him to his feet and guiding him toward the window. The lad sagged against his father's broad chest, still not in full command of his faculties. With an exasperated sound, the earl propped Max against the wall and grabbed up a decanter of brandy from a bowed side table. Yanking out the crystal stopper, he turned and flung the contents over Max's face.

The shock of the cold liquid had the desired effect. The lad's shoulders snapped to attention as he shook his head a few times to clear the remaining cobwebs.

"Can you manage to climb down by yourself?" demanded the earl. "I fear the rope may not hold the weight of two of us."

Max wiped at his face. "Yes, sir."

"Then do so!" he ordered. "Now!"

The clatter of feet on the stairs indicated that the servants below had heard the scuffle and were on the way. Wrexham strode to the door and kicked it shut, then grabbed the desk chair and wedged it under the knob. "That should hold them for a bit," he muttered. As he turned back toward his son, the footman felled by Allegra's blow had risen to his knees. The earl paused for a brief moment. His fist flashed forward, landing a clean shot to the jaw that laid the fellow out cold.

Max had hauled himself up over the windowsill. Only the upper part of his body was visible as he fumbled for a good grip. Wrexham leaned out and took him by both shoulders. "Be careful," he said softly, before pushing him on his way.

The door rattled as the group of men outside tried to force it open.

"Is that loaded?" Wrexham pointed at the pistol on the desk.

Allegra nodded.

His eyes narrowed as he took it up. "Kindly keep an eye on Max's progress. As soon as he is on the ground, get yourself out."

"My lord, I should be the last to—"

"Oh, no, ladies first," he said with scathing politeness.

"But—"

A shoulder slammed into the door, nearly knocking the chair from its position.

"I am in no mood to argue! Go!"

She ceased her protests and rushed to the window. "He's made it," she called after a moment. Relief was evident in her voice.

This time two men took a run at the door, nearly springing it from its hinges.

"Go!"

She disappeared into the blackness. The earl then aimed at the very top of the door and squeezed off a shot. A grim smile passed over his lips at the scrambling sound of the hasty retreat. With any luck, that should hold them off long enough. He tucked the pistol in the pocket of his coat and swung himself out onto the ledge. Allegra had just reached the ground. Without looking up, she pushed Max into a dead run and headed off in the direction of the gate.

"But Father . . ." gasped Max as his boots crunched over the graveled path.

"Don't worry about your father—he is doing quite well on his own," she answered without breaking stride.

Indeed, the earl was halfway down the rope, pleased that Allegra had at least shown enough good sense to get his son moving. It was looking as if they might yet extract themselves from this coil without further mishap since he doubted that a pursuit could be mounted before they were well away from Westwood Manor.

Shouts from above alerted him that Lord Sandhill's servants had more daring than he had reckoned with. They were back in force, and, as Wrexham looked up, one of them was bold enough to stick his head out the open window. The long barrel of a pistol appeared immediately afterward. With a muffled oath, the earl let go of the rope just as a shot rang out. The bullet grazed the back of his hand, but he was hardly aware of its impact as he dropped the remaining ten feet and hit the ground with a resounding thud.

At the sound of the shot, Max skidded to a halt. "Father!" he cried as he made to dash back to the house.

Allegra grabbed him by the shoulders to restrain him. She had already seen that the earl had recovered his feet and was weaving in and out of the bushes in order to present less of a target as he worked his way toward them. "Your father is unscathed," she assured him. "Come on, we must hurry—he won't appreciate it if we let ourselves get caught now!"

The sight of the earl's lean form moving quickly through the shadows convinced Max that his father needed no aid, and he let himself be dragged on in the direction of the horses. Wrexham caught up with them at the gate. With another string of choice oaths, he urged them to greater speed. As Max and Allegra vaulted into their saddles, they needed no further words to set their horses into a full gallop. The earl's big stallion fell in beside them, and the pounding of the hooves echoed off the soft earth as the three shapes were swallowed up by the blackness.

Wrexham reined his mount to a walk a short distance from the stables. The stallion's flanks were lathered in sweat, and the earl patted the horse's muscled neck in appreciation. "Well done, Ulysses," he murmured.

Not a word was addressed to Allegra and Max, who followed behind in single file. A grim silence hung over the small party as Wrexham gave a wide berth to the wing of the stables where the grooms slept. On reaching the other end, the earl dismounted and slid the door open. Allegra and Max led their horses in behind him.

The light of a single flame flared up as the earl lit a lantern and hung it from a peg above the first stall. He threw the reins of his stallion at Max.

"See that the horses are properly cared for," he said in a near whisper that didn't hide the fury in his tone. "Then I shall see both of you in the library."

As he turned to go, his knee buckled so that he was forced to grab onto the edge of the stall to steady himself. The string of curses that followed left both Max and Allegra with ringing ears well after the earl moved off with a pronounced limp and disappeared out the door.

Max's face was ashen. He swallowed once or twice before he could speak. "I . . . I don't think I've ever seen Father that angry."

Allegra slumped against some bales of hay. "With good reason," she replied with a heavy sigh. "I'm sure he's never had such provocation." She raked her hand through the mass of curls that had come undone during the mad flight. "Oh, Max, I'm truly sorry for having brought this down around your head. I knew I should not have allowed you to put yourself at risk."

Max smiled gamely. "I left you little choice," he reminded her. "I'm old enough to face the consequences of my actions." He shrugged. "Besides, how bad can they be?" Despite the bravado of his words, his expression showed he was not quite as sanguine as he wished her to believe.

Allegra didn't answer, but unbuckled the girth of her saddle and carried it over to its rack. She began sponging her horse down while Max was putting away the tack of the other two. Finally, she broke the silence.

"Dear heavens," she murmured. "I hope on top of everything else, your father isn't badly hurt."

"His leg? It's an old injury," said Max. "It pains him occasionally when he overexerts himself."

"Well, I imagine tonight's activities might be termed that," she answered dryly. "Especially when you take into account that he had to let go of the rope at a fair distance from the ground."

Her attempt to lighten the mood served its purpose.

The bleak expression on Max's face was replaced by a grin. "For an old dog, Father acquitted himself pretty well."

"Indeed." She sought to keep his mind off the impending confrontation. "How did he injure his leg in the first place?"

Max rubbed at his chin. "Let me see, it was nearly six years ago, I think, during haying time. Something spooked the horses of one of the wagons, and the team bolted while the driver was helping with the loading. There were two children in the back. Father was riding by and heard the cries. He set off after them, for the horses were headed for a steep ravine. There was no time to try to head them off, so he leaped between the team and managed to get the two animals under control. His leg was badly twisted in the process."

Allegra's eyes widened with amazement. "You mean to say your father risked his life for two of his tenant's children?"

He looked at her blankly. "They were *children*, Mrs. Proctor. Of course he did."

She looked down at the toes of her scuffed boots.

Max finished rubbing down the earl's stallion and led him off to his stall. He jammed his hands in the pockets of his jacket and kicked at a tuft of hay as he returned. "Well, I suppose there's no sense in putting it off any longer." He had gone a bit green around the gills.

Allegra brushed the dirt from the seat of her breeches and put on a resolute look.

"Let me do the talking."

Chapter Five

The earl glowered at the two of them from across the wide expanse of his desk. His windblown raven locks and angled black brows only accentuated the color of his current mood.

"Perhaps you will kindly tell me what in the devil's name was going on this evening." Wrexham's angry eyes were fixed on Allegra, his words all the more ominous in that his voice was barely above a whisper. "I agreed against my better judgment to hire you to supervise my son's education, and how is my trust repaid? It seems you have seen fit to add housebreaking and thievery—not to speak of perhaps murder—to his curriculum."

"I can explain, Father!" cried Max, nearly jumping out of his chair. "It was not—"

"Please, Max," interrupted Allegra. "I appreciate your desire to help, but your father is speaking to me." She turned to face the earl. "You are entirely justified in your anger, sir. I had no right to involve Max in such a dangerous undertaking—"

"She had no choice! I blackmailed her."

Wrexham's left eyebrow raised slightly.

"I found the rope and pistol in her trunk and forced her to tell me the whole story," continued the lad. "Then I told her if she didn't let me help her, I would come and tell you everything."

"Max," she repeated gently, "that is no excuse for my actions." Again she forced herself to face the earl. "I have no right to expect any quarter from you, my lord, but might I at least ask you not to inform the magistrate about who was responsible for tonight's activities. I shall pack my trunk immediately, and if you wish, I shall take myself from your house without delay, though I would be grateful if I may wait until first light—"

The lad couldn't restrain himself any longer. "Lord Sandhill is a bloody scoundrel! He stole a very valuable book from Miss Allegra's father, and she needs to get it back so she can use the proceeds from its sale to set herself up as an independent lady," he exclaimed. "You have always told me that a gentleman should act honorably and that it is his duty to see that those less fortunate than he are protected from wrong. If you knew the truth, you wouldn't be angry with me!"

"Your father isn't concerned with the details, Max. Nor should he be. And I hardly think he is in the mood to be regaled with a tale of my personal woes. It is very late, and I think we all wish the night to be over."

"But—"

Allegra heaved an exasperated sigh. "Max, may I have a word in private with your father?"

The lad's eyes darted from the earl's stern countenance to Allegra's rigid features.

"Very well," he muttered. "But I shall wait right outside in case you should need me."

Wrexham repressed a twitching at the corners of his mouth.

As soon as Max had left the room, Allegra drew in a long breath. "Please, my lord, the fault is all mine in this affair. Max was only trying to do what he thought was right. If anyone is to be birched, it should be me."

"I have never in my life birched Max, Mrs. Proctor. In my experience, any living creature treated in such a manner either learns to hate the person wielding the rod or becomes broken in spirit. Neither is a condition I would wish on my son." There was a slight pause. "Nor have I ever birched a female," he added. "Though in this instance I am sorely tempted." His eyes narrowed as he uttered under his breath, "I understand in certain circles it is considered quite . . . stimulating."

Two spots of color came to her cheeks, and her chin rose a fraction. "It is most ungentlemanly to mention such a thing, no matter how much I deserve your scorn," she said with as much dignity as she could muster.

The earl's lips compressed as he remembered that however frayed his patience might be, he was still speaking to the daughter of a respectable clergyman. "Your pardon," he muttered.

His fingers began to drum on the polished surface of his desk.

She expected another scathing set-down to follow, but Wrexham remained silent for what seemed to be an inordinately long time. Instead, it was she who ventured to speak again.

"As for not birching Max, let me say that you are an even better father than I had thought."

He looked surprised. "You think me a good father?"

"A most excellent one, my lord. You have taken the time and consideration to raise a son any gentleman would be proud of. I only hope you will not be too severe with him over his misplaced sense of chivalry. His intentions were all that is honorable. As I said, the lack of judgment was mine."

With a harried sigh, Wrexham leaned back in his chair. "He's a good lad," he allowed. Unconsciously, his right leg stretched out toward the warmth of the fire. Allegra didn't miss the slight grimace that pulled at his mouth, and her brows drew together in concern.

"I'm truly sorry. I've caused you to aggravate your leg."

He started to change position. "No!" she cried. "Please, try to remain comfortable." Her voice was tinged with genuine concern.

"It's nothing, really," he said, flexing it gingerly. "Must have twisted it when I landed."

"It *was* quite a height," she said gravely.

His lips twitched at the corners. "You need not remind me of how high it was, Mrs. Proctor," he said dryly. In fact, it took a concerted effort to retain a stern countenance at the recollection of his earlier predicament.

She ducked her head to hide a smile of her own at

the image of the Earl of Wrexham dangling ten feet in the air from the end of a rope.

"Well." His tone had softened somewhat. "I suppose I had better hear the whole of it, else Max will accuse me of being unjust."

Allegra contemplated the toes of her boots. "I hardly think it necessary, sir. What difference could it possibly make? I acknowledge my wrong in involving Max, and I shall explain to him that you are entirely in the right in turning me out. Besides," she added, "I have humiliated myself enough in your eyes tonight—I never intended to impose my personal problems on you."

"Mrs. Proctor, let me be the judge of what I would like to hear. Since my recent actions—and those of my son—are deserving of transportation, at the very least, if the authorities got wind of them, I feel I have earned the right to know why."

Allegra twisted uncomfortably in her seat, and her fingers played with the worn buttons on her oversize coat.

"Well?"

It was with a visible effort that she forced herself to speak. "I . . . I am searching for a way to tell you without seeming overly melodramatic."

At that the earl gave a bark of laughter. "Finding my son and a female disguised as a man scaling the walls of a lord's manor in the dead of night to break into a hidden safe is already the stuff of horrid novels, so you needn't worry about being melodramatic."

She couldn't help but give a ghost of a smile. "Oh, dear, I suppose it did appear rather gothic."

"Quite." His eyes betrayed a flash of real humor. "Besides, I admit that my curiosity is now piqued."

"Very well." Her voice was barely above a whisper. "I suppose the story really began a little over a year ago. Lord Sandhill has a large estate in Kent, in the neighborhood of the rectory where my family lived, and my father owed his living to him. His lordship's son is— I shall be blunt—an unbridled, unprincipled young man whose propensity for reckless behavior is matched only by his father's amusement at what he views as harmless

sowing of oats by his heir. In vain did my father try to
counsel some temperance of behavior, only to be laughed
at by both of them.

"One day my younger brother tried to stop the viscount from . . . forcing himself upon one of the local
girls. Robert was hardly older than Max, and was never
a sturdy lad, but he had spirit." There was a catch in
her throat, then she went on. "Of course he was no
match for the viscount. My brother was beaten within
an inch of his life. He never really recovered from his
injuries, and some weeks later caught an inflammation
of the lungs and died."

Wrexham interrupted her. "One of the local girls?"
he asked softly.

Her face drained of color as she avoided his eyes.
"Yes."

"How did he dare touch you, the vicar's daughter, and
a married woman as well?" The anger had disappeared
from his voice.

She sighed, surprised that the earl had been so perceptive. "I believe his words were something to the effect
that no one would care about an old hag who had already been . . . used before."

The earl's lips compressed in a tight line. "Please, go
on."

"My father was broken with grief. Within a matter of
months, he, too, passed away." Her hands were clenched
so tightly together in her lap that the nails nearly drew
blood.

"What of the rest of your family? Your . . . husband?"
As Wrexham spoke, he realized with a start that he
knew nothing about the particulars of her marriage. She
had never made mention of it.

She blinked. "My mother died when Robert was born,
and my husband had been gone for quite some time.
There was no one else."

The earl remained mute.

"Forgive me if I seem to have digressed, but it has a
bearing on what has taken place tonight. My father was
hardly in his grave when I returned to the rectory to
find all my belongings piled in the dust with Lord Sand-

hill's orders to take myself off by dusk—he ordered me to be off from my home of twenty-eight years without so much as a day's notice.

"There was just one thing. Lord Sandhill had always lusted after a particularly rare book that he knew to be in my father's possession. It had been passed down through my family for generations, and naturally my father refused to part with it, no matter the price he was offered. Does it surprise you when I say the book was nowhere to be found among my things?" Allegra finally raised her eyes to meet Wrexham's, a look of defiance turning their color a hard malachite. "I vowed then and there to get back what was rightfully mine. I went to live with a widowed cousin of mine in London and tried to figure out how to gain entry to Sandhill's town house. Before I could make any headway, I learned he had taken himself off to his estate in Yorkshire for the summer. I was at my wits' end on how to proceed, other than languish in town for months, taking advantage of my cousin's generosity. Then I saw your ad for a tutor— or rather, Max's ad—and, well, you know the rest."

The earl's jaw worked once or twice. "Hell's teeth," he muttered as he stared into the dying embers. An unreadable emotion flashed in his eyes.

"I hope I might prevail on you to permit me one last favor, my lord—that is, assuming you will agree to not turning me over to the authorities," she ventured. "May I be permitted to have John Coachman convey my trunk to the inn? I can ill afford to lose what possessions I have with me."

There was a long pause before he answered. "Go to bed, Mrs. Proctor," he said softly. "I shall expect to see you present yourself in the breakfast room at eight."

"Thank you, sir. I am well aware of how generous you are being." She made to rise, then started as she caught sight of the back of his hand. "Why, you're hurt!"

He stared down at the ugly red furrow. "Oh, that." He had forgotten about the pistol shot. "It's nought but a scratch."

"Nonsense!" Without thinking, she reached for his

hand and gently pushed back the cuff of his shirt. "It needs to be cleaned and bandaged, my lord."

He began to protest, but she cut him off.

"Don't stir from that chair. I shall be back in a moment," she ordered in her best schoolroom manner, then hurried toward the door.

Wrexham heaved a sigh and settled back in his chair, trying to put out of his head the vision of those long legs clad in skintight breeches.

In a short time, Allegra returned with a basin of steaming water, a length of clean linen and some basilicum powder. Setting these down on the desk, she fetched another branch of candles and moved her chair around next to his.

"Sir, kindly remove your jacket."

Wrexham shrugged out of the garment and let it drop to the carpet.

Without further ado she rolled the sleeve of his shirt up to the elbow. Taking up a soft sponge from the hot water, she began to clean the wound. The earl watched her slender fingers move deftly at the task. Their touch was firm, yet gossamer soft—a most pleasant sensation.

His brows came together as he sought to banish the notion. "Don't think to turn me up sweet with your attention," he growled.

She looked up at him with utter surprise. Then slowly, as it dawned on her what he meant, a look of amusement spread over her face. To the earl's amazement she started to laugh.

"Forgive me, my lord," she managed to sputter after a moment. "I can imagine you have no high opinion of me, but I would have hoped you had not thought me a complete imbecile." As his brows came together, she went on. "I've dragged your son into illegal activities, not to speak of putting him at risk of bodily harm. You have had to ride neck and leather, scale manor walls, engage in fisticuffs with a rather large footman and be the target of gunshots. Really, I would have to be a candidate for Bedlam to think there is *anything* I might do to gain your good graces!"

Wrexham couldn't still the twitch of his lips. "You

forgot the book, Mrs. Proctor. Could you not have picked a less weighty tome? My ribs will no doubt bear the mark for some days."

"I suppose I could have grabbed something less weighty than Shakespeare." Her eyes took on a decided twinkle. "But it seemed like a good omen—it was *All's Well That Ends Well.*"

At that, the earl gave a bark of laughter himself.

She sprinkled some of the basilicum powder over the raw flesh and began to bind his hand with a strip of fresh linen. "Now that we have settled your suspicions, sir, let me also add that Max found your performance tonight quite admirable."

Wrexham cocked one eyebrow. "Indeed?"

"Yes, he said for an old dog, you acquitted yourself pretty well." She tucked the end of the linen snugly into place and rose from her chair. "I must say, I have to agree with him—you were most impressive, my lord, especially for a man of advanced years."

"Good night, Mrs. Proctor," he replied, struggling to keep a straight face. He waited until the she had left before he permitted himself a chuckle.

Then his face turned very grave.

Max speared another piece of bacon. "I won't allow him to turn you out. It isn't fair."

"Your father has been more than reasonable about the matter, all things considered. I'll not have you kicking up a dust with him, Max, do you hear? You are not the only one willing to pay for the consequences of his actions. I knew there were risks involved, and I feel I will have gotten off quite lightly if all your father does is turn me out without reference."

Max's face took on a mulish expression, but he didn't say anything further. Allegra took a sip of her tea and crumbled a bit of toast between her fingers. She had little appetite, despite knowing she should fortify herself for the arduous coach journey back to London—if not jail. Max had no such problem. He requested another helping of kippered herring, then turned his attention to the generous slice of sirloin on his plate. She was grateful that he appeared to be suffering no ill effects from the blow to the head.

The door to the breakfast room opened, and the earl entered, dressed with his usual perfect correctness. Allegra did not miss, however, that he still moved with a slight limp. He took his seat at the head of the table without saying a word and motioned for the footman to fill his cup. A newspaper, lately arrived from London, lay folded by his plate, and he began to peruse the pages as he drank his tea. A simple assortment of toast and preserves appeared from the kitchen and was placed before him.

There was no sound but the clink of cutlery and the rustling of paper for what seemed like an age. Finally, Max began to chafe under the strained silence. He cleared his throat loudly, but drew no response from his father. A stern look from Allegra quelled any further attempt to gain the earl's attention. The lad pulled a face, but contented himself with propping his chin on one hand and stabbing at the remains on his plate with the other.

"Max, kindly remove your elbows from the table," came Wrexham's muffled voice from behind the paper.

Max dropped his fork and straightened in his chair. "Sir, when—"

The page turned with a decided snap, just as Allegra delivered a swift kick to Max's shin. "Let your father finish his breakfast in peace," she whispered when he turned to look at her in surprise.

He pulled a face again, but ceased his squirming.

"Wilkins, bring a fresh pot of tea, then you may leave us."

Max restrained himself from speaking until the servant had departed. "Well, what have you decided?" he demanded. "I care nought for whatever punishment you wish to mete out to me, but it would be grossly unfair of you to turn Mrs. Proctor over to the magistrates—"

"I have no intention of turning Mrs. Proctor over to the authorities," he answered. A ghost of a smile came to his lips. "Even if I did, I should have to include both of us, and I, for one, do not enjoy long sea voyages."

The earl laid his paper aside, the morning sun glinting off the bandage on his hand. "As for you, Mrs. Proctor has seen fit to explain the particulars behind last night's escapade. While I laud your sense of justice, however misplaced, you will have to learn to exercise better judgment in the future. We will discuss this more fully in private, but be assured you will have ample time to contemplate my advice as you help Willy and Jem muck out the stables for the next two weeks."

"Yes, sir," mumbled Max. Then his head came up. "But—" His father's piercing gaze caused him to fall silent.

The earl steepled his fingers and turned his eyes on Allegra. "The charges you have leveled at Lord Sandhill are of a most serious nature."

"Yes, my lord, they are." Her voice was as level as his.

Wrexham pursed his lips. When it was evident she had nothing further to add, he went on. "Despite your questionable behavior in some regards, I have no reason to doubt your story. I intend to make some inquiries of my own into the matter. As for your situation, you may remain here as Max's tutor—"

"I knew you would—"

The earl held up his hand. "Let me finish, Max. If I can be of some assistance in seeing that Mrs. Proctor's property is returned to its rightful owner I will do so, but it will be handled as *I* see fit. There will be no repeat of incidents such as occurred last night. Do both of you understand me clearly?"

Both of them nodded solemnly.

"Good. There is one other matter to settle. I have decided on making a trip to London shortly, and allowing you to come along, Max. Mrs. Proctor shall also accompany us, so that she may travel in a more comfortable manner than by the mail coach. But once in London, I shall engage a more suitable tutor to return home with us."

Max all but leaped out of his chair. "But I don't want another tutor, I want Mrs. Proctor to stay—"

"Sit down, Max," said Allegra sharply. "Your father's

offer is more than fair, and you will cease cutting up his peace over it any longer.''

Max fell back in his seat with an injured expression, but he said no more.

She turned to the earl. "Thank you, sir. You are being most magnanimous.''

Wrexham shifted in his seat, uncomfortably aware that his decision to dismiss her had nothing to do with the events of the previous night. "You have no need to thank me. I am merely doing what any gentleman would feel obligated to do,'' he growled.

A discreet knock came at the door. The earl's butler opened it halfway, but before he could announce the reason for his presence, a heavyset figure of medium height shouldered past him, ignoring all pretenses at politeness.

"Excuse the interruption, Wrexham, but I thought I should warn you of the shocking event that took place last night. A band of thieves attempted to rob West-wood Manor!''

Not a muscle twitched in the earl's face. "Indeed?''

"Aye. Three big, brawny brutes by the account of Sandhill's servants. And vicious, too. Threatened to murder them all. The biggest one hit the head footman a wicked blow to the temple—''

Allegra coughed.

"—while the leader thrashed him to within an inch of his life when he tried to save the female servants from ravishment.''

Wrexham's eyebrows lifted slightly. "Shocking,'' he murmured.

"Only the selfless bravery of the butler and the other footmen enabled them to finally fight the villains off. Naturally we are scouring the area for the thugs, but you had best be on guard.''

"My thanks, Tristley. I shall, but in all likelihood the criminals have thought better of attempting their dastardly deeds around here,'' replied the earl dryly. "I don't imagine they will be heard from again.''

Squire Tristley scowled. "You're probably right—the cowards have probably fled, though I'd dearly love to get my hands on them. They'd soon be sorry they ever showed their ugly faces where I am magistrate."

"I have no doubt of that." Wrexham refilled his cup. "Would you care for some tea?"

"No, thank you for the offer, but I'd best be on my way and warn Baron Knightley at Hillington. Pray, don't disturb yourself," he added hastily as the earl made to rise. "I can see myself out." He caught sight of the bandage on the earl's hand. "I trust you haven't suffered a serious injury, my lord?"

"Not at all," replied Wrexham smoothly. "You know how it is—I was doing something I shouldn't have been doing, but luckily the consequences were not greater. I should suffer no lasting ill effects."

Tristley frowned in slight confusion. "Yes, one must have a care in the country. Well, good day to you, my lord."

As soon as Tristley was gone from the room, Max let out a burble of laughter. "Murderers, ravishers!"

"Max," warned Allegra in a low voice. "Let us drop the subject."

His eyes danced with mirth. "Far be it from me to argue with the biggest, toughest brute of them all."

Allegra put down her napkin. "I think it's time for your lessons, young man."

Wrexham picked up the paper to hide the glint of unholy amusement in his own eyes.

Allegra set her basket down and took a seat on the overgrown stone fence to rest for a moment. She was still trying to make sense of all that had happened. In retrospect, the whole plan to break into Westwood Manor had been a crazy scheme, with little chance of success. Only the earl's timely interference had saved things from becoming an unmitigated disaster. She was lucky not to be moldering in the county jail, with the only prospect for the future a trip to the penal colonies of Australia.

Yes, she certainly owed the earl a debt of gratitude.

Of course there was no question that part of his actions stemmed from his desire to protect his son. Yet that didn't explain everything. He didn't have to let her remain in his household, and he certainly didn't have to offer to help her. That she had never expected—but then, there was a great deal about the Earl of Wrexham that surprised her.

He shrugged off his actions as being what any gentleman would consider doing his duty, but in her experience, most gentlemen seemed inclined to do aught but what suited their own whims. The earl, on the other hand, appeared to be that rare person with a true sense of integrity, of honor. She imagined that he would be a stalwart friend to those he cared for, just as she was sure he would also make a formidable foe. Somehow it had mattered more than she cared to admit that he had believed her tale. The idea of not measuring up in his eyes had been of more concern than any of the consequences he could mete out. Those had been more than fair, she admitted, all things considered.

Allegra shook her head slightly, as if as baffled by her own mixed feelings as well as the actions of his lordship. Why, she found that along with a growing respect for the man, she was actually beginning to . . . like him, despite her resolve to the contrary.

He was aloof to the point of arrogance, overbearing and had little regard for polite manners, she reminded herself. Suddenly, the image came to mind of the earl planting a facer to Lord Sandhill's burly footman, and Allegra smiled in spite of herself. No one could question his physical prowess, she thought, as she pictured the way he had handled the situation with cool aplomb, carrying his son to safety and negotiating the tricky descent while under fire. Those broad shoulders and long, muscled legs had . . .

Two spots of color appeared on her cheeks. That was quite far enough for her thoughts to stray. She could not deny that the Earl of Wrexham was what any female would consider a most attractive man, but that didn't interest her in the least. Men were more trouble than they were worth. The rewards simply didn't justify the sacrifices—in truth, in her experience, the rewards had proven to be . . . rather disappointing.

She gathered up her basket and surveyed the varied leaves and textures of the herbs and flowers. She had nearly everything she needed. It was only a matter of locating some St. John's wort, but the afternoon promised to remain a most pleasant one for a walk through the fields.

Later that evening, Allegra knocked softly on the library door.

"Come in," snapped Wrexham, his eyes not stirring from the book in his lap. "Confound it, Rusher, could not whatever it is wait until—" He looked up at her in surprise.

"Pray, forgive me for intruding on you, my lord. I . . ." Suddenly, she felt foolish and awkward. What had appeared in the light of day a reasonable idea now seemed patently ridiculous. If she could have retreated with a shred of dignity intact, she would have done so.

"Well?"

There was nothing for it but to go on. She placed a glass of liquid on the round table by the side of his wing chair. Wrexham regarded the frothy green contents and wrinkled his nose slightly at the herbaceous odor.

"What in the name of heaven is that, Mrs. Proctor?"

"I . . . well, I spent a considerable time with an elderly woman in our parish who was known for her healing skills. She taught me quite a lot about herbal remedies. This one is particularly good for pain and inflammation. I . . . thought it might be of some help for your knee."

The earl stared at her, then the glass.

"Max told me that you are loath to use laudanum because of its ill effects over time," she continued in a hesitant voice. "This herbal tisane has no such drawbacks and is nearly as effective. I have given the recipe to Cook."

Still he said nothing.

Allegra gave a ghost of a smile. "You need not fear that nightshade is one of the ingredients."

That brought a smile to his lips as well. "Not trying to hasten me to an early demise? It would be most imaginative, and, as I have said, you have no lack of imagination."

"I like to think I have no lack of common sense either, sir. You see, I would have nothing to gain by doing such a thing."

He picked up the glass and eyed its contents. "And what do you hope to gain by this?" he asked softly.

She stiffened. "Its ingredients do not include honey or sugar either," she said tartly. "I have already told you, I have no notion of trying to sweeten you up. If you do not wish to drink it, then by all means, do not." She turned to go. "However, you would be a fool. It works. Good night, my lord."

Her hand was nearly on the door knob when he spoke.

"A moment, Mrs. Proctor."

She turned with a wary expression on her face.

"Thank you."

The color of her eyes lightened. "You are welcome, sir." She regarded his leg propped up on a plump hassock in front of the fire. "I trust that it will bring you some immediate relief."

The door flung open, nearly clipping her on the chin. "Oh, there you are, Mrs. Proctor." Max entered the room, a wedge of apple tart in his hand. "I have been looking all over for you."

"It seems you have been quite thorough in your search. Did you imagine she was locked in the larder?" remarked his father lightly.

Max grinned. "It has been at least two hours since supper," he said as he polished off the last bite. As he wiped his hands on the seat of his pantaloons, the earl rolled his eyes heavenward. "Max, I hope you will not put me to blush with such behavior in London. Your aunts will truly ring a peal over my head for raising a heathen."

The lad caught himself in mid-gesture and reddened. "Sorry," he stammered.

"What did you want to see me about?" asked Allegra quickly.

The lad looked relieved to have the subject changed. "Oh, as to that, I wanted to ask you—" He stopped abruptly. "Ah, perhaps now is not a good time," he went on, slanting a sideways glance at his father.

Allegra took note of the slight hardening of the earl's features. "Not at all," she replied calmly. "Your father and I have just finished with our business."

Max appeared to be studying the subtle patterns of the Oriental rug.

"I'm sure there is nothing you wish to discuss with me that cannot be said here," she continued pointedly.

The lad shifted his weight uncomfortably from foot to foot. "Well, it concerns a certain skill with opening locks," he mumbled. "I . . . was wondering how you learned to do that."

"Never mind," she snapped, now sorry she had pressed him. The earl had more than enough sins to lay at her door, besides thinking she was encouraging his son to further mischief.

To her surprise, Wrexham's mouth began twitching at the corners. "Come now, Mrs. Proctor, surely you don't mean to deprive us of what promises to be a most interesting story. I admit, my curiosity is piqued on how a gently bred female came to add such unusual skills to the normal repertoire of sewing and sketching."

Max's face brightened at the unexpected support. "It would further my education in the ways of the world, would it not?" he said slyly.

It was Allegra's turn to color under the combined scrutiny of father and son. "Really, my lord," she muttered. "I wouldn't think you would wish to encourage such an improper topic."

The earl chuckled. "Improper? In the light of recent events, I might as well give up trying to run a proper household."

She found herself unable to maintain a straight face. "Well, if you put it that way." On taking in Max's eager expression, she relented. "Oh, very well. My cousin Lucy has in her employ a coachman who, along with a special knack for horseflesh, possesses certain other talents. In his youth he . . . tried a few other professions before deciding that his present position offered the best prospects for a long and comfortable life."

"Your cousin sounds like a most fascinating person," remarked the earl.

"Oh, she is," assured Allegra.

"What does her husband think of her—"

"Naturally, she is a widow."

The earl's eyebrow arched in question.

"A man wouldn't allow her to exercise her own judgment in such things."

"Perhaps in this case he would be justified," he murmured.

"A typical male response!" shot back Allegra, feeling there was little need to temper her tongue. After all, she was already turned out. And besides, the earl had asked for it. "John is the most loyal, resourceful servant a person could wish for. Why, he has saved Lucy from any number of unpleasant situations by using his wits and his experience. Of course, a more prejudiced mind would never have given him a chance."

Rather than provoking a fit of anger, her heated words only increased the glint of amusement in Wrexham's eyes.

"Pray, how did she meet this paragon of a retainer?"

Allegra cleared her throat. "She made his acquaintance one night in . . . in the study of her town house. After a rather lengthy discussion, John decided that a change of employers was a most attractive idea."

"I am surprised he was willing to . . . er, enter into such a discourse."

"One doesn't argue too strenuously with a brace of pistols, my lord."

Wrexham gave a shout of laughter. "Remind me to return one of them to your keeping—once we are in London."

"So it was John who showed you how to work the picks?" demanded Max, impatient to hear the particulars.

Allegra nodded. "When I came to stay with Lucy and told her of my plan to retrieve my rightful property from Lord Sandhill, we enlisted John's advice."

"He approved of your plan?" asked Wrexham.

"No, he did not," she admitted. "He informed me that

it was a harebrained scheme likely to land me in the suds, but since he couldn't talk me out of it, he said I may as well be prepared to deal with the obstacles I would face."

"The man had some sense, at least. You should have listened—"

"Is it difficult?" interrupted Max. "The actual task of getting the lock to open?"

Wrexham noted with a wry smile that he couldn't recall seeing his quiet, bookish son so animated on a topic that didn't concern the nuances of an archaic grammar. Somehow he wasn't as displeased as he supposed he ought to be. Why, even he had to admit the subject was getting rather interesting. . . .

"Actually it is not. Once one understands the principles by which the tumblers work, it is a matter of patience and touch," answered Allegra. She tried to repress a little smile of satisfaction. "John said I had a real knack for it."

"Oh, will you give us a demonstration?" Max cast a glance at his father's desk. "Could you, say, open the top drawer?"

"Certainly not!" She forced herself to meet the earl's gaze. "Be assured, sir, I would never—"

"You would be sadly disappointed. No stolen treasures, no purse of gold."

"No passionate billets-doux?" She was immediately aghast at her words.

The earl's jaw tightened. "I am not given to fits of passion, Mrs. Proctor. That sort of romantic fool exists on the pages of Lord Byron's verse, perhaps, but I am not one of them. Now fetch your picks, Mrs. Proctor, assuming you were not forced to abandon them in Sandhill's library. Neither of us shall have a moment's peace until you satisfy Max's curiosity."

She could only hope her face was not as scarlet as it felt. "I will, my lord, on one condition."

Wrexham's brows came together.

She pointed to the glass, standing forgotten on the side table. "Please drink that."

He hesitated for a moment, then drained the contents.

Max made a face as he watched the green liquid disappear. "What was that?"

The earl set the glass down with a thump. "Mrs. Proctor is under the impression that her vast array of skills also includes medicinal ones. In this instance I shall humor her in order that we may see the real display."

Allegra shot him an indignant look before she turned to Max. "It was an herbal tisane that I trust will help alleviate the pain in your father's knee." As she made for the door, she added something else under her breath, drawing a grin from Max. "A pity it does nothing to improve a person's disposition."

When she returned, she undid the ties of the canvas pouch and laid a number of thin metal implements out on the earl's desk.

"It is a matter of feeling the positions of the tumblers, then exerting the right pressure to move them." She went on to explain in great detail certain of the techniques and tricks her cousin's coachman had taught her. By the time the demonstration was over, the earl's desk drawer had been neatly sprung more than a few times.

"Here," she said after the last successful attempt. "Would you care to try?"

Max took the proffered tool and set to work with the sort of rapt expression he usually reserved for translating Virgil. It took a good deal of fumbling and one or two muttered curses, but the lock finally gave way to his efforts.

He looked up, flushed with elation. "I did it!" He snapped the drawer shut. "Let me see if I can do it quicker this time. I'm sure with practice I could have it open in a trice."

Allegra glanced at the earl with a look that announced quite clearly who should bear the blame for the turn things had taken.

On the next try, Max succeeded in manipulating the tumblers nearly as quickly as Allegra had. "Excellent!" He stepped away from his handiwork and offered the thin piece of metal to the earl. "Aren't you going to try your hand, Father?"

Wrexham looked for a moment as if he might refuse

to dignify the proceedings with his participation, but he couldn't resist the challenge. He took the pick and regarded the closed drawer for moment, then with a few deft movements of his long fingers, he caused the drawer to spring open in half the time it had taken the others.

Max's jaw dropped in amazement.

"You are very good at this, sir," she murmured. "Why do I have the feeling that tonight is not the first time you have done this."

The earl schooled his expression to be deliberately bland. "Indeed? I cannot imagine what would lead you to think that." He placed the pick back alongside the others and returned to his wing chair. To his surprise, when he moved, the pain in his leg had lessened considerably. Not only that, when he sank into the soft leather, he felt deliciously relaxed, free of the nagging tension that usually crept upon him late at night.

"Now, if the two of you don't mind, I would like to finish the chapter of my book without further interruption."

"Good night, Father. That was an impressive display." A touch of awe in the lad's tone only increased the earl's feeling of well-being.

Allegra waited until Max had left the room. "Better?" she inquired quietly, noting that the tautness around the earl's eyes had eased somewhat.

"Much." He let out a small sigh as he stretched his limbs out toward the warmth of the flames. "You are truly a female of . . . unusual talents," he murmured.

"Good night, my lord."

His eyes had fallen closed, so he missed the wisp of a smile as she stole from the room.

Chapter Six

At breakfast the next morning, Max failed to inquire about the particulars of the morning lessons for the first time since Allegra had arrived at the Hall. Instead, he badgered her to be allowed to abandon the books for the day and hone his budding skills with the lock picks.

"Perhaps we could try a different sort of lock, like that of the wine cellar."

"Max! I beg of you, don't let your father hear such talk—"

The earl strolled into the breakfast room. "Too late, I'm afraid. I trust you keep your instruments under lock and key, Mrs. Proctor," he said dryly. "I value my supply of French brandy and would take it greatly amiss if anything were to happen to it."

Allegra couldn't help but note there wasn't a trace of a limp to his step. "My lord, you have to admit I'm not entirely to blame for this. Really, I never meant to encourage Max to take up such a . . ."

"Hobby?" he suggested. Motioning for the footman to bring him some tea, he picked up the newspaper by his plate and began to read.

Allegra rose and withdrew something from the pocket of her gown. She marched over and placed the set of picks onto the earl's plate. "You may return those to me when we reach London, along with my pistol," she said in response to Wrexham's startled expression. "I have no intention of fostering any more unacceptable behavior in your son, sir—of that you may be sure."

"I don't believe I made any such accusation," he replied, returning the packet to her hands. "I see no harm in Max expanding his education to include matters of a more practical nature. One never knows when such things may come in handy." He fixed his son with a level gaze. "Naturally, I have your word that you will not take advantage of my trust and trespass where you know you should not be."

"Oh, yes, sir."

"Good." The earl returned to his paper, quite satisfied with how he had handled the situation.

Yes, he thought to himself, it was doing the lad good to take an interest in things other than his studies. Already there was a new spark of enthusiasm about him that had been lacking until . . . well, until the new tutor had arrived. He quickly pushed aside that disquieting thought. It was merely the frisson of adventure that had the lad's eyes agleam. It would be the same in London, with new sights and new acquaintances at every turn. Just because he, too, had a new spring in his step was no reason to admit that life had been a touch flat until the arrival of Mrs. Proctor and her madcap schemes.

He frowned and turned the page with rather more force than necessary, causing Max and Allegra to exchange puzzled glances. The notion of a new spring in his step made him uncomfortably aware of the debt of gratitude he owed her. For the first time in an age he had slept soundly, and this morning his knee was indeed less stiff and painful. And how was he to repay her? By sacking her from a position for which she was eminently qualified? Remembering her remark on prejudiced minds only exacerbated his darkening mood.

Leaving his shirred eggs and bacon untouched, he rose abruptly and left the room without a word to either of them.

Allegra watched him depart with a look of consternation. She had been about to ask after his leg, but the look on his face forestalled any questioning. Good Lord, the man was quixotic—pleasant one moment, irritable as a wounded bear the next. There seemed to be no understanding him—not that it mattered. She wouldn't be around long enough for it to make any difference whether she could fathom the Earl of Wrexham's strange moods.

"Why don't we practice on the old gate leading down to the rose garden?" suggested Max as they crossed from the main entrance and headed for the broad path bordered on either side by tall boxwood hedges leading down through the formal gardens. "The years of rust will only add to the challenge."

The sound of carriage wheels on the gravel drive interrupted Allegra's reply. Both of them turned to observe who was approaching. A smart black phaeton, its wheels and trim picked out in a shade of dark yellow tooled around the bend, drawn by a perfectly matched pair of greys. Max stopped, a smile on his face as he waved a greeting to the fashionably dressed driver.

"Lord Bingham! Father didn't tell me you were planning a visit."

The gentleman drew his team to a halt by the main entrance and jumped down from his perch with an easy grace, motioning for the groom to lead the horses away. "Good day, Max. Some urgent business came up near the border that requires my presence. I'm afraid I sent no warning of my coming, and I must be off again in the morning." His gaze subtly shifted to the stranger, and his eyebrow raised a fraction. "I hope this isn't an . . . inconvenient time."

"I'm sure Father will be delighted to see you," exclaimed Max. Quickly remembering his manners, he turned to Allegra. "Lord Bingham, may I present my . . . er, my new tutor, Mrs. Proctor. Mrs. Proctor, this is Lord Bingham, one of Father's oldest friends."

Lord Bingham swept the curly brimmed beaver hat from his golden locks and inclined a bow in her direction. "A pleasure, Mrs. Proctor." He was much too well-bred to express any overt surprise at Max's announcement, but his eyes fairly danced with interest as he took in Allegra's tall, willowy form and the errant honeyed curls that had eluded the severe bun at the nape of her neck. "You have my sympathy, ma'am," he said with a grin. "I have known Max since he was in the cradle, and

I know what you are up against. I am glad to see that he occasionally releases you from the schoolroom."

In spite of her opinions concerning titled gentlemen, Allegra found herself responding to his open countenance and friendly manner. She returned his smile. "Oh, Max and I have come to an understanding that I believe is mutually agreeable to both of us. I assure you, I do not let him bully me overly."

He regarded her thoughtfully for a moment, then spoke to Max. "Your father is ensconced in the library, no doubt?"

Max nodded.

"Good Lord, Leo is in danger of becoming a dull old dog. Come, let's roust him and have a good gallop before nuncheon—that is, if I am not interrupting lessons?"

"I believe Max will suffer no ill effect by putting off his . . . current studies until a later date," said Allegra.

Lord Bingham winked at Max. "You know, I found my lessons deucedly boring, but I did not have the advantage of such an amiable tutor."

Max grinned. "Oh, Mrs. Proctor is never boring, I assure you."

Once more, Lord Bingham bowed politely to Allegra. "That is an extraordinary compliment, ma'am, coming from Max. I look forward to hearing more about the progress of his studies."

He and Max then took their leave, and she watched the two of them head back to the Hall, a steady stream of friendly banter trailing in their wake.

Rather than return indoors herself, she decided to continue on through the gardens, welcoming the chance of a solitary walk to order her thoughts. A pensive look crossed her brow as she set out down one of the well-tended paths. When she had arrived at Stormaway Hall, she had been so sure of her opinions, especially those regarding the aristocracy. After all, as a woman of mature years, she felt she had experienced enough of human nature to make such judgments. But somehow young Max—and his father—were shaking the very foundation of her assumptions. The lad was the opposite

of a spoiled, willful child of privilege. And while there
was no question that the earl was maddeningly arrogant,
opinionated and used to having no opposition to his dic-
tates, he was also principled, capable of compassion and,
most of all, fair. Her thoughts lingered for a moment on
the way he had dropped the hulking footman with one
blow, then handled their hasty retreat from the library
with cool aplomb—why, it was quite unfair of his friend
to tease him with being a dull old dog! He had cut rather
a dashing figure throughout the entire mad escapade and
had displayed both quick wit and physical prowess in
extricating all of them from danger.

She sighed. It had been much simpler when she had
been able to regard all of the *ton* as unworthy of respect
or regard. Now she had the uneasy feeling that to dismiss
the Earl of Wrexham as such would prove no simple
matter. A stone bench set back from a circular pool
offered a welcome respite from her trampings, and she
took a seat while continuing to wrestle with her feelings.

Allegra was so deep in thought that she didn't hear
the crunch of gravel until the approaching footsteps were
quite close. Her head came up with a start, but before
she had a chance to reveal her presence, a voice floated
clearly through the tall boxwood hedge that separated
her resting place from the other path. A flush stole over
her face as she realized the topic of conversation. Now
it was too awkward to speak up, and she could only
pray that they would move on quickly. To her dismay,
however, the footsteps ceased.

"Max introduced me to his new tutor." Lord Bingham's voice was rich with humor. There was the chink
of a flint as he lit a cheroot. "How very interesting. Pray,
how did that come about?"

"It is a long story, Edmund," replied the earl through
gritted teeth. "Do not roast me over it—I assure you, it
is trying enough."

Bingham laughed. "You shan't escape so easily, my
friend. I look forward to hearing all the particulars tonight." The pungent scent of tobacco wafted through the
air as he paused to savor the heady aroma. "If I didn't
know you better, Leo, I should ask you whether you are

studying anatomy at night with the tutor," he added lightly.

"Certainly not!" came the strangled reply.

"No, I know you are too much the gentleman to take advantage of someone under your roof, but you could hardly be blamed. She is a most attractive young woman."

"I hadn't noticed," growled Wrexham.

His friend slowly blew out a ring of smoke, then gave a chuckle. "Leo! Not notice those intriguing emerald eyes and interesting curves? You *are* in danger of becoming a dull old dog up here. What do you do for excitement?"

There was an uncomfortable silence.

"Poor Leo. You used to be quite the dashing fellow. But then, I suppose you are getting on in years—"

"I'm only three years older than you," snapped the earl. "And still well able to plant you a facer if you wish to try to draw my cork. Besides," he added, thinking with a note of satisfaction on the past evening, "I am not so far along in my dotage that I can't rise to the occasion when it is required—things are not quite so sadly flat around here as you might imagine."

Bingham raised a hand in mock surrender. "Cry truce! You know I am merely teasing. Though in truth, I should think that a change of scene once in a while might do you good. You know, I am sometimes concerned about how you hide yourself."

"As to that, I'm planning a journey to Town shortly. Max has been pestering me for an age to show him the sights, and I have some other pressing matters to attend to."

"Well, I shall look forward to your company. And shall the intriguing Mrs. Proctor accompany you as well?"

"Save your amorous pursuits for the legion of ladies willing to succumb to your charms," said the earl rather sharply. "I trust you will not try to seduce Mrs. Proctor. Besides," he added with a grimace, "she has no great opinion of any gentlemen with money and titles. Thinks we all have the character and morals of a weasel."

"Indeed? Surely as your employee, she is a bit more charitable toward you—"

"Oh, me in particular she finds arrogant, ill-tempered, high-handed and prejudiced."

"How perceptive," murmured Bingham.

Wrexham merely shot him a black look. "In any case, yes, she will accompany us to London. But only because one of those pressing concerns of mine is to engage a more suitable tutor."

Bingham said nothing for a moment as he rolled the aged cheroot absently between his fingers. "Ah, well, I suppose it couldn't really be expected that a female would be capable of the sort of intellect needed to deal with Max. No doubt the lad is being kind in not announcing she doesn't really pass muster."

"Mrs. Proctor is more knowledgeable, articulate and perceptive than most of the members of White's— though that is not saying much, I fear." The words had come out before Wrexham was aware of what he was saying.

Bingham regarded his friend with a curious look. "Perhaps not. But if that is the case, why do you need a new tutor? Max seems quite satisfied with the arrangement."

A frown creased Wrexham's brow as he stared at the patterns of light and shadow playing over the tall hedge. "It's . . . dash it all, it's not right, that's why. She is a female!"

"Ah, I thought you hadn't noticed."

"You know what I mean," snapped the earl.

"Rather arbitrary of you, Leo," drawled Bingham. "Actually, I should think a gently bred female might be a rather nice civilizing influence on Max as well as yourself, given that the two of you stay hidden away in the wilds here most of the time."

"Hah!" Wrexham nearly choked. "Civilized? You don't know the half!" When his friend raised an eyebrow in silent inquiry, he merely shook his head. "Perhaps over brandy tonight, you shall hear the whole of it, if Mrs. Proctor gives me leave, for as a matter of fact, I wish to ask what you hear of Lord Sandhill in Town."

"Your neighbor? What does—"

"I told you, it is a long story, one in which my son's tutor figures quite prominently."

"Things become more interesting by the minute." He grinned. "Perhaps I've been too hasty in consigning you to the ranks of those past their prime."

Wrexham refused to rise to the bait this time. He merely pulled a face and tapped his crop impatiently against the side of his riding boot. "Put out that vile thing and come along. Max will be waiting at the stables for us."

As their steps faded away, Allegra hoped her face would at some point soon return to its normal hue.

Allegra took a moment to smooth the folds of her navy merino gown before entering the drawing room. The gown was hardly of the latest fashion, but it was presentable enough to sit down to dine with the earl and his guest. When Max had knocked on her door and announced with ill-concealed enthusiasm that both of them were invited to entertain Lord Bingham, she had been loath to accept. Even now, her face burned with embarrassment as she recalled the earlier conversation between the two gentlemen. However, she hadn't had quick enough wits to come up with a plausible excuse, nor had she the heart to disappoint the lad, for his eager expression had told her that he counted on her presence.

Her hand went from the soft wool to check the pins that held her hair. She had dressed it in a style less severe than usual, though no doubt unremarkable compared to the elegant coifs of the belles of the *ton*. Still, she felt less like a governess. Her fingers grazed a few errant curls. Why, Lord Bingham had actually implied that she might be . . . attractive. But recalling the earl's remark brought her feet firmly down to earth. Of course he hadn't noticed. She was nine-and-twenty—well past the age that gentlemen took any interest in a female. With that lowering thought, she gave a wry smile at the very silliness of giving a care to her appearance and entered the room.

The two gentlemen, though not dressed formally for

dinner, looked impeccable with their perfectly tied cravats, tailored coats and pantaloons. For a moment she felt awkward and dowdy in the face of such elegance. Then her chin came up a fraction. They may have money and privilege, she reminded herself, but strip away the trappings of their class and there was precious little to admire.

Wrexham turned from speaking to his friend. An unreadable expression flashed in his eyes before he nodded a curt greeting and inquired whether she would take a glass of sherry. Lord Bingham's reaction was less difficult to decipher. There was a frank approval in his gaze as he bowed and brought her hand lightly to his lips.

"How kind of you to join us, Mrs. Proctor, and save us from appearing crusty old misogynists." He gave her a slight wink as he raised his head, and she couldn't help but respond to his smile. It was genuine, causing the fair skin around his pale blue eyes to crinkle.

His good spirits were infectious, and she found herself relaxing enough to answer him with the same light tone. "I shall endeavor to keep you entertained, sir, but I warn you, I have little of the social graces to which you are accustomed."

Bingham laughed. "Good Lord, I should hope not! Wrexham and Max have assured me I can expect rational conversation from you rather than inane chatter about the weather or the latest French modiste."

She couldn't resist the opening. "But I thought that in your circles no true lady of breeding was supposed to have a serious thought in her head."

Wrexham returned from the sideboard with her sherry. "Unfortunately you are correct. Perhaps it is because most of the gentlemen are equally featherbrained."

Bingham repressed the twitching of his lips. "Ah, is that why you have fled the drawing rooms of Town to rusticate here in the wilds? It is a wonder you allow such a frivolous fellow as me to cross your threshold."

"Mrs. Proctor is not the least interested in why I choose to live where I do," said Wrexham stiffly. "And despite appearances to the contrary, you do have a brain, when you choose to use it."

"I shall do so now. I can see that further comment along those lines will only put you into an ill temper, and this is meant to be a pleasant evening." He turned back to Allegra. "Wrexham is not actually as dull a dog as he might seem. He can be quite lively when he isn't barricaded in his study."

For some reason it bothered her that the earl's friend seemed to think him past his prime. Without thinking about it, she came to his defense. "That is most unfair of you, sir. I assure you, Lord Wrexham is not, as you put it, a dull dog in the least. He does not spend *all* of his time in the library—"

The sound of choked laughter interrupted her words as Max entered the room. "Actually, Father has been spending more time than he would like in libraries." That remark caused Allegra to stifle a laugh. "But not as you might think," she added.

Even Wrexham allowed himself a ghost of a smile.

Bingham cocked one eyebrow. "Well, Leo, you seem to be a lucky dog in having such staunch admirers. There seems to be an interesting story here if you will see fit to tell it."

"That is up to Mrs. Proctor," replied the earl. His eyes met Allegra's. "However, I can vouch for Lord Bingham's discretion, and with his broad circle of acquaintances in Town he may have heard something useful regarding Sandhill."

She nodded her assent. "I trust your judgment in this, my lord. You have my leave to tell him whatever you feel is necessary."

Bingham regarded both of them thoughtfully before speaking. "Why the sudden interest in your neighbor? Thought you couldn't abide the fellow—not that I blame you. Dashed rum sort, if you ask me."

"What do you hear of him in Town?"

"Well, now that you mention it, there have been a few disturbing rumors floating around." Bingham stopped to clear his throat, throwing a pointed look at Max and Allegra.

"Oh, you may as well go ahead," said Wrexham with a sigh of resignation. "No doubt they would find a way to make my life intolerable until I told them."

"Well, over the past few years, Sandhill has begun to play quite deeply at . . . certain gaming establishments. Though he wins occasionally, it is not near enough to cover the losses, which, from what I've heard, have become more and more frequent. Apparently the son is an even worse profligate, and at times the amount of their vowels have reached staggering proportions. The thing is, it's well known the family fortune is on its last legs. And yet the blunt comes from somewhere to pay the debts, for paid they are." He paused, and his mien became quite serious. "The first odd occurrence happened about a year ago. Do you recall how the Duchess of Courtland's emerald necklace disappeared at a house party given by Rockham at his Devonshire estate?"

Wrexham's brows came together. "I vaguely remember reading of it—you know I pay little attention to that sort of thing. But if I recall, there was no evidence of any intruder, and the lady in question is featherbrained enough to have mislaid the bauble."

"Even Her Grace would manage to remember where she put down something worth nearly twenty thousand pounds," said Bingham dryly. "Sandhill was present on that occasion, as he was when the next piece of jewelry was discovered missing at Hiltshire's gathering."

"I imagine a number of the same people made up both parties," pointed out the earl.

His friend nodded. "True enough. But after that, the *modus operandi* changed. Thefts began to occur with regularity among the *ton*, always when the victims were engaged for the evening and the servants either given leave for the evening or occupied in another part of the house—whoever masterminded things had an uncanny knowledge of the habits and schedule of Society." His voice dropped low enough that Allegra had to strain to hear his next words. "You know I enjoy a rather broad circle of friends. Well, whispers have reached me that two men, one older, one much younger, are the ones responsible. My source describes them as 'right flash coves what talk funny'—in short, gentlemen. He tells me the loot is taken by cutter to the Continent, where it is fenced, usually in Paris or in Amsterdam. When pressed for further description of the ringleaders, he claims never to have actually seen them, but from what little he has heard, the pair fits your neighbors."

Max began to say something, but his father cut him off. "Have you notified the authorities about this?"

Bingham shrugged. "You know as well as I that without hard evidence or someone willing to give testimony, it is not a charge that would be taken seriously. But my advice is to stay well clear of the man. He is a nasty piece of business."

"But—" blurted out Max.

Wrexham shot him a warning look as the butler entered to announce that dinner was served, causing the lad to swallow his words. It was with ill-disguised impatience that he managed to keep still until the first covers were removed and the footmen had left the dining room.

"Mrs. Proctor has also been a victim of Lord Sandhill and his son!"

For an instant, Bingham's expression betrayed a flicker of surprise before he composed his features back into the mask of a perfect gentleman. "Indeed?" He slanted a glance at Wrexham. "I would not have thought him so clumsy as to risk preying on a member of your household, Leo. What—"

"What could he have possibly wanted from an impoverished widow?" finished Allegra with an ironic smile. "As it happens, my father possessed a very rare book. When he died, Lord Sandhill contrived to have it . . . fall into his own hands rather than mine. As it was some time ago, I was not in the employ of Lord Wrexham."

Despite the brevity of her explanation, delivered in a calm, steady tone, it was clear that Bingham sensed there were many more layers to the story beneath the simple veneer of her words. He took a sip of claret while regarding her with a penetrating look. "What a shock you must have experienced, to find yourself in the vicinity of your nemesis when you came to take up your position here," he murmured.

A tight smile crossed Allegra's lips once again. "I'm sure you are well aware it is no coincidence that I am here, though it was only by a fortuitous stroke of luck that my cousin saw Max's notice concerning a tutor."

"Max's notice? What the—" exclaimed Bingham. "Dash it all, Leo, I think it is time I hear the whole of this if I am to be any use."

Wrexham didn't miss the slight flush that had stolen over Allegra's features at the prospect of having to endure the telling of all her misadventures. "And you shall be," he replied, "over our port."

Allegra flashed him a look of gratitude from under her lashes, which made him feel oddly pleased.

"But—" remonstrated Max.

"I believe you had promised to tell me of your current studies, Max," said Bingham, smoothly following his host's lead. "I am most intrigued to hear just what sort of challenges Mrs. Proctor is putting before you."

The conversation turned to books. Despite his air of nonchalance, Lord Bingham turned out to be as well read as the earl, and Allegra found her earlier misgivings melting away as he drew her into the conversation. His easy manners also brought out a side of Wrexham she had not seen before. The earl relaxed his usual reserved manner to trade quips and good-natured barbs with his friend. Why, he even laughed at times, the fine lines around his eyes crinkling in mirth, the dark brows relaxed rather than drawn together in a predatory scowl. It was a good thing she was not in the least susceptible to girlish infatuations, she thought, for there was no denying that the earl's smile was rather devastating.

By the end of the meal, Allegra realized that not only had the evening not been the sore trial she expected, but that she had enjoyed herself immensely. Far from treating her as a featherbrain, the two gentlemen had accorded her opinions and remarks the same attention as they gave each other. With a slight pang of longing, she wondered what it would be like to experience such stimulating conversation every evening. But no sooner had the notion crossed her mind than she banished it from her thoughts. In a short time, she would be back in

London, forced to impose on her cousin Lucy's generous hospitality or to find another position, one which surely would not include sitting down to dine with her employer and his titled guests as if she were one of them.

Yes, that would be her fate—unless she could retrieve her father's book.

She stole a sideways glance at the angular planes of Wrexham's face, softened somewhat as he grinned in response to his friend's latest sally. Would he truly help her, or would his words prove no more than idle promises?

Wrexham seemed to sense her scrutiny and turned slightly in his chair. For an instant there was a strange intensity in his eyes before they broke away and he inquired what she thought of Bingham's unflattering comments concerning a noted scholar of the day. With a mental shake of her head, Allegra put aside her musings to rejoin the animated discussion. As Max was quick to add his own lively opinion, his voice warbling between bass and alto in his haste to get out his words, it was another long while before Wrexham pushed his chair back from the table, signaling an end to the meal.

"Why don't we take our port in the library," he suggested to his friend, drawing an indignant look from Max at not being included in the invitation.

"I'm not a child anymore," he grumbled.

Bingham smiled in sympathy at the lad's injured expression. "Patience, Max. You are almost of age. And besides, if you were to join us, you should leave Mrs. Proctor abandoned, which would be most unmannerly."

Max's face brightened considerably. He turned to Allegra. "Would you care for a game of chess before you retire?"

She accepted with pleasure, and the two of them withdrew to the drawing room after a round of polite good nights, leaving the gentlemen free to retreat to the masculine comfort of the earl's library.

Lord Bingham could hardly refrain from laughing. "They did *what*?"

Wrexham smiled himself. "It was not quite so funny

at the time, I assure you, to observe my son and his tutor scaling the walls of Lord Sandhill's manor house in the dead of night."

Another chuckle came from the other man. "I take back all I said earlier about your dull existence. Why, it's quite the stuff of a Radcliffe—or Quicksilver—novel. You were actually shot at?"

The earl held up his bandaged hand. "Any worse and I might have had some rather awkward explaining to do to the local magistrate. Believe me, the two of them heard in no uncertain terms what I thought of such a risky scheme. It's a wonder we aren't all locked up in jail."

"Actually it's a wonder they didn't manage to pull it off, for the fact is, it sounds remarkably well planned." His expression then became very serious as he poured himself another glass of the earl's excellent port. "Mrs. Proctor's explanation is a most disturbing story—if it is true."

Wrexham's eyes narrowed. "I do not doubt her veracity. You have met her—do you?"

Bingham shook his head. "No," he admitted. "Still, I see little that can be done about the matter. It is unlikely that she will ever be able to recover her property, for most likely the book has long ago been sold."

The earl's expression became even more grim. "You don't imagine I intend to let Sandhill get away with such behavior?"

Bingham swirled the tawny contents of his glass, then rose and began to peruse the titles on the nearest shelf. After a lengthy silence he turned back to the earl.

"Leo, I have known you long enough to sense it is not the mere theft of a book that has roused you to such anger."

Wrexham didn't answer for a moment. "The younger Sandhill tried to rape her," he finally said, his voice barely louder than a whisper. "When her younger brother, a lad no older than Max, tried to stop him, Sandhill beat him badly enough to cause his death. Her life has been shattered by a so-called gentleman, one of our own. You expect me to turn away and do nothing?"

"Riding to the aid of a damsel in distress?" His friend smiled faintly. "It seems that deep at heart, you are still a romantic."

"Don't be ridiculous," growled the earl. "I am nothing of the sort. I simply dislike seeing an injustice done, especially by one who already enjoys a privileged life."

"Why not simply give her the money she would have received from the book rather than embark on some risky course of action? Lord knows, you're rich as Croesus and can well afford it."

"That's not the point," replied the earl doggedly. "Sandhill and his son must be punished for what they have done. Besides," he added with a grimace, "I doubt she would accept anything from me. Why, she's made it perfectly clear that she doesn't like me any more than she does Sandhill."

Bingham's eyebrow shot up for a moment, then his dry sense of humor reasserted itself. "Good heavens, Leo, you used to have a modicum of charm."

The earl shot him a black look.

"I suppose that means you have informed her you mean to give her the sack?"

Wrexham shifted uncomfortably in his chair. "Wouldn't be right to be less than honest about my intentions," he muttered. "But in any case, she has no great regard for any gentleman of title—not that I blame her."

Bingham finished off the contents of his glass. "Well, I can see there is no use trying to change your mind on this. When I return to Town, I shall see what else I can discover for you. But have a care, Leo. Sandhill and son will not take any interference into their affairs lightly. And do not underestimate them—I fear they are very dangerous men."

Chapter Seven

Allegra heard the wheels of Lord Bingham's carriage roll away from the entrance of the Hall at some ungodly hour near dawn. Sleep proved elusive after that, as she found herself mulling over the events of the past evening. Her feelings were decidedly mixed. That the conversation had been both stimulating and amusing was undeniable. And that the two gentlemen had treated her with such courtesy, even kindness, was more than she had ever have expected. But more than that, their lordships seemed to be truly concerned over her plight.

She bit her lip in consternation. That didn't make sense. They weren't supposed to care for anything but their own pleasure. Surely, Wrexham would lose interest as soon as it became tedious or inconvenient to think about the matter. And no doubt Lord Bingham, despite his warm manner and friendly words, would forget such an insignificant person as a female tutor long before he returned to his busy life in London. As she had learned more than once over the past year, it wouldn't do to get her hopes up that anyone, except perhaps her dear cousin Lucy, would care enough about her troubles to help.

As she recalled Wrexham's promise to tell his friend the full story over their port, a faint blush once again colored her features. For the second time that day she had become the topic of conversation between the two gentlemen—a most unsettling realization. It was most difficult to have one's personal problems laid bare before strangers. Did they think her a fool? A weakling? Or worse, an object of pity?

But remembering Lord Bingham's words in the garden caused the heat to rise to her cheeks. *Intriguing eyes and interesting curves!* She shook her head slightly. His lordship was no doubt merely teasing his friend when he had called her a most attractive young woman. She knew she was neither. And if she had had any delusions to the contrary, they would have been quickly dashed by Wrexham's reply. An ironic smile played on her lips. The earl's words summed up the matter quite neatly—*I hadn't noticed.*

Indeed, why should he?

And why should it bother her in the least that he hadn't? It didn't, she assured herself as she flung back the covers with a touch more vehemence than necessary. Further sleep was nigh on impossible, so she dressed and quietly left her room, hoping that a brisk early morning walk might chase away such disquieting thoughts.

When Allegra returned and entered the breakfast room, she felt much better and was about to greet Max with a cheery good morning when, to her surprise, she noted the glum expression. Even more revealing of his depressed spirits was the way he was merely pushing the food around on his plate, and the plate of scones that sat untouched by his elbow.

She buttered a piece of toast and sipped at her tea before breaking the silence. "Why the long face? Or would you prefer I didn't ask?"

An elbow found its way onto the table to prop up a jutting chin. "I . . . I wish that Lord Bingham could have stayed longer. It can be rather flat around here without any visitors. Father prefers it that way, but . . . it's so quiet." He heaved a sigh and jabbed at a slice of Yorkshire ham. "Rusher said that when my mother was alive, our London town house was always filled with guests, and there were parties and balls."

Allegra measured her words carefully. "I think you would find such an existence might lose its shine rather quickly—there is rarely an idea of substance discussed or honest opinion given."

Max's brows came together at that.

"You must also realize that maybe it is hard for your father—perhaps such things remind him too much of his loss. Was he . . . very much in love with your mother?"

Max considered the question for some time. "He never speaks of her," he finally answered in a small voice. "But he must have been. I've overheard the servants saying she was called the darling of Society."

She was probably diminutive, with porcelain skin, rosebud lips and raven tresses—not tall and gangly with sun-darkened cheeks and hair neither blond nor brown thought Allegra with a touch of waspishness. And Lord Wrexham probably doted on her every vacuous word.

Then, with a start, she suddenly realized there was no portrait of the lady anywhere in the Hall. That seemed strange, but she shrugged it off and forced her attention back to Max. "Well, I'm sure you will come to appreciate that your father has taught you to value intelligent conversation over the fripperies of Society. I'm sorry you are feeling blue-deviled at the moment, but remember, you will soon have a chance to judge for yourself, for soon you will be journeying to London. There you will get all the excitement that you desire."

His eyes lit up a bit. "I cannot wait, save for that it also means that you—"

"Kindly remove your elbow from your plate, Max." The earl stepped in through the French doors. He looked as if he had just returned from a hard gallop, his hair ruffled around the collar of his riding jacket, the color of his wind-whipped cheeks only emphasizing the rich blue of his eyes. Right now they were fixed with a penetrating intensity on his son. "And sit up straight."

Max's lower lip jutted out. Already in a testy mood, he was quick to take umbrage at the mild reproof. Quite deliberately, he slumped even more in his chair and began to mash his shirred eggs into an unappetizing lump with some bits of kippers.

Wrexham sat down as one of the servants brought him a cup of tea.

Allegra bit her lip, wondering just how much the earl had overheard. But rather than dwell on her own possible embarrassment at having discussed his personal life, she sought to stave off any unpleasant confrontation between father and son. "Max, if you are finished, perhaps we should begin our lessons now. What would you—"

"Max," warned the earl as he looked up.

The lad threw down his fork. "Why bother having manners? There's no one here to see them!" he said bitterly.

"You will apologize to Mrs. Proctor for such a churlish remark," said Wrexham quietly. "Then you will forgo lessons for the morning and take yourself off to your room. If you insist on acting like a child, you will be treated as one."

The lad threw an angry look at his father as he pushed away from the table. "Why can't you be more like Lord Bingham!" he cried hotly. "*He* doesn't treat me as if I am still eight years old. *He* would let me see something of the world." His wildly roving eyes fell on Allegra. "And *he* is not rude to Mrs. Proctor. He wouldn't turn her out just because I wish for her to stay!"

Stifling what sounded suspiciously like a sob, he threw down his napkin and fled from the room.

Though his features were rigidly under control, Wrexham's face turned a shade paler, and his eyes betrayed both hurt and bewilderment.

Allegra shot the earl a look of sympathy. "Pray, do not give Max's outburst too much heed, my lord. I fear he was already out of sorts before you came in. Your words were merely an excuse to give vent to his feelings."

The earl's brow creased. "I hadn't realized he was so . . . unhappy."

She shook her head. "I don't think it is that at all, sir. Lads of his age are at a most difficult stage, neither child nor adult. I suppose they must flail about and challenge authority simply in order to test their own growing muscle."

Wrexham regarded her thoughtfully. "That is quite perceptive of you, Mrs. Proctor."

"My brother—" she began, before abruptly cutting off her words and starting anew. "With your leave, I shall go up and have a word with Max. I'm sure he's already regretting his unwarranted outburst."

Wexham's fingers drummed on the table. "If you think it best." He hesitated a moment. "I would have thought you might enjoy seeing Max and me at daggers drawn."

"Perhaps you find it hard to believe, but I would never wish to see you at odds with your son, sir. Max is . . . well, Max is a very special young man, and you have been an admirable father to him."

The earl looked a bit startled, then his lips compressed into a rueful smile. "But not, it seems, as admirable as my friend." He went on, more to himself than to Allegra, "Edmund has always found it an easy thing to make people like him. You found him pleasant, did you not?"

"Quite," she agreed. "Intelligent and witty as well."

Wexham's eyes narrowed slightly. "Ladies find him extremely attractive."

She couldn't resist. "Oh? I hadn't noticed. But then again, females of my advanced years don't take note of such things."

He looked as if to say something, then pushed away his empty cup and stood up. "I mean to ride over to Lord Sandhill's this morning."

It was Allegra's turn to look startled. "Please, sir, you needn't let Max's words goad you into—"

"Mrs. Proctor, I told you earlier that I meant to look into this matter. Contrary to what you might think of me, I don't require my son's reminder to keep my word." With that, he stalked from the room

It appeared that neither of the Sloanes were in the best of humors this morning.

Max dropped his book and peered out the window. "He's back," he announced, unable to contain the note of anticipation in his voice.

The earl tossed the reins of his stallion to a waiting groom and came inside.

"I wonder what he has learned."

"Perhaps you should wait a bit before—" But the lad was already headed for the stairs. With a sigh, Allegra rose and followed him. If Wrexham was going to be pestered into telling what he had discovered, she might as well hear it, too. But on reaching the door to the library, she paused, seeing that Max was shifting uncomfortably from foot to foot behind the earl's back, uncertain of how to approach his father.

Finally, he swallowed hard and spoke. "Ahh, Father."

Wrexham turned sharply, apparently unaware that his son had entered the room.

"I . . . wish to apologize for my behavior this morning. Mrs. Proctor has—well, it was wrong of me."

"Apologies accepted," said the earl gruffly. "I trust you have offered the same to Mrs. Proctor?"

Max bowed his head. "Yes, sir."

"Then the matter is forgotten."

"There is something else."

Wrexham remained silent.

"What I said this morning," stammered Max, his eyes full of remorse. "I . . . I didn't mean it, not any of it."

The earl's features softened. "It's quite all right."

"No it isn't," said Max doggedly. "I'm sorry I ever said such things. I don't wish Lord Bingham was my father, truly I don't."

"I'm sorry as well if I have seemed unaware of your feelings, Max. And I should hope you would feel free to talk to me about anything that is on your mind. You may be sure I shall give it the attention it deserves. Agreed?"

Max nodded.

"Good. Then let us put this morning behind us." Without turning in her direction, the earl called out to Allegra. "You might as well join us now, Mrs. Proctor. There is little point in keeping either of you in suspense about my visit to Sandhill. No doubt the two of you would worm it out of me shortly in any case."

Allegra stepped guiltily into the room. "I didn't mean . . ."

Wrexham waved her into silence as he perched on the edge of his massive desk. "Don't bother trying to gammon me into thinking you were merely passing by the door," he said with a quirk of his lips.

Allegra looked indignant. "I was going to do no such

thing, sir. I followed Max, but only to make sure that he did not pester you unduly if you did not choose to tell us what happened."

"I see." He cracked a smile, but it was quickly replaced by a more serious expression. "Well, unfortunately, I have little good news to report. Though I gained admittance to Sandhill's library with the excuse of wanting to borrow a certain reference book I knew he possessed, I saw no sign of your rare volume, Mrs. Proctor. And," he added, "I managed a good look at all the shelves."

"You didn't have a chance to check the safe, though," said Max quickly.

The earl shot his son a look that warned him not to contemplate anything along those lines. "No, I did not."

"But you do not think it is there," stated Allegra.

"No," he admitted. "I do not."

She took a deep breath. "I have been thinking on what Lord Bingham told us regarding Lord Sandhill's activities. Do you think it likely that my book is still in his possession at all?"

The earl hesitated only a fraction before shaking his head.

Allegra's hands tightened into fists at her side. "No, I think not either. Well then, I suppose that is that. I thank you for your help, sir, but there appears to be little point in pursuing the matter further. There is nothing to be done." She made to leave, realizing with chagrin that her eyes were stinging.

"Not exactly, Mrs. Proctor."

The earl's words stopped her in mid-step.

"When Bingham returns to Town, we shall see what more he can learn of the rig Sandhill is running. If it can be discovered exactly how the stolen property is disposed of, perhaps there is a chance of recovering some of it."

Allegra's lips curled into a disdainful smile. "Really, my lord, we both know that the authorities won't investigate a man of Lord Sandhill's rank and wealth."

Max's eyes fixed expectantly on his father's face.

"We shall see," replied Wrexham in a low voice. He

stood up and walked toward the fire. "I did learn that Sandhill leaves for London shortly. We shall not be far behind."

The evening was well advanced. Wrexham had been settled in front of the fire with a new scientific text from London for some time when the door of the library opened and his son quietly entered the room.

"Father, you said I might, you know, discuss anything that was on my mind with you."

Wrexham reluctantly wrenched his attention away from the page he was reading. *Damnation.* He was just getting to the critical part of the experiment. "Hmmm?"

"Well, I was wondering, when was the, ah . . . the first time . . ."

"Hmmm?" repeated the earl.

"When was the first time you were with . . . a lady?"

"They were around all the time," he replied impatiently. "I have two older sisters, remember? And my own mother was alive until four years ago." He eyes strayed back to the printed words.

"That's not what I meant." The toe of Max's boot scuffed at the carpet. "You know, *with* a lady. Alone."

The book snapped shut. Max had his full attention now.

"How did it . . . happen?" persisted his son.

"Errr." The earl was caught by surprise. He hadn't expected to have this conversation for another little while.

Max was watching him expectantly. Wrexham closed his eyes for a moment. There was nothing for it but to go on.

"Er, your grandfather took me to . . . to a certain establishment in Town."

The lad's eyebrows came together. "And?"

"Well, there are females—experienced females—who, er, show you how it's done."

Max looked a touch perplexed. "Is it that difficult? From observing things around the stable, I wouldn't have thought . . ."

Wrexham's face became a shade redder. "In regard to men and women, there are certain techniques . . ."

"Techniques?"

The earl wondered why it was that his neckcloth suddenly felt two sizes too small. "I mean, there are ways to ensure that . . . both parties find it . . . pleasurable," he said in a strangled voice.

His son looked utterly fascinated. "Like what?"

Wrexham swallowed hard, regretting his hasty words. "The sorts of things that . . . I mean, well, there are books on that sort of thing."

"Books?" Max's eyes eagerly sought the shelves above his father's head.

"Not here, for God's sake," muttered the earl. "Locked away."

"I should like to have a look at them."

Wrexham forced his eyes toward his son. The lad was nearly as tall as he was, though perhaps not quite as broad in the chest. His features were beginning to take on the chiseled edge of manhood—there was no denying that the opposite sex would find what was happening attractive, to say the least. He heaved a sigh. There really was no way to put it off. Besides, Max now had the means to circumvent the little matter of a locked cabinet.

"Oh, very well."

Then his mouth tightened as he thought about the possible temptations, now that his son was . . . aware of such things. He wouldn't tolerate liberties with the maids or the daughters of his tenants. A true gentleman must understand the code of conduct. A sigh escaped his lips.

"Max, sit down. We had better have a little talk."

Wrexham wiped the beads of sweat from his forehead and poured himself a stiff brandy. It went down in one gulp.

It could have been worse, he mused. He could have had a daughter.

With that chilling thought in mind, he quickly helped himself to another brandy, offering up a silent prayer of thanks as he tossed that one back as well. Slowly, his insides began to relax, and he picked up his book from where it had fallen to the floor. There would have been a touch of humor to the whole situation—if it hadn't been himself having to do the explaining. Well, now that it was over and done with, at least he could try to enjoy the rest of the evening.

A knock came at the door.

The earl's jaw clenched. Surely Max couldn't have any questions as yet. "Come in," he snapped.

Allegra entered the room. "I wondered if I might borrow your copy of Cicero's—is something wrong, my lord?"

"*Nothing* is wrong," muttered the earl, turning the page with a decided snap.

Her brows shot up, but she refrained from further comment. "May I borrow it?" she repeated.

He looked up blankly.

"The copy of Cicero."

He gave a curt wave at the bookcase.

Allegra spent a few minutes searching for the title. "I just passed Max upstairs. Is there a particular reason he was grinning like a Bedlamite?" she asked as she bent over to check another shelf.

"Do I have to endure questions from you, too?" exploded Wrexham. "Is it too much to ask for a little *bloody* peace and quiet in my own home?"

Allegra straightened in surprise. "Forgive me for intruding on you," she said quietly. She started for the door, book in hand.

"Sorry," he muttered. "Forgive my language."

"It's not necessary to apologize. I shouldn't have disturbed you."

"It wasn't that."

She stopped. "Is everything all right with Max? I hope you did not have another trying time with him."

He gave a harried laugh. "I'm afraid everything is *too* right with Max!" His hand raked through his hair. "Can you imagine, he asked me about . . ." Too late, he realized what he was saying.

"About what?"

The earl grimaced. "About . . . relations between a man and a woman."

"Oh, dear," said Allegra, though there was a gleam of amusement in her eyes. "Pray, how did you handle that one?"

"I explained certain . . . er, rudimentary things. And I gave him a few books."

"Books? What sort of books?"

The earl's face turned a most interesting shade of puce. "On, well, techniques and . . . you know what I mean."

She wished she did.

"I see," she remarked blandly. A certain sly sense of humor prompted her to go on. After all, she had nothing to lose—she was already sacked. "How lucky you had such material at hand, my lord. But I suppose at your advanced age there is no harm in at least reading about it."

Before the earl's jaw could return to its normal position, she swept out of the library, making a mental note to check the shelves of Max's study one night after he had gone to bed.

Max carefully placed the polished brass telescope into the small leather bag and slung it over his shoulder. "Are you sure you don't mind coming along? The way is rather rough."

Allegra glanced at his worn clothing, more befitting a stable boy than the son of an earl, then down at her own gown, the oldest she possessed. "I imagine a tear or a streak of mud will be well worth the chance to see these magnificent birds of yours in their nesting place."

He nodded vigorously. "It isn't every day one gets to observe peregrine falcons with their young. It was only by merest chance that I happened to spot the site on Dunster Crag. Now I mean to get a closer look. But I imagine we shall be gone most of the day."

Allegra regarded the bulging package that had appeared from the kitchen. "Cook seems to think we shall be gone considerably longer," she remarked.

Max grinned. "We have to go a good ways on foot,

so we'll need ample sustenance." He tied the bundle up behind his saddle, and the two of them set off on horseback toward the looming moors to the north.

It was a glorious day, and Allegra enjoyed the feel of the fresh breeze on her face as they urged their mounts into a steady canter. An owl let out its ghostly hoot, and high above a hawk circled in solitary search for prey. The furze was beginning to bloom, softening slightly the rugged contours of the rocky landscape. Even without the dash of color, she found the stark wildness appealed to all her senses. Perhaps, she mused, it was because she, too, refused to be meekly tamed by the whim of man.

They rode for sometime without conversation, comfortable with their own thoughts. The trail gradually became steeper, and the horses had to slow their pace in order to manage the tricky footing. When they reached the top of the ridge, Max fell back abreast of her and suggested they stop for a brief rest. Allegra was only too happy to agree, for the view was spectacular. He helped her dismount and they went to sit on a ledge overlooking a stand of thick pine trees that gave way to rough sheep pastures in the distance. Max's attention was grabbed by a rush of wings.

"A merlin, I wager," he murmured as he reached in his bag for the telescope. "I wonder if he has caught a hare down there." He trained the lens on the wooded ravine at their feet. Then suddenly his whole body stiffened as he focused on something to his left.

"What is it?" asked Allegra. She craned her neck over the edge, but could see nothing.

Max's hand shot out and yanked her back to the shelter of a large outcropping of granite. Before she could voice her surprise, he pressed a finger to his lips, then passed her the telescope and pointed to a rough cart path that threaded along the edge of the trees.

"Sandhill's son," whispered Max in her ear, though she needed no help in identifying the tall, stocky figure who had just dismounted from his horse. He seemed to be consulting a piece of paper in his hands.

Her mouth compressed in a tight line as she passed the brass instrument back to Max. The visage of Vis-

count Glenbury was not one she cared to see in person—
she saw it often enough in her nightmares. She couldn't
imagine what he was doing out in this isolated spot. He
did not strike her as a gentleman much interested in
flora or fauna, unless, of course, the fauna wore skirts
and had no one around to provide protection.

The same thought appeared to have occurred to Max.
His brow furrowed in unconscious imitation of his father. "What the devil is he up to?" he muttered as he
observed the other man continue slowly along the rutted path.

Allegra felt a chill come over her. "I don't know, but
let us get away from here."

"Wait!" Max brushed away her hand from his sleeve.
Through the lens of his glass, he saw the shape of another man stepping out from the shadows. "Why, he's
meeting someone!"

She tugged once more on his jacket with some urgency. "Please, Max."

"But this is important. I'm sure there is something
havey-cavey going on here."

"Then let us go tell your father. He'll decide what
to do."

Max snapped the telescope shut and replaced it in his
bag. His face took on a mulish expression. "It will be
too late," he argued. "We'll miss the chance to discover
what their business is."

"Dear God, you can't mean—" Before she realized
what he was doing, Max had twisted out of her reach
and was already over the side of the precipice.

"I mean to follow them. Don't worry—I can take care
of myself." Only the shock of his dark hair was still
visible. "Wait here."

"Oh, Max," she whispered to herself, pressing her
cheek up against the cold slab of stone.

It took her only an instant to make up her mind.

She hurried back to their horses and grabbed up the
reins of Max's stallion. Thrusting her half boot into the
stirrup, she flung herself onto his saddle, hiking her skirts
up so that she could sit astride. As soon as the animal
had negotiated the tricky descent down from the ridge,

she urged it into a full gallop, giving silent thanks that she had overheard the earl arrange a meeting with his bailiff at one of the tenant farms not far off.

She cared not a whit what a hoydenish figure she must have cut as she pulled her lathered mount to a halt in front of the stone cottage, her ankles and more in full view of several astonished men. The earl was among them. With no more than a slight lift of his eyebrows, he stepped forward and took hold of the stallion's bridle.

"Max!" she managed to gasp before he could say a word. "I tried to stop him! Then thought it best to come tell you right away."

The earl regarded her frightened look. "Tell me what?" he demanded, choking down his own rising fears. "Steady now, Mrs. Proctor, I beg of you. Tell me what?"

She caught her breath. "Have no fear, I'm not turning missish on you, sir." Then she quickly explained to him what had taken place.

"Hell's teeth," said Wrexham, his jaw clenched. "Can you show me where?"

She nodded.

He had already signaled for one of the men to bring Ulysses to him, and as soon as he was in the saddle, he waved at her to lead the way.

Conversation was impossible. It was all she could do to keep control of Max's big stallion, driving the tired animal into a breakneck pace back toward the looming moors, the pounding of the horse's hooves echoing the sound of her racing heart. *Dear God,* she prayed, *let him be all right.*

At the point where the trail began to wind upward, she pulled the stallion to a skitterish halt. "We spotted the viscount from there," she called, pointing to the ridge. "But Max climbed down the other side. There is a rough cart track—"

"I know it," said the earl. Without another word, he turned Ulysses and spurred forward. Allegra put her heels into her own mount's quivering flanks and followed him. They skirted a thick copse of stunted oak and Scotch pine and came upon the path where it cut into a narrow ravine between two hills.

Allegra recognized the spot where Max had first seen Sandhill's son and pointed it out to the earl.

He sprung down from his saddle. "Go on back to the Hall," he said curtly.

She slipped to the ground as well. "I'm going with you."

His lips compressed, but he wasted no time in arguing with her. Turning on his heel, he moved off in the direction she had indicated. Allegra picked up the hem of her skirts, cursing once again the constraints of female dress, and hurried after him. They walked in grim silence, the only sound the scrabbling of their feet over the loose rocks and rutted ground. Ignoring her presence, the earl scanned the surrounding woods and hills for any sign of his son.

"Hell and damnation," he muttered under his breath. A slight limp was now evident in his step, but his pace never wavered. "Where the devil is he?"

A few minutes later, Allegra nearly collided with the earl's broad back as he came to a sudden stop. The path took a dip down a steep incline, its surface littered with loose scree. Allegra immediately sensed the problem and came alongside him.

"Put your arm around my shoulder, sir," she said as she slipped her arm around his waist. With her support, he was able to negotiate the unstable footing without mishap.

"Thank you," he muttered. "I—" His voice cut off as he spied what appeared to be a pile of rags up ahead.

She gave a little cry.

Wrexham broke into an awkward run, Allegra right on his heels.

Max was lying facedown. A small pool of blood had formed beneath him, an ugly splotch of dull red on the ochre dirt, and his limbs were utterly still. The earl fell to his knees. Stifling a low groan, he took his son by the shoulders and gently turned him over.

Allegra had to bite down on her knuckle to keep from letting out another cry. Both of the lad's eyes were swollen shut and his cheeks were already beginning to mottle with bruises. His lower lip was badly split, and a trickle of dried blood clung to his scraped chin. The state of his ripped and muddied clothing only hinted at what damage might have been done below.

In the next instant she was on the ground, cradling Max's head in her lap while Wrexham felt gently at the lad's neck for any sign of a pulse.

"Oh, Max," she whispered in anguish as she smoothed the tangled curls from his brow.

As if in answer to her plea, a faint groan escaped from his lips.

The sound caused the earl to let out his breath in an audible rush.

"Thank God." His eyes sought out Allegra's as he removed his coat and covered Max's chest. "I fear that with this damnable leg of mine, I shan't be able to carry him." He glanced back down at his son's battered form. "Besides, without knowing what bones are broken, it may be too dangerous to move—"

"A cart," she said quickly. "We must fetch a cart."

He nodded in agreement, yet seemed frozen in place.

"You can ride faster than I. I'll stay with Max." She looked up at his drawn face. "I promise you, I will guard him with my life. Now go!"

Her words seemed to shake him out of his lethargy. He paused only long enough to give her arm a quick squeeze, then scrambled to his feet and set off, teeth gritted against the searing pain in his leg.

Chapter Eight

Heavy grey clouds scudded in from the west, and the day that had begun so promisingly turned ominous. Allegra added her own short spencer to the earl's garment so that Max would not take a chill. She had already torn several lengths of cloth from the hem of her skirt, then soaked them in the icy waters of a nearby brook in order to clean the worst of the grime from his face and apply a cold compress to the nasty swelling around his eyes. Once or twice he stirred under her touch, his lips moving ever so slightly, as if he were trying to speak. But even that slight effort seemed to exhaust his meager strength. There was no further sign of life, save for the faint rasp of his labored breathing.

It seemed like an eternity before she heard the clatter of wheels coming toward them. The earl leaped down from beside the driver and stumbled over to Allegra.

"Still much the same," she said quickly in answer to the stark question in his eyes. "He hasn't regained consciousness. You have sent for a doctor?"

"Of course I have." He raked his hand through his hair. "It was a lucky thing that work was being done on Renfew's roof. One of the men has taken Ulysses to bring Dr. Graham to the Hall while Watson already had his cart hitched in order to fetch supplies from Hingham. We've brought a board, so that Max may be moved with the least disturbance."

His gaze had never left his son's battered face. As the driver of the cart turned his team and dragged a section of planking from the back of the conveyance, Wrexham took Max's lifeless hand and bent low over his ear. "Steady, lad," he whispered hoarsely. "I'm here with you now."

The two men then carefully shifted Max onto the board and placed it on a hastily arranged pile of straw. Wrexham and Allegra climbed in on either side while the other man hurried to take up the reins. The cart moved off with a lurch.

Wrexham's face betrayed his frustration with the painfully slow progress over the ruts and rocks. He grimaced with every jolt, his hands clamped tightly on the board to absorb as much of the jostling as he could. Allegra put her head down and did the same. In a short time, her hands were raw and bleeding from the considerable effort, but she hardly noticed. All of her attention was riveted on the bruised face that lay so utterly still.

Neither of them spoke a word. What was there to say?

At last the cart track intersected with one of the main roads and the driver dared urge the horses into an easy trot. Still, it was another long while before they turned up the winding drive leading to the Hall. The doctor was already pacing anxiously by the front entrance, and several of the footmen, their faces creased with concern for the younger Sloane, hurried to assist the earl in carrying his son up to his chamber. Allegra trailed in their wake, along with the housekeeper, who carried a large tray with all the items the doctor had requested.

Once Max was laid in his bed, the doctor ordered everyone from the room. "You as well, my lord," he added, indicating that he expected Wrexham to quit the chamber.

"The devil I will," cried the earl. "I mean to stay with my son."

Dr. Graham heaved a sigh, then shut the door behind them.

Allegra stared for a moment at the polished oak that swung closed only inches from her nose, then turned to encounter the worried faces of footmen and the housekeeper, as well as Rusher and a number of the maids who had gathered to await news on Max's condition.

"Rusher, Mrs. Gooding, I think it best if you and everyone else returned to your duties. I shall inform both of you as soon as there is any word concerning Max's condition, but it does no one any good to be milling around here," she said firmly. "Lord Wrexham has worries enough without having to confront a sea of long faces."

No one thought to question her authority to make such decisions. The crowd of servants slowly dispersed, leaving her alone to pace the hallway in silent vigil.

Wrexham held his breath as the doctor carefully cut away Max's bloodied shirt and began his examination. He probed gently around the abdomen, then applied his ear to the lad's chest for a long enough time that the earl feared he may have fallen asleep. Next, his skilled fingers moved slowly over the raw face and made a careful inspection of the skull. Finally, he straightened and sat back on the edge of the bed.

"Several ribs are cracked, but there appears to be no danger of a puncture to the lungs. Neither is there any indication of a rupture to any of the other organs. He's taken a nasty crack to the head, but his pupils are not badly dilated, so I don't believe it dangerous." He returned several instruments to the small leather valise by his side. "Despite the multitude of cuts and bruises, I can find no other serious damage. Max is a hearty young fellow. He will be in considerable pain for the next few days, but I see no reason why he won't make a full recovery."

The earl let out his breath in a rush of relief.

"Of course, head injuries must always be watched for the first few days, and we must guard against his taking a fever or inflammation of the chest in his weakened condition. I shall stop by first thing in the morning, but of course you must send for me during the night if there is any change for the worse." He adjusted the gold-rimmed spectacles perched on his long nose and dropped his voice a level as he began to wind a long bandage around Max's chest. "Have you any idea who could be responsible for such a vicious attack?"

Wrexham's mouth thinned to a tight line, but he didn't answer.

Dr. Graham cleared his throat and removed a small bottle from his bag. He squeezed a number of drops into a glass of water. "Here is a draught of laudanum for when Max awakes. I shall tell Mrs. Gooding the exact dosage on my way out—"

"F . . . Father . . ." came a weak voice.

Wrexham rushed to the side of the bed. "I'm here, Max."

"I'm . . . sorry I disobeyed. . . ."

"It's all right."

The lad's eyes fluttered open, and he essayed a wan smile through his bruised lips. "I suppose I deserve to be birched."

Wrexham smoothed his son's matted locks off his forehead. "We shall discuss that some other time, shall we? Right now I want you to rest."

"He . . . he—" Max's words broke off as he winced in pain.

The earl already had the glass to Max's lips. "Here, drink this," he urged.

Despite a weak protest, he wouldn't allow the lad to push it aside until the last drops were choked down.

"Vile stuff," said Max with a grimace. The expression only deepened as he tried to move his head. "Hurts like the very devil," he muttered as the earl sought to adjust the feather pillows. But in another few moments, his eyes fell shut and he drifted back into sleep.

The doctor lay a hand on Wrexham's arm. "With that amount of laudanum, he should rest comfortably for another few hours, my lord. I suggest you lie down yourself. If you'll forgive me for saying so, you look all done in. I'll send Mrs. Gooding up to sit with the lad for a while."

Wrexham stared down at his disheveled clothing and scraped hands. "Yes, of course," he mumbled, but he made no effort to rise.

"Much as I value your patronage, Lord Wrexham, I have no desire for a second Sloane patient," said Dr. Graham. "Get some rest, sir."

The earl's mouth crooked in a wry smile. "Very well. I promise I shall summon Mrs. Gooding to stand watch for a time."

Knowing he would have to be satisfied with that, the doctor shut his bag and quietly left the room. He was in such a hurry to fetch the housekeeper he didn't notice Allegra standing in the shadows, hands clasped to her breast. Nor did Mrs Gooding, whose ample bulk was, a few minutes later, moving up the stairs as rapidly as the doctor's had descended them. Muttering a steady stream of invocations under her breath, she pushed open the door to Max's chamber and disappeared inside.

It was only when the earl's tall form limped into the hallway that she found the courage to speak.

"How . . . is he?" Allegra's throat was so tight, the words came out as a croaked whisper.

Wrexham's head jerked around. He made a quick nod.

"Oh!" Her hands flew to her face as she took several deep breaths. "Thank God."

The earl moved slowly toward her, his eyes taking in her muddied face, the hair tumbling in disarray from the loosened pins and lopsided state of her dress, with the ragged tear exposing a good deal of one ankle. His brows came together slightly before he spoke. "Max is extraordinarily lucky. His injuries are not as bad as they look, and Dr. Graham expects that he shall make a full recovery."

"That is good news, indeed." Allegra hadn't failed to notice his look. She glanced down at her gown and swallowed. "Forgive my shocking appearance, my lord. I . . . I couldn't bear to go and change until I had news of Max."

"You think I mean to criticize the state of your gown?" he growled as he stopped in front of her. "Mrs. Proctor, without your actions, Lord knows how long Max would have lain there—and what the consequences would have been."

Her mouth quivered. "But, my lord, it's all my fault to begin with. I had no right to involve your son. I was so afraid that Max was—" A sob burst forth as she could hold in her pent-up emotions no longer. To her added mortification, she felt a wetness on her cheeks. "Oh, dear, I . . . I never cry," she mumbled, brushing angrily at her face with her sleeve. But the tears wouldn't stop.

Suddenly, her head was buried in the soft linen of the earl's shirt, and his long fingers were gently stroking her windblown curls. It was a few minutes before her shoulders stopped heaving and she managed to lift her chin from the solid warmth of his shoulder.

"I'm sorry, my lord, I don't know what came over me. I'm not usually such a watering pot."

"No, I don't imagine you are," he murmured, strangely reluctant to release his hold of her.

She straightened and began smoothing at the wrinkles on her sleeve to cover her embarrassment. Wrexham reached out and took one of her hands. He regarded the raw scrapes for moment, then took her firmly by the arm and marched her toward the stairs.

"My lord—" she began.

The earl ignored her protest and guided their steps to the library, where he sat her in one of the large wing chairs by the roaring fire. Moving to the sideboard, he poured a generous amount of spirits into two glasses and thrust one of them into her hands.

"Drink this," he ordered.

She took a tentative swallow and nearly choked. "Wh . . .what . . ." she sputtered.

"Brandy." He drained his own glass. "Every drop, Mrs. Proctor," he added, indicating the contents of her snifter. "I insist—I think we both are in need of it."

She did as she was bade, swallowing the rest of the amber liquid in one gulp. "Oh!" she exclaimed. "It does warm the insides, does it not?"

Wrexham's mouth quirked in a slight smile. He refilled both their glasses and went to stand by the fire.

"Please, my lord," she said softly.

He cocked an eyebrow in question.

"Please sit down. Your leg must be aching abominably—I can't bear to see you standing."

A flicker of surprise crossed his features. After a slight hesitation, he shuffled to the other chair and took a seat. His eyes closed for a moment as he settled into the welcome softness of the leather, then they popped open again.

"What are you doing?" he sputtered.

Allegra was kneeling in front of him. "I am removing your boots, my lord. I'm sure you will much much more comfortable without them." Her fingers began massaging at his bad knee, drawing an involuntary sigh of relief from the earl.

"Better?"

He stretched his stockinged toes out toward the fire. "Much," he admitted. Then he started. "Hell's teeth, your hands, Mrs. Proctor."

She looked down at the various cuts and scrapes as if aware of them for the first time. "It's really nothing. They don't bother me—"

"You will kindly sit back in the chair, Mrs. Proctor." There was no mistaking it was an order.

Allegra reluctantly rose and returned to her seat, tucking her feet up under her as she nestled against the over-stuffed arm. She watched as the earl took another swallow of his brandy and let out another sigh. Their eyes met.

"I meant what I said earlier, my lord," she said softly. "I am so truly sorry for what took place today. Max has become very special to me. If he had been—" Her voice caught, and she shook her head. "I would never have forgiven myself."

"Don't go raking yourself over the coals. You are hardly to blame for the evil nature of Sandhill's son," he answered. "And Max is going to be fine—though it appears I should do well to stand him a few lessons with Gentleman Jackson himself when we reach London," he added lightly, in an attempt to assuage her obvious distress.

"He never would have been in such a situation if it hadn't been for me! I had no right to intrude upon your household and involve Max—and you—in all of this, no matter that I meant no harm to either of you. Be assured that I mean to remove my presence from here immediately so that Max will not take it into his head to do anything so foolish again."

"The devil you will," he snapped. "Whether you like it or not, Mrs. Proctor, I am now as deeply involved in this as you are. Do you think me so fainthearted that I would be run off by the likes of Sandhill and son? I told you before, I meant to keep my promise to help you. And now that they have chosen to strike out at my family as well—" His jaw tightened. "I would follow those two bastards to hell itself in order to see justice done."

A mixture of hope as well as regret sprung into Allegra's eyes.

"So let me hear no more talk of quitting your position here until *I* decide on how we shall proceed."

At that, she essayed a slight smile. "I thought I was already given the sack."

"Not until we have reached London," he reminded her in a gruff voice. "Until then, I still expect you to abide by my wishes."

Allegra took a sip of her brandy to avoid having to give an answer. After all that he had done, it seemed churlish not to agree, but she, too, took her word seriously. The omission did not escape the earl's notice and drew a soft chuckle from him.

"I suppose that is too much to ask," he drawled. "Well, at least let us agree to work together to ensure that those two curs cannot cause any more suffering."

To that she could concur wholeheartedly. Then she started to rise. "I shall go sit with Max—"

"Sit down, Mrs. Proctor. He will not waken for several hours." He regarded her drawn face and the dark smudges under her eyes. "You will take yourself off to your own bed—and I shall brook no argument. Besides, it is not your duty to serve as nurse. I shall stay with him tonight."

"I'm not at all tired," she lied. "I wish to help with Max. Please."

The flinty blue of Wrexham's eyes softened considerably. "Oh, very well. We shall spell each other."

He swirled the remaining brandy in his glass, and his attention seemed to drift to the crackling fire. He stared, lids half closed, into the fire, a pensive look on his face. Allegra curled even deeper into the comfort of the wing chair, unmindful of how frightfully improper a picture she must have presented. Somehow, the earl's presence was oddly comforting—or perhaps it was merely the brandy beginning to take effect. The knot in her stomach began to loosen, and a pleasant warmth started to seep throughout her limbs. Her chin dropped a fraction, then her shoulders began to tilt ever so slightly to the side.

Wrexham smiled to himself at the sight of Allegra fast asleep in his favorite chair. The firelight glinted off the golden highlights in her hair and played over the smooth, high cheekbones and long lashes. Hardly the image of a female of advanced years, he couldn't helping thinking. Why, in repose she looked barely out of the schoolroom herself. There was something achingly vulnerable about the arch of her neck and the way her slender hands clutched together in her lap.

Her lips twitched, and she made a slight cry in her sleep. His smile disappeared as he thought about all she had endured. Yet it hadn't diminished her courage or her determination. Well, he had promised to do all he could to help her put those nightmares behind her, and he meant to keep that pledge.

With a sigh, he took her in his arms and carried her up to her room. And then it was time to turn his attention to his son.

Wrexham's head jerked up with a start. He must have dozed off for just an instant, he thought, as he rubbed wearily at his eyes. The soft flicker of a candle came into focus. Allegra stood over his chair, her face cleaned of the mud and dust, her windblown hair now neatly arranged, her tattered gown replaced by one that smelled faintly of lavender and sunlight.

"I think it is time you heeded your own admonitions, my lord," she said softly. "Go to your own chamber. I shall stay with Max."

"No need. Just closed my eyes for a moment," he mumbled thickly.

Her skeptical expression conveyed what she thought of that farididdle.

"You'll do Max no good if you push yourself to a

state of collapse," she pointed out. Her hand touched his shoulder. "Now go, sir. That's an order. You know you may trust Max to me."

He made a wry face. "I thought *I* gave the orders here." However, he couldn't argue with the sense of her suggestion. He rose stiffly, grimacing slightly as every joint seemed to cry out in fatigue. He gestured to the glass on the small table by the bedside. "When he wakes, try to have him drink that. Check his brow regularly for any sign of fever. And see that the pillows don't shift—"

She took his arm and guided him toward the door, her grip tightening as his knee buckled slightly. "I am no stranger to the sickroom. Rest assured I'll see to everything."

He managed a smile. "I know—what's this?" He stared at the glass she had placed into his hand.

"I made a draught for you. For your leg."

"Good Lord, you needn't feel you have to take care of *both* of us," he muttered as he limped toward the door.

"I don't mind," she whispered at his retreating back.

Max's face took on a mutinous expression. "I don't want to drink another glass of the odious stuff. And I don't want to stay cooped up in bed, with Mrs. Gooding and you fussing over me as if I were not able to lift a finger for myself."

Allegra laid aside the book she was reading out loud to him and fixed him with a steady gaze. At least, she noted, his features were returning to normal, despite the petulant cloud hanging over them at that moment. The nasty swelling had disappeared, the cuts were healing nicely and the worst of the bruises had faded to a dull grey.

"I'm sure you don't. But until Dr. Graham gives leave for you to rise, you will stay where you are, even if I am forced to fetch a length of rope to tie you to the bedposts."

He tried to scowl, but a grin materialized instead. "You would, wouldn't you?"

"Of course." She looked at the stack of other books that lay piled on the floor. "Would you care to hear something else, or would you rather I put the candle out. You must be getting tired since Mrs. Gooding told me you didn't nap before supper was brought up."

"I'm *not* tired—" He made to sit up, but the movement sent a spasm of pain through his ribs, causing him to bite off his words with a sharp intake of breath.

Allegra raised one eyebrow. "You are sure you don't wish to drink the medicine?"

"Well, perhaps one more time," he said through gritted teeth.

She passed him the glass, then stood up. "If you don't mind, *I* am tired. I shall see you in the morning."

"Sorry to be such a bother," he mumbled. "I know it must be deucedly flat to sit here with me for hours on end—I don't mean to be such an ill-tempered companion."

"You know I don't mind."

He flashed her a grateful smile. "Good night then, Mrs. Proctor. And thank you."

"Good night, Max."

It was not really very late, nor was she really as tired as she had led Max to believe. Before retiring to her own chamber, she decided to visit the library to borrow a book she had been meaning to start. There were so many wonderful volumes in the earl's collection. She wished she had a chance to devour them all, for she doubted she would ever have access to such a vast choice ever again. A sigh escaped her lips at that depressing thought. At least the earl had been kind enough to let her run tame among them while she was here.

She was busy perusing the shelves next to the fireplace when the sound of the door opening interrupted her thoughts. She turned around with a guilty start.

Wrexham was standing in the doorway. He had removed his coat and the knot of his cravat was loosened in a casual manner. A book was tucked under his arm.

"Oh! I thought you had already gone upstairs, my lord. I didn't mean to intrude on your—"

"You are always welcome to avail yourself of any book here." He came into the room and stirred the fire until a flame leaped from the banked coals. "Has Max kept you captive till this hour? I'm sorry if he is making life a sore trial for you."

She let out a little laugh. "It is a delight rather than a trial to see him recovering so quickly. But I fear we are not going to be able to keep him abed much longer. I've already had to resort to threats of tying him to the bedposts."

Wrexham chuckled. "Which no doubt you would do."

"Now that is exactly what *he* said. Am I such a harridan, then?"

"Not at all." He put the book down on his desk and strolled over to the sideboard to fix a glass of brandy. "Merely someone with, shall we say, strong ideas and the resolve to see them carried out."

"Ah. Worse than a harridan—a managing female."

The earl's mouth twitched at the corners. "I see I should cease trying to cross verbal swords with you tonight, Mrs. Proctor, for no doubt I will end up neatly skewered in no time." He gestured toward the arrangement of bottles. "Would you care to join me? A brandy, perhaps?"

Allegra shook her head. "You might be required to lug me upstairs again like a sack of grain. I don't believe I have ever apologized to you for that."

"Rest assured you are quite unlike a sack of grain."

Faint color stole to her cheeks. She quickly bent her head and made a show of studying the gilt titles.

"A sherry, then," he continued. Without waiting for a reply, he poured out a glass for her along with a brandy for himself and carried them toward the fire.

She took a moment to select a slim volume of Shakespeare's sonnets from one of the lower shelves, then came around to accept the glass and take a seat by the hearth. As Wrexham sat, stretching out his long legs toward the blazing logs, the grizzled deerhound rose from where he had been slumbering in the shadows and padded toward the earl, stopping first to deposit a rather wet token of his affection on Allegra's hand before greeting his master with a contented whoof.

Wrexham's fingers ruffled the silky fur. "You are one

of the chosen few, you know. Sasha usually tolerates only Max and myself."

"I told you, animals seem to like me."

"Animals and children," murmured the earl with a hint of a smile. He cleared his throat. "I don't believe I have properly thanked you for all you have done for Max. Your quick thinking quite possibly saved his life, and the constant concern and attention with which you attend the sickroom—"

She lowered her eyes. "You need not thank me as if I am performing some duty, my lord. I have become very . . . fond of Max."

He nodded, a strange expression on his face. "I suppose it is that for which I am grateful. My son has not had . . ." His words trailed off as he stroked Sasha's massive chest. The dog wriggled in pleasure. "You—" began the earl, before he stopped abruptly, a tinge of red rising to his cheeks.

Allegra's curiosity was certainly piqued. The notion that Wrexham could be discomfited was intriguing to say the least. "What?"

He shook his head. "Never mind. I was about to make a rather cow-handed remark."

She smiled at that. "Surely you know by now that there is little that can offend me."

His lips twitched in return. "Very well, I was going to say I am sorry that your marriage did not result in your own children. You would be a very good mother."

A stab of sadness and some other emotion altered her face for the briefest of moments, and he inwardly cursed himself for causing her pain. Just as quickly, though, she composed her features. "That is . . . most kind of you to say, sir. However it will never be."

"You may remarry, Mrs. Proctor," he said quietly.

Her face became quite pale. "I have told you, I don't intend taking on the bonds of matrimony again, but if I did, there is no reason to believe I would be any more capable of giving my husband a child than I was before."

He didn't miss the longing behind the matter-of-fact words. Though he knew perhaps it would be best to let the subject drop, he went on, driven by a sudden need to know more about her and her life before she came to Stormaway Hall. "How long were you married?"

Allegra took a deep breath. "Six months. An influenza epidemic swept through our village, and my husband insisted on tending to many of the parishioners. His was not a strong constitution to begin with, so when he contracted a case himself, there was little the doctor could do."

"I'm sorry."

"Max has told me your wife also succumbed to the fever—"

"Yes." The earl's voice was clipped. He immediately steered the conversation back to her. "Your bereavement is . . . recent?"

She shook her head. "Quite some time ago, when I was young. I married at eighteen."

"A childhood acquaintance?" he persisted.

"No. He was my father's curate." A wry expression played on her lips. "He was the first person I had ever met besides my family who expressed an interest in books or ideas. I took his long silences for deep thought and a sensitive intellect. Once we were married, I found out that they were merely long silences."

Wrexham gave a choke of laughter. "Forgive me," he apologized. "I am not making light of it—"

She flashed him a look of understanding. "Absurd isn't it, how foolish we can be in our youth." She hesitated a fraction. "Though I don't imagine you would know anything of that. Max has also told me his mother was both beautiful and lively—everything a gentleman could wish. You must miss her very much."

Allegra wondered if perhaps she had gone too far, for the earl's mouth hardened and he turned to stare into the fire. It seemed as if he did not mean to answer, when finally he spoke. "My wife, Mrs. Proctor, was the most selfish and shallow lady imaginable. I was perhaps a greater fool than you in thinking she would ever care for aught but the next ball or flowery compliment."

She looked confused. "But Max thinks—"

"I see no reason why Max should know of how little his mother cared for his existence." He gave a bitter laugh. "Why, when Max was four, he nearly died from a raging fever. I remember holding him in my arms one evening, his body racked by vomiting, his skin burning to the touch. My wife looked in at his room, dressed to go out, and her main concern was not to sully her new ball gown." His black brows drew together in an angry line at the memory. "No, Mrs. Proctor, I do not miss my wife in the least." A sigh followed. "For two halfway intelligent people, we seem, as you say, to have made some rather ridiculous mistakes in our younger years. I, for one, do not intend to ever again repeat such folly as letting the heart overrrule the head." He wrenched his gaze from the flickering flames of the fire and turned to regard her intently. "But you—do not despair of having children, Mrs. Proctor," he said, abruptly changing the subject. "From my extensive scientific readings and from . . . practical experience on an estate, it can sometime take longer . . ." He broke off, not quite sure how to continue on such a delicate topic.

She smiled tightly. "It is kind of you to imply I may not be . . . barren. But it seems unlikely. Six months should be . . . adequate." A burning curiosity warred with her sense of propriety. "Shouldn't it?" she couldn't help but add in barely a whisper

"Er, that would depend on the, er, frequency . . ."

Allegra sighed. "I imagine that three times is quite—"

Wrexham stared at her in disbelief. "What?"

Her cheeks turned a vivid shade of crimson as her gaze slid to where her hands lay knotted in her lap. "No doubt you think me a wanton, on top of everything else," she stammered. "Is that . . . a lot? Harry felt it was his duty to suppress any weakness of the flesh, but on occasion he could not."

"Good Lord, the fellow must have been a bigger gudgeon than you have indicated," he muttered with some force. "Mrs. Proctor, let me assure you that chances are quite good that you are childless through no fault of your own."

Her eyes came up with a flicker of hope. "You mean . . . was not his behavior . . . normal?"

"Most certainly not. There is nothing shameful or sinful in a husband and wife sharing intimacies."

"I had wondered about that," she said in a small voice. "My mother died when I was quite young, and so there was never a chance to—even with my cousin Lucy, well, it is not the sort of thing one discusses over breakfast."

The earl gave a harried laugh. "No, I should think not," he agreed.

Her hands began to smooth at imaginary wrinkles in her gown in order to cover her jumbled emotions. She suddenly stood up, the book she had chosen clasped to her breast.

"Thank you for the sherry, my lord." Her chin rose slightly, as if to bolster her flagging spirits. "Once again, I have need to apologize to you. I'm afraid I've shown a shocking want of sensibility in discussing such private matters with you. But I suppose by now my highly improper behavior comes as no great shock to you." She drew a long breath. "If you don't mind, I think I shall retire for the night. It has been a long day."

Before he had time to reply, she had fled the room.

He stared at her untouched glass on the side table. She may not need a drink, but he certainly did—perhaps more than one.

The flames had flickered down to mere embers, but the earl had still not stirred from his chair. Not for the first time, his hand raked through his locks, as if in search of exactly what it was that had him so overwrought.

Hell's teeth, she was nearly an innocent, he thought, feeling nothing but contempt for the late Mr. Proctor. And her fears and vulnerability were touchingly like those of a young and inexperienced girl. He would never have expected it from the self-assured, worldly female she chose to appear. But then, he had never really attempted to look behind the mask—after all, she had merely been an employee. He had been smugly satisfied with his own assessment of her character and it had only been by merest chance that he had learned the true details of her life—details that painted an entirely different picture of his son's tutor. It didn't take the gnawing feeling in the pit of his stomach to make him realize he was thoroughly ashamed of himself.

His hand tightened around his glass. Had he really become so blind? First he had missed the subtle changes in his own son, and then he had failed to sense the complex emotions underneath the acerbic intellect of this unusual female who had appeared at his door. Perhaps Bingham's gentle barbs were on the mark. Perhaps in locking away a part of himself he was becoming a different person, one he wasn't sure he liked.

A muttered oath drew the sleeping hound's attention. The big dog raised his shaggy head, then scrabbled to his feet and came to lay his muzzle on his master's lap.

"I'm not sure I deserve your loyalty, old fellow," murmured Wrexham as he scratched behind the animal's ears. "I've been a pompous ass."

His thoughts turned back to Mrs. Proctor. He wasn't sure what about her disturbed him so. It wasn't as if he was unaware of life's vagaries. She had been forced to endure more than her share of pain and suffering—but so had a great many people in the world. That life was not fair was hardly a shock to him. Why, if anything, his own experiences had made him more cynical in that regard.

Yet somehow he found himself feeling she deserved more. Instead of feeling sorry for herself, she had shown spirit and courage in the face of adversity, he thought with an uncomfortable twinge. And her own hardships had not dulled her capacity for compassion, even lo—

His mind froze on the word. Yet there was no doubt that she cared as much for Max as if he were her own child. *Damnation,* she should have children of her own! Why the devil hadn't some man had the good sense to recognize what a unique female she was, a caring, capable woman who wouldn't bore a man after a week of marriage. And damnably attractive too. Contrary to what he had told Bingham, he *had* noticed—more than once.

With a heavy sigh, he wrested his thoughts away from that direction.

Besides, he knew the answer to his question. Most men didn't want a unique female. The rare one who might appreciate her qualities she was highly unlikely to meet, given her situation.

The gnawing within became a little sharper. That his plans for her would only exacerbate her problems did nothing to assuage his already tender conscience. But there was nothing for it. She simply couldn't remain as Max's tutor, though why, he still couldn't explain. It simply wouldn't do. However, he vowed to himself, he would see her comfortably settled before all of this was over. He would make sure she had her precious independence and would not have to take a position of servitude again.

So why didn't that make him feel any better?

It was quite a time later before the large hound heard the tread of his master's footsteps retreating up the stairs to his bedchamber.

Chapter Nine

$\backsim$

Wrexham stared in consternation at the letter in his hands. He had already read it a second time, and his scowl had only deepened. What the devil, he thought, could Edmund be thinking to—

"Good morning, Father." Max limped into the breakfast room, leaning heavily on a cane, Allegra hovering anxiously at his elbow.

The earl's expression brightened considerably, though his brows still puckered in concern. "Hello, Max. Are you sure you should be moving about so much? I should be happy to have a tray brought to your room and have my tea with you."

"I am heartily sick of a tray in my room," grumbled Max. "I don't need to be treated like an invalid anymore."

Allegra rolled her eyes in mock despair. "Well, Dr. Graham did allow as he could get up if he felt able. Unless, sir, you would like to locate a length of rope. . . ."

Wrexham chuckled. "No, I suppose we needn't resort to that." He turned to his son. "As long as you show some sense and do not tire yourself unduly."

The lad nodded a vigorous assent as he slid into his chair. A moment later he was digging into a plate heaped high with gammon, shirred eggs, broiled kidney and a slice of pigeon pie that one of the footman had prepared for him. "Heartily sick of porridge, too," he mumbled between bites.

Allegra and Wrexham exchanges amused looks.

As Max sent his plate back for a second helping of everything, he glanced at the folded sheets of paper lying next to the earl's cup.

"Who is the letter from? Anything of interest?"

Wrexham had momentarily forgotten the pages he had laid aside. "What? Oh, it's from Bingham. Naturally, he inquires as to how you are coming along. He—" The earl stopped short. "He hopes you are feeling better," he finished lamely.

Max laid down his fork. "What else does he say?" he demanded.

Wrexham was uncomfortably aware of two sets of eyes boring into him. "Nothing of note," he muttered. "Sandhill has returned to Town, but we knew that."

Max pulled a face. "There is something you are not telling us."

His father made a show of taking up the freshly ironed newspaper and opening it with a decided snap. Max shot a disgruntled glance at Allegra, but remained silent as he began to chew thoughtfully on a piece of sirloin.

She didn't like the look in his eye—not one bit.

Later that morning, Max made his way into the school-room, where she sat comparing two different translations of Homer. His expression was still cause for concern— Allegra had come to know him well enough to recognize when he was bursting with something to tell her, though at the moment he was taking great pains to appear nonchalant.

She regarded him warily as he gingerly settled onto the comfortable settee by the window.

"Have you read any of E. M. Quicksilver's novels?" he inquired casually.

"Why, Max, I hadn't imagined that sort of horrid novel would have any interest for you. You know, they are supposed to appeal to frivolous ladies of the *ton* who have nothing better to do with their afternoons than immerse themselves in outlandish plots with rather silly heroines and brick-headed heroes who should have more sense than to fall in love with such brainless widgets."

He grinned. "I've read them all."

"So have I," she admitted. "He is better than most, but not quite as evocative as Mrs. Radcliffe."

"I shall give him your opinion next time I see him—he's always interested in what the critics think."

"Hmmm," was her noncommittal reply as she kept her head bent over the texts.

"It's Lord Bingham," he announced after a dramatic pause. "Quicksilver, that is."

Her pen stopped its scratching.

"Nobody knows except my father . . . well, and me, of course," he continued, a note of triumph creeping into his voice at having finally garnered her complete attention. "He has a vivid imagination, does he not? And he knows all sorts of interesting people in Town. For research, he says."

"Does he?" Her voice remained noncommittal. Was it her imagination, or was the lad playing her like a trout on a line? And where had he learned to be so sly in his machinations. A month ago he would have blurted out what was on his mind without . . . She swallowed hard, trying not to feel guilty as she recalled that Lord Wrexham had been worried that Max was *too* staid. Well, that concern could be tossed out the window.

"That's very interesting, Max. It appears Lord Bingham is a man of many talents—"

"Oh, more than you know!" he crowed. "Why, you would be astounded by his latest plot!"

She began to write again. "Then I shall look forward to reading his next volume."

The lad abandoned his show of nonchalance. "Aren't you even a bit interested in what I've learned?" he demanded.

Allegra opened her mouth, but before she could answer, Max continued on, unable to contain his enthusiasm. "It's the most fantastic plan—"

"What is?" she interrupted.

"Why, the plan Lord Bingham has come up with to ensnare Sandhill and son."

She put her pen down. "Is that what is in Lord Bingham's letter?"

"Yes! That's what I've been trying to tell you."

"And you convinced your father to share it with you?"

The lad's eyes dropped toward the floor.

"Max?"

"Not exactly" he mumbled. "But don't be angry with me! We have a right to know what is being discussed. Why, just because you are a female and I am a few years shy of a certain age doesn't mean we should be treated as if we were imbeciles."

On that she had no argument, which, she knew, was what Max was counting on. The lad was fast bridging the gap between child and adult—too fast in this case!

She heaved a sigh.

"I went to see Father in the library and, well, the letter was lying on his desk," he explained. "I . . . I suddenly felt a sharp pain in my side and had to sit down for a moment. Father insisted on fetching my medicine from my bedchamber, and in his absence—"

"Max! That's enough!"

He took on an injured expression. "But you haven't heard the best part!" he protested.

"Nor will I," she said firmly. "That was an underhanded trick to play on your father, one not worthy of a gentleman."

Max had the grace to color.

"And furthermore, I promised your father that I would not engage in any more escapades with you. Lord knows, he's endured more than enough worry over your well-being in the last little while."

"This doesn't involve me," countered Max. "And you agreed not to act on your own here at the Hall. Lord Bingham's plan is contingent on being in London." His eyes took on a gleam as he added one last point. "And remember, Father has already informed you that when we reach London, you will no longer be in his employ."

"Good Lord, your reasoning would put Machiavelli to blush," she muttered. Nevertheless, he had a point. And she had to admit she was intrigued.

Max didn't fail to sense it and sought to press home his advantage. "At least listen to the plan, Mrs. Proctor. What harm is there in that?"

Her last defenses crumbled in the face of curiosity.
"Oh, very well."

Wrexham eyed the clock on the mantel. He had a meeting with his steward out by the south pastures, but there was ample time for taking Ulysses out for a good gallop beforehand. Both of them had spent far too much time cooped up inside of late. He was about to rise when a knock came at the door.

"Come in," he called curtly, adding a curse under his breath. He had been looking forward to the wind in his face.

Allegra entered with Max in tow.

He took one look at their solemn faces and and felt a stab of alarm. "What is wrong? Should I summon Dr. Graham—"

"No, my lord," said Allegra quickly. "There is nothing the matter with Max's health. However, there is something he would like to tell you."

The earl's look of concern changed to one of wariness as he turned to regard his son. "Yes?"

Max fell into a rather prolonged fit of coughing.

"That won't fadge," scolded Allegra. "Neither your father nor I were born yesterday, so you might as well get on with it."

The noise stopped, and the lad shifted his weight uncomfortably from foot to foot. "Ah, Father, I am to apologize for a most ungentlemanly trick. I contrived to have you fetch my medicine so that I could sneak a look at Lord Bingham's letter."

The earl's dark brows rose.

"I know it was wrong," continued Max. "But . . . but you should have shared Lord Bingham's plan with us! Mrs. Proctor has a right to know all that is being discussed about her problem."

Wrexham ignored his son's last outburst and fixed his gaze on Allegra. "I take it Max wasted no time in conveying to you what he had read?"

She nodded.

He let out his breath in an exasperated sigh. "Well, thank the Lord that someone besides me has a modicum of reason in this affair. It is gratifying to see you exhibiting the good sense I have come to expect from you, rather than succumbing to harebrained schemes that—''

"Actually, I think it is a brilliant plan."

Wrexham stared at her, dumfounded.

"I do not approve of Max's violation of your trust, sir. And as I have told you, I do not intend on doing so myself while under your roof. But once I am in London, I fully intend to inform Lord Bingham that I wish to put his idea into action."

"The devil you will!" exploded the earl. "Are you mad? Why, Bingham's plan is no better than something out of one of his horrid novels—''

"They are very good, you know," interjected Allegra. "Though as I said to Max, perhaps not quite up to Mrs. Radcliffe's writing."

"This is no laughing matter, Mrs. Proctor. I don't think you have any notion of the risk involved. It's far too dangerous—I forbid you to entertain even the thought of it!"

Allegra's eyes took on a decided gleam. "Forbid me? And under what authority do you propose to do that?"

He was taken aback for a second.

"May I remind you, my lord, as I am not your—not a member of your family, you have no right to do any such thing." She smiled grimly as she followed up on her advantage. "Have you forgotten that once we reach London, I will not even be in your employment anymore?"

Wrexham's fist came down on his desk. "Then perhaps I shall leave you here in Yorkshire," he said through gritted teeth.

"Then I shall take the mail coach. I have the funds," she replied calmly.

"Oh, hell," swore the earl under his breath. "Sit down, both of you," he demanded. "Let us attempt to discuss this in a rational manner."

"That is a useful idea, my lord, especially if you will stop shouting," murmured Allegra.

"I am *not* shouting," retorted the earl. And, indeed, his tone did modulate to somewhere in the vicinity of a normal conversational level. He regarded the two figures now seated before him with a steely gaze and his long fingers began to drum on the tooled blotter. The tinge on Max's cheeks betrayed his discomfort under his father's quelling scrutiny, but Allegra met the earl's angry eyes without flinching.

He finally broke the uncomfortable silence. "Mrs. Proctor, surely when you take a moment to examine Bingham's idea more carefully, you will see that it is completely out of the question for any number of reasons."

Allegra kept her jaw clamped shut, ignoring the plea of reason in his voice.

When the earl saw that she meant not to answer, he let out a heavy sigh and went on. "First of all, the notion that I should bring you to Town masquerading as a distant cousin, recently bereaved and left a fortune by the obliging deceased, is outside of enough—"

"And why is that?" she inquired rather acidly. "I may not be a proper lady, my lord, but I was raised with a modicum of manners, and have dined out enough in country society to be fairly certain I wouldn't disgrace myself in some drawing room or ballroom. Or perhaps you believe that those of us without title or fortune will always reveal ourselves as inferior in the presence of our betters, no matter what the dressing?" For some reason, the idea that the earl found the very thought of her as a fine lady perpostrous piqued her more than she could explain.

Wrexham's brows came together in confusion. "That is not at all what I meant. That is, I . . . ." His words trailed off as he wondered how in the devil he had been put on the defensive so quickly. "Good Lord, you know very well that I believe no such thing—why you are much more . . ." Again he stumbled over his choice of words. ". . . sensible to be around than most of the *ton*," he finished lamely.

Sensible? Hardly mollifying, she thought, but apparently it would have to do.

The earl was beginning to recover his equilibrium. "It has to do with habits and such—things that would be difficult for you to be aware of. There are any number of pitfalls, Mrs. Proctor, that could give you away—"

"But that's why Lord Bingham has suggested enlisting Aunt Olivia's help!" interrupted Max. "You've always said she has a good head on her shoulders and can be trusted to come through in a pinch. With her help, Mrs. Proctor won't have any trouble learning what she needs to know to be accepted as who she says she is."

Wrexham's eyes closed for a moment, trying to suppress the feeling that, had Bingham been present, he would have cheerfully throttled his friend's neck. Unfortunately, Max was right. His Aunt Olivia was certainly a perfect choice for aiding them in this endeavor. Not only was she clever and capable, but she had an odd adventurous streak that would no doubt lead her to look upon the whole thing as fun! That her husband was away on a diplomatic mission in St. Petersburg for another few months and had taken their two grown sons with him only made matters worse, for there would be no other voice of male reason to moderate what he was sure would be her enthusiasm for the plan.

Why, he wondered balefully as he stole another look at his son's eager face, was he the only member of the family who exhibited any common sense and refused to succumb to wild extremes of emotion?

Clearing his throat, he tried a different tack. "That may be so, Max. But Mrs. Proctor, have you truly considered the real dangers? These are ruthless men you mean to toy with, and they are by no means slowtops. One careless slip of the tongue could put your life at risk. Doesn't that frighten you?"

Allegra's expression didn't waver. "I would be a fool not to realize there are risks, my lord. But I feel that the odds are decidedly on my side."

"And why is that?" His eyes narrowed, and his voice took on a touch of sarcasm. "Do you mean to slip that ancient pistol into your reticule and imagine yourself safe?"

She shook her head. "Certainly not. It is *you,* sir, who tips the balance."

He was completely taken aback.

"Me!" he exclaimed as he scanned her face for any sign that the words were some sort of joke.

Her expression remained quite serious. "Yes, my lord. I think the risk is worth taking, for it is my opinion that Sandhill and his son are no match for us if you will consent to be a part of the plan."

Wrexham started to speak when he caught the look in his son's eyes. He felt a sudden constriction in his chest.

"Of course they aren't," said Max with a note of pride. "If anyone can bring them to justice, it is Father. He is smarter and braver than either of those bast . . . uh, villains."

The earl shifted uncomfortably in his chair. "I . . . suppose Edmund is not entirely out of his head. With certain modifications, it might be possible . . ."

"I knew you would not let them get away with what they have done!" cried Max triumphantly.

Wrexham felt things slipping away from him. "I warn you both that if I agree to go along with this, it is *I* who will decide exactly how we proceed. Is that clear?"

Both of them nodded solemnly.

"And if I feel it is becoming too dangerous, I will put a stop to the whole thing in an instant."

Neither of them raised a word in argument.

"When do we leave for London?" demanded Max, barely able to contain his exuberance.

"I haven't made a final decision," snapped the earl irritably, though he knew quite well what the outcome would be. "And certainly not until you are fit enough to travel," he added, a touch less sharply. "So I suggest you take yourself off and lie down. It appears you've had more than enough exertion for this morning."

Max showed eminent good sense by rising and limping from the room without further argument, though he did give Allegra a surreptitious wink as he went by.

She waited until the lad had shut the library door. "I'm sorry, my lord. I acted in haste without realizing that I might be putting you in an awkward position with Max. I should have discussed the matter with you in private." She sighed. "I know there really is no earthly reason for you to expose your family and yourself to further danger. I would only ask that you do not actively interfere if Lord Bingham agrees to help me put his plan into effect."

"Bingham lacks a practical turn of mind. He's liable to forget some detail or another that could lead to serious trouble," growled the earl.

Allegra regarded him gravely. "He may not be as capable as you, my lord, but please understand that I cannot let the matter rest. I will do whatever I must."

Wrexham cleared his throat. "I have told you before I am quite immune to flattery."

She looked a bit startled, then lowered her lashes. "Flattery? I am well aware that I have little of the wiles or the charms with which to attempt such a thing with a gentleman."

He made no answer, but began drumming his fingers on the desk once again. "Oh, hell," he finally muttered. "I should no doubt be hauled off to Bedlam, but if I'm to keep all of you out of the suds, I suppose I shall have to take charge."

Her eyes came alight with a certain glow. "Thank you, sir," she said simply.

The earl nodded curtly and dismissed her with a brusque wave of his hand.

As he watched her retreating form, the realization dawned on him that his son and his tutor had somehow contrived to have him take on the role of one of those ghastly heroes in Bingham's novels.

He supposed he should feel ill-used, indeed, but somehow the thought of it only brought a quirk of a smile to his lips.

Allegra surveyed the trunks and neatly corded boxes stacked in the corner of the entry hall, which tomorrow morning at first light would be loaded into one of the carriages for the trip to London. The moment was finally here. During the past two weeks she had almost wondered if his grudging acquiescence to Lord Bingham's plan had been conveniently forgotten. He had never brought it up again since the initial discussion and deftly turned aside any of Max's efforts to broach the subject.

Instead, he had immersed himself in estate affairs, spending the days out with his bailiff in the fields and the evenings at his desk in the library, dealing with his ledgers and correspondence.

For her own part, she refrained from raising any further questions on the few occasions she saw him, partly out of guilt for the rather underhanded way in which his promise of help had been secured. But that didn't dampen her curiosity as to what he was thinking about the matter, for she was sure one as sharp as the earl did not move into action without a plan of his own.

Drat the man. Surely, he knew he would have to tell her at some point. Why couldn't he share what—

"Mrs. Proctor."

Allegra started at the sound of his deep voice, causing her candle to flicker wildly in the shadows.

"It's getting late. You should be in your bed. We leave at an early hour."

"Yes, my lord. I . . . I just came down to fix some chamomile tea."

He regarded the steaming cup in her hand, then fixed her with a questioning look. "Will you join me in the library?" It was more a command than a request. Indeed, he didn't wait for a reply but turned on his heel and left her to follow in his wake.

Allegra sat rather stiffly in one of the wingback chairs while he poured himself a brandy and came to stand in front of the crackling fire. She sipped at her herbal tea while he swirled the amber spirits in his glass. A taut silence reigned before Wrexham cleared his throat and spoke.

"I am well aware that chamomile is used when one is experiencing agitated nerves and having trouble falling asleep. If you are having second thoughts, you needn't go through with this, you know."

She put her cup down.

"You would only be showing good sense, nothing else, should you decide to abandon this dangerous scheme."

"You are quite mistaken if you think I mean to back away now. Why, I am more determined than ever to see this out, my lord."

He muttered something incoherent, of which she caught the words "stubborn" and "mule."

Ignoring the interruption, she continued. "If it is you who are regretting your involvement, you certainly may feel free to withdraw."

His dark brows drew together. "I don't go back on my promises, Mrs. Proctor."

"Well, neither do I," she shot back. She could see that her words took him by surprise. "I promised myself that I wouldn't let Sandhill get away with his crimes. I have no intention of stopping now."

The earl muttered something else—this time it sounded suspiciously like an oath—then put his drink down on the mantel and stalked over to his desk.

"Neither, it seems, do any of the other participants in this gothic melodrama!" He gestured to a sheet of paper lying on the blotter. "My sister writes that she is already on her way to take up residence in my town house so that she will be there when we arrive."

Allegra blinked. "I most certainly understand, sir, your irritation at having any more members of your family involved in this."

"I am not irritated, Mrs. Proctor. I am furious."

"Surely, you can explain to her that her presence is not at all necessary—"

"Not necessary! My dear Mrs. Proctor, if you are so blithely unaware of the rules of Society that you think I could take up residence with an unattached, unchaperoned female under my roof, then this proposed charade of yours will not last more than a day," he exclaimed.

"I am well aware of the rules," she said defensively. "I just meant, perhaps we could find someone else."

"Oh? And who might that be?" he inquired, his voiced edged with sarcasm. "I assure you, Bingham will not do."

Her lips pressed together in a tight line.

"And as for knowledge of the rules—I hope I needn't remind you that to be caught in a situation like this, alone in a room with a gentleman, would have the direst of consequences once we are in Town," he couldn't help but add.

A flush of color came to her cheeks. "You have made your point, sir. If your wish is to humiliate me, you may, of course, continue."

He glared at her, but left off, and went on to other matters. "Olivia has already begun to make arrangements for her modiste to be ready to make up a suitable wardrobe as soon as you arrive."

"Wardrobe?" repeated Allegra.

"You can hardly appear in Society in those mousy governess things you insist on wearing here. Not if you wish to be taken for a rich widow."

"I . . . I hadn't thought of that."

"I'm sure there is a great deal you have not thought of concerning this foolish plan," he said acidly.

Allegra's face had gone quite pale, but her chin came up a fraction. "Does your sister mention an amount that she considers sufficient to cover what is necessary. I shall have to inquire of my cousin—"

Wrexham took in the unflinching dignity in her tone as well as the slight tremor of her jaw. "I have already arranged to take care of it," he said quietly.

"No!" She shot to her feet and came toward the desk. "On no account will I accept a farthing of your . . . charity—"

"Consider it a bonus for the outstanding work you have done with my son. It is a common practice for an employer to reward a job well done."

Allegra bit her lip. She couldn't argue with the earl about the need for suitable gowns and such. Her cousin Lucy would no doubt be willing to come to her aid once again, but she had already been obliged to do so much. . . .

"Very well," she said in a tight voice, blinking back a tear of frustration. "We shall decide on an appropriate sum, but any amount over that I shall pay back to you at a . . . future date, if that is acceptable to you."

Wrexham watched the war of emotions on her face and couldn't help but be reminded that she was alone in the world, with no wealth or position to protect her from harm—nothing but her own courage and determination.

His tone softened considerably. "That is quite acceptable."

She was standing close, close enough for him to see how the candlelight refracted off the smoky green of her eyes. He drew in an involuntary breath as she lifted her head and spoke again.

"Perhaps you are right sir," she said in a near whisper. "Perhaps I must give up this plan if it means I must become a burden to others. I—" Her voice caught as a single tear spilled down her cheek. She angrily brushed it away. "Oh, damnation."

The muttered oath caused Wrexham to smile. He took a step closer to her and his long fingers came up to brush away another errant drop. In the flickering light she looked achingly vulnerable. He wanted nothing so much as to soothe away the troubled look on her expressive face. "You cannot face every adversity in life alone, Mrs. Proctor. There is no shame in allowing friends to help you. I am only trying to point out to you how many pitfalls—and dangers—there are to this plan."

Allegra made to speak again, but as her mouth opened, the earl's lips came down upon hers.

The initial shock caused her to go rigid, but as his kiss deepened, she made a soft sound and melted against his broad chest. As his arms tightened around her waist, her arms were suddenly, of their own accord, around his neck, her fingers reveling in the silky feel of his long, raven locks.

"Allegra," he murmured against her throat, pressing a string of kisses along the line of her jaw. " 'Tis a lovely name. I have wished to say it aloud for some time now." He took possession of her mouth once again. This time her lips parted wide for him, and he tasted the lingering sweetness of herbs as his tongue slid deep inside. Hesitantly, her own tongue came up to meet his, and its gossamer touch caused the last shreds of the earl's rigid self-control to unravel.

His hand came up to touch her breast. He felt the nipple harden through the thin fabric of her dress, and the thought that she was responding to his touch fanned the flames of his desire even higher. He pulled her even closer, molding their bodies together.

"My lord," she cried softly.

"Leo," he urged. "I should like to hear my name on your lips."

Her fingers twisted in his hair. "Leo," she whispered near his ear. "Oh, Leo."

Wrexham took two quick steps forward, pushing her right up against his massive oak desk. His hands lifted her onto the polished wood. Then he stepped between her legs, pressing up against her most intimately. The logs on the fire hissed and crackled, echoing the rising heat between them.

As their mouths met in another deep embrace, he pulled at her skirts, hiking them up above her knees. The shapely legs in their demure stockings and garters nearly took his breath away.

"Dear God," he murmured as his palm ran up the inside of her thigh.

Allegra's nails dug into his muscled back. "Leo?" she whispered. "What is happening? I . . . I have never felt like this before."

He gave a low groan. "I'm not sure I have either." Then his hand began to reach down for the fastenings of his breeches. . . .

"Father? Are you down there in the library?"

Wrexham wrenched his lids open. "Dear God in Heaven."

Max's footsteps echoed from the head of the stairs.

With desperate haste, he set Allegra on her feet and stepped away to straighten his coat and the disarray of his shirtfront and cravat. She shook out her skirts and sought to rearrange the front of her dress. His fingers raked through his disheveled hair. She sought to fix the worst of the slipped hairpins. As the door swung open, the earl managed to take up a position by the fireplace while Allegra made a show of studying one of the books around on the other side of the desk.

"Father," said Max. "I was wondering if—oh, I'm sorry. I didn't realize you were here, Mrs. Proctor." He

looked back at his father's rigid face. "Am I interrupting something?"

"Of course not," snapped Wrexham. "That is, we
were merely discussing . . . upcoming strategy."

"Oh." Max frowned slightly. "It's rather warm in here,
don't you think? Perhaps you should bank the fire a bit."

Taking up a poker, the earl jabbed at the logs with
more force than necessary.

"Have you decided on any course of action?" demanded Max. "It's not fair if you keep anything hidden
from me."

"Nothing has been resolved," said the earl in a tight
voice.

Allegra took up a slim, leather-bound volume, then
cleared her throat. "If you will excuse me, my lord, I
believe there is nothing further for us to discuss tonight.
As you said, we must be off at dawn, so I think I shall
leave you two and retire."

Wrexham's head jerked around, but her face was in
shadow, and he couldn't discern her expression.

"Good night, Max." There was the barest of hesita-
tions. "Good night, my lord."

"Good night, Mrs. Proctor." The earl managed to
choke out the words, hoping his voice had some semblance of its normal tone.

The door closed quietly behind her.

"Are you sure the two of you haven't quarreled?"
asked Max with some concern as he approached the fire.

"We have *not* quarreled." Wrexham retreated to the
sideboard. He poured himself a fresh brandy and was
shocked to see the decanter shake ever so slightly in
his hand.

Bloody hell.

"What sort of strategy were you discussing? Maybe I
could—what happened to your neck?"

His hand flew to cover a red mark just above the
collar of his shirt. "Nothing—I must have scraped myself
shaving." Then he threw back the contents of the glass
in one swallow and turned to refill it. "Damnation,
Max." He was perilously close to shouting. "I simply am
in no mood for further questions tonight. Tomorrow is

going to be a long and tiring day. If you don't mind, I'm going to bed as well. I suggest you do the same."

He took up the decanter along with the glass and stalked from the room, leaving his son feeling both puzzled and just a bit miffed.

After the fourth glass, the brandy at last began to take effect, finally loosening the knot in his stomach—not to speak of his groin. With a ragged sigh, Wrexham sat on the edge of his bed and took his head in his hands. Good Lord, how things had come about as they had was still a shock to him. Never in his entire life had he lost control of his emotions like that.

He hadn't meant to kiss her. And he certainly hadn't meant to . . .

A wave of nausea passed over him as he realized that in another few minutes his breeches would have been down around his knees and Max would have walked in on the sight of his father merrily breaking every code of gentlemanly behavior that he had so rigidly drummed into his son's head. He couldn't begin to imagine what Max might have thought. His hands raked through his hair.

And what must Allegra—Mrs. Proctor—be thinking? She had been upset, vulnerable. He had only meant to comfort her, but somehow the light of the candle playing off her quixotic eyes, the glitter of the tear on her cheek, the curve of those full, sensuous lips had, in an instant, transformed his warm words into fiery deeds.

Though there was precious little left, he poured another glass of brandy, hoping to wash away the sweet taste of her mouth on his.

It was no use. It lingered even when his fingers came up to brush over his lips, still bruised with the passion of their embraces.

With a groan he sank back against the pillows. Sleep would be impossible. The best he could hope for was oblivion.

Chapter Ten

The next day dawned grey and chilly, which mirrored the mood surrounding the departure. Max still wore an injured expression over his father's sharp words from the night before, while the earl and Allegra both had the drawn faces and dark smudges under their eyes that bespoke of a sleepless night. Neither of them uttered so much as a word during the loading of the baggage carriage, and, when the time came to set off, Wrexham signaled for his stallion to be brought around instead of climbing into the traveling carriage along with the other two.

Allegra settled herself across from Max, studiously avoiding his questioning look, and let her eyes fall shut. At least for a time she could put off any demand for conversation by pretending to doze off. Though her exhaustion was all too real, she had little hope that sleep would bring a welcome escape from her thoughts, given her agitated state of mind.

What must the earl be thinking of her shocking behavior? Her throat constricted as she recalled his grim expression as he had stalked down the stairs to oversee the preparation of the carriages. Why, he had looked positively sick at the sight of her. She could hardly blame him. When she considered what had taken place last night in the library, she was as appalled with herself as he must be. That a man was subject to certain urges was understood, but that she should have responded with equal abandon was beyond the pale.

She had been aware of what he had been about to

do, and she knew she would have allowed him to take what liberties he desired—nay, if she were brutally honest with herself, she had to admit she would have welcomed them. Surely, he must have sensed that. There could be no question that he now thought of her as no better than Haymarket ware.

She felt the sting of tears against her lids. It hurt to have lost his good opinion of her character. Despite their frequent differences of opinion, the earl had always shown her a certain respect. Why, for a time it even appeared that they had become . . . friends. But now there was nothing to do for it but muster up the courage to comport herself with at least a shred of dignity for the rest of the journey. After that, it hardly mattered. She couldn't imagine she would be around a moment longer than it took the servants to toss down her trunk from the carriage carrying the baggage.

Her thoughts were interrupted by the sound of Max closing his book with a decided thump in the hopes of gaining her attention. A wave of guilt washed over her. Dear God, how could she look Max in the eye? If he had any inkling of what had taken place, he would no doubt be filled with disgust, too. It took all of her considerable resolve to keep from turning into a veritable watering pot. She couldn't, however, stave off the beginnings of a splitting headache that threatened to make the journey even more uncomfortable.

To make matters worse, a spitting rain began to fall, forcing the earl to abandon his mount and take refuge inside the carriage. Muttering a few choice words, he shook the drops of water from the brim of his hat, then flung himself back against the squabs with a grunt and and drew a slim book from the pocket of his coat. Ignoring the others, he snapped it open and focused his gaze on the printed pages.

It was not, she noted, a volume of romantic poetry.

After another hour of jostling along the toll road, the tension within the carriage was as palpable as the damp chill that permeated the air. Finally, Max could tolerate it no longer.

"What is wrong?" he demanded of his father. "Why

are you and Mrs. Proctor acting as if something is amiss if you haven't quarreled?"

The earl didn't raise his eyes from his book. "I don't know what you are talking about."

"What fustian!" said Max, unwilling to let the matter drop.

His father looked up with narrowed eyes. "I would prefer it that you don't indulge in a fit of sullens simply because I choose to read rather than converse at this early hour. It is a long journey, Max. Try to exhibit a little self-control."

"Don't patronize me as if I am a schoolboy," retorted Max. "As if I can't tell something is wrong," he added under his breath.

"Then stop acting like one," snapped Wrexham. "Else I'll order the carriage turned around this instant and take you back to the nursery."

Max let out a gasp of outrage, but Allegra managed to forestall a further outburst by shooting him a warning look. Still, the situation was volatile enough that she felt she had to intervene to head off a real explosion.

"My lord," she said hesitantly. "In all fairness, Max hardly deserves to be spoken to in such—"

The earl's voice rose a notch. "Kindly refrain from telling me how to deal with my son, Mrs. Proctor."

"Don't yell at Mrs. Proctor!" cried Max. "She has done nothing to—"

"That's enough," said Allegra quietly, yet her tone caused Max to fall silent. "Let us not fall to brangling among ourselves." She took a deep breath. "Max, you must try to accept that there are a number of, ah, complex issues concerning this entire venture about which your father and I must come to a mutual understanding. It is not that we have . . . quarreled, it is just that we do not entirely agree on certain things and must work it out between ourselves. You may not understand it, but you must make allowances for it. Rest assured that you will be included in discussions that have bearing on our actual course of action."

Max appeared mollified by her words. "Very well," he said, picking up one of the books at his side. After a moment he added, "I apologize for my outburst, Father."

Wrexham sighed. "I'm sorry I snapped at you, Max. It was indeed uncalled for."

The mood inside the carriage lightened somewhat. Allegra forced a smile to her lips. "What are you reading, Max?" she inquired, initiating a discussion that further coaxed the lad into his normal good humor.

Wrexham stared down at his book, mechanically turning the pages every so often, though they may as well have been written in Hindi for all that he was comprehending. He couldn't help but marvel at how well Allegra dealt with Max. It was uncanny how she had just the right feel for his mercurial moods and was able to coax him back into a good humor rather than having him fly into the boughs at the least provocation. Unlike himself, he thought with a grimace, who lately seemed to elicit only the worst behavior from his son. Well, he seemed to be making a mull of most things these days.

He stole a glance at Allegra as she conversed with Max. *Confound it,* he wished he could tell what she was thinking! Her countenance revealed only her usual outward composure, but he had come to know her well enough to hear the coil of tension in her voice. That, and her steadfast refusal to meet his gaze in the forthright manner he had come to expect was a sign that she was not as unmoved by recent events as she would like to appear.

Did she think him an unprincipled rake—or worse— for his pawing advances? His hands tightened their hold on his book. It was impossible to explain what had come over him in those few moments. Lord knows, he had never experienced such a loss of control before, and it made him rather angry—angry with himself for such incomprehensible behavior, angry with her for turning him so topsy-turvy. . . .

The carriage hit a rut, jostling Allegra's skirts and revealing a touch of ankle. Wrexham's mouth went slightly dry as he recalled the shapely legs beneath the woolen fabric, the way his palm had glided over their silky length.

To his utter dismay, he began to feel a tightness in his groin. Giving thanks that the rain had slackened to a mere drizzle, he rapped abruptly on the trap to bring the carriage to a halt and stumbled out the door. Perhaps a hard gallop in this weather could dampen both his anger and his desire.

The sun was finally breaking through the scudding grey clouds when the horses trotted into the yard of the inn. The ostlers sprang forward to change the team, and Max and Allegra climbed down from their conveyance as the earl bespoke a private parlor from the obsequious landlord. Conversation over nuncheon was excruciatingly civil, the words as stiff as their travel-worn limbs. As soon as was decently possible, Allegra excused herself, voicing the need to take a short stroll before having to submit once again to the confined space of the carriage.

There was a large walled garden behind the inn, and she slipped inside the iron gate, grateful for a modicum of privacy with which to order her thoughts. She had little time to reflect, however, before the crunch of boots on gravel caused her head to come up. The earl came to a stop before her. There were a few moments of awkward silence before he forced himself to speak.

"I feel beholden to offer apologies for my beastly behavior last night."

She noted more anger than contrition in his voice, as she averted her eyes from his black scowl. "You needn't apologize, my lord," she said tightly. "I am well aware that the fault is entirely mine for what occurred."

"What?" he exclaimed, taken completely aback.

"Once again I have shown myself to be quite beyond the pale. My behavior was little better than that of a . . . a lightskirt," she elaborated. "You have every reason to feel that your low opinion of my judgment and my person are entirely justified." She squared her shoulders, unwilling to let him see how wretched she felt. "I . . . I deserve your scorn."

He gave an incredulous shake of his head. "That is hardly what I feel," he answered in a low voice.

"And I could hardly blame you if you wish to rid yourself of my presence as soon as we reach Town. I cannot imagine that you would wish your sister to be exposed to—"

"I told you, I don't go back on my promises. I have no intention of altering our plans."

"But . . ." she began

Any flare of anger in his voice had faded, replaced by a different emotion. "Since your limited experiences have given you an odd understanding of relations between a man and a woman, you must take my word that the blame does not rest with anything *you* did. My actions—" he stopped short, suddenly aware that he had no idea how to explain his actions.

A horn sounded in the courtyard, signaling the arrival of the mail coach. At the piercing note, a number of people began to emerge from the taproom. Out of the corner of his eye, he noticed that Max had also come outside and was looking around in all directions.

He swore in frustration. "Damnation! This is hardly the place to engage in a discussion of this sort—"

"I agree, sir," she interrupted, sparing him the need to go on. "In truth, there is really no need to discuss it any further at all. I'm sure both of us regret the appalling lapse of judgment and will never let such an unfortunate thing happen again." She took a sharp breath. "Perhaps it would be best if we could simply agree to forget the entire sordid incident and proceed with the important matter at hand if you are truly still willing."

His mouth compressed. So she found his attentions "appalling" and the incident "sordid." He stood silent, feeling utterly at a loss as to how to allay her misconceptions, how to express all that he wished to say. With a grunt of frustration, he gave up and nodded curtly. "Very well. Let us not mention it again."

Her eyes still avoided meeting his. "I shall endeavor not to give you any further reason to question my judgment."

Somehow, those words left him feeling precious little satisfaction.

*   *   *

It was a great relief to everyone when the carriage finally pulled up in front of the earl's town house in South Audley Street. The rest of the journey had been rendered even more uncomfortable by unremitting bad weather and a broken wheel spoke that had caused almost a day's delay. The constant jostling and cramped confinement had subdued their spirits even further. By the last day of travel, hardly a word was spoken until they reached the outskirts of the city, where Max, at least, was able to muster up some enthusiasm as the sights and sounds of London began to unroll before him.

Wrexham gave a series of terse orders to the two footmen who hastened down the marble steps to assist their descent from the carriage, then led Max and Allegra into the tastefully appointed entrance hall, where the earl's butler greeted them with a formal bow.

"Welcome back, my lord. I trust you will find everything in order for your visit. Lady Alston informs me that you will staying longer than usual."

Any reply from the earl was forestalled by the rustle of silk as a tall, elegantly gowned lady hurried down the curved stairs.

"Leo! So you have arrived at last." She laid her 'long, slender fingers on the earl's shoulder and presented her cheek for a kiss. "You are looking well. Country life must still agree with you."

"As are you, my dear," murmured Wrexham as he finished his embrace. Despite his fatigue from the days of traveling, his lips curved into a fond smile. "I trust James is well and the boys are not getting into more mischief than usual."

"They will be sorry to have missed your visit—you are in Town so rarely these days." Her attention was distracted by the tall, coltish figure standing behind the earl. "Max!" she cried, abandoning all pretense of ladylike reserve. She flung her arms around the lad's neck and hugged him tightly. "How you have grown! Good Lord, I scarcely recognize you—you are nearly as tall as your father, and just as handsome."

"Aunt Olivia," said Max with a self-conscious grin, "it's nice to see you, too."

Her arm still entwined with that of her nephew, she then turned to Allegra. "And you must be Mrs. Proctor. I trust you will forgive my shocking lack of manners, but I so rarely see my baby brother and dear Max that I cannot refrain from embarrassing them with my hugs and kisses." There was a decided twinkle in her eyes as she extended her hand. "I am Leo's sister, Olivia. I have heard a great deal about you from Lord Bingham, as well as from Leo's letters, and I have been looking forward to making your acquaintance."

Allegra's mouth twitched at the lady's reference to the tall, broad-shouldered earl as her baby brother. The family connection, however, could hardly be missed. Lady Alston had the same arched brows and raven locks as her brother, though hers were more liberally threaded with silver than the earl's. The eyes were perhaps a shade lighter, but radiated the same piercing intelligence. Allegra had the feeling that, like her brother's, they missed very little. With a slight swallow of nervousness, she responded to the other lady's greeting.

"That is very kind of you—especially given what his lordship must have written," she said softly. "I only hope I am not half so troublesome as he says."

Lady Alston gave a delighted laugh. "Oh, I have long since learned that Leo's bark is far worse than his bite."

The earl let out a decided "hmmph."

"But of course," she continued, a glint of amusement in her eyes, "he is far too much a gentleman to write anything disparaging about a lady. He has only told me what a splendid tutor you have been for Max."

Allegra colored slightly. "I can hardly take credit for any of Max's abilities. Rather it is I who must struggle to keep up with his prodigious intellect." She essayed a slight smile. "Slow wits do not seem to be a Sloane family trait."

Lady Alston regarded her thoughtfully for a moment before speaking again. "This promises to become a most interesting conversation, Mrs. Proctor. But I fear I'm being frightfully remiss in my duties as a hostess. I'm sure you must be thoroughly worn out from your journey and would like to freshen up before supper. Let me show you to your room." With that, she released her nephew's arm and led Allegra toward the stairs. "Leo," she called over her shoulder, "Hawkins has everything in order for you and Max. I shall see you both later."

Allegra had not quite known what to expect on meeting the sister of an earl and wife of a marquess. She couldn't help but imagine someone rather intimidating and cool, so it was with great relief that she found Lady Alston to be as charming as her brother was reserved. In fact, she found herself immediately liking the other woman. A sly sense of humor was already quite evident, and despite the light tone, something about her manner left little doubt as to the keenness of her observations. No, Lady Alston was not at all the type of empty-headed female Allegra had feared meeting.

Thanks to Lady Alston's efforts, dinner was a more pleasant meal than any that had been endured during the journey to London. She kept Allegra and Max engrossed with colorful descriptions of all the attractions she meant to show her nephew. Indeed, the lad could soon scarce sit still in his chair as he listened to all of the sights in store for him. She even managed to coax a few smiles from the earl with her pithy comments concerning the latest scandals among the *ton*. However, his moody silence throughout most of the meal drew a raised eyebrow or two from her, though she forbore to make mention of it.

When the last of the courses were removed, Wrexham lost no time in announcing that he would take his brandy in the library.

"I shall come along with you, Leo," she said, ignoring the frown that flitted over his features. "Max, since I would hope your father has not yet encouraged you to partake in that habit, I shall see you in the morning. I think we can manage a trip to see Lord Elgin's marbles after my modiste finishes taking Mrs. Proctor's measure." She turned to Allegra. "Would you care to join us?"

Allegra shook her head. "That is very kind of you, Lady Alston, but I think I shall retire early tonight. It has been a rather . . . tiring journey. Besides, I am sure you and your brother have much to catch up on and would prefer some time alone, so I shall bid you good night now." Without looking at the earl, she added, "Good night, my lord."

Wrexham inclined his head a fraction, then abruptly pushed back his chair and got to his feet.

Allegra's mouth tightened in concern as her eyes followed his retreating form.

"Dear me," murmured Lady Alston as she, too, watched the earl quit the room. "Leo appears to be in a black humor—it is most unlike him. I wonder what has him in such a taking."

Allegra's lips crooked into a pinched smile. "Oh, you needn't look far for the cause," she answered softly. "I fear he is quite ruing the day I appeared on the steps of Stormaway Hall."

"You may pour me a sherry while you are there," said Lady Alston as she took a seat on the brocade sofa that faced the blazing fire. Patting the plump cushion beside her, she added, "Then come sit here beside me and let us have a comfortable coze."

Wrexham turned from the sideboard, a mulish expression on his face. "One which, no doubt, will include waxing poetic over Edmund's fanciful plot," he said waspishly. "Really, Olivia, I would have expected more sense from you. This is no childish game—the dangers are all too real."

Her eyes narrowed. "I am well aware of that, Leo. I saw the marks on Max's face, faded though they are. And Edmund mentioned the shot that grazed your hand. But this monster must be stopped before he hurts more innocent people. If you have a better plan, I am quite willing to listen."

"Damnation," he growled as he handed his sister her sherry. "As of yet, I haven't—that is to say, there have been . . . a number of distractions. But I am sure there is a way I may trap the villain without involving—"

"The ladies?" finished Lady Alston with an arch of her brow. "I don't see why that is such a cause for worry. Mrs. Proctor strikes me as an extremely competent sort of person." Taking Wrexham's silence for a grudging surrender on that point, she continued, "I doubt that either she or I will do anything buffleheaded enough to endanger you—"

"I am hardly concerned about the danger to myself," said the earl through gritted teeth. "Edmund's plan calls for All—Mrs. Proctor to be the one most exposed to Sandhill's wrath should anything go wrong. I cannot countenance such a thing."

"Well, she is not some silly widget of a girl, Leo. I imagine she has considered the consequences. She has a right to decide for herself, whether you like it or not."

The earl's expression only darkened at his sister's words, and he muttered something under his breath as he took a long sip of his brandy. Further comment was forestalled, however, by a light knock on the door.

Wrexham put his glass down with a thump. "Come in," he snapped.

Allegra slowly opened the door. "Forgive me for intruding on you," she said hesitantly, her eyes carefully avoiding those of the earl. Wisps of steam curled up from the large cup in her hands, giving off a pungent scent of woody herbs. "I . . . I saw that your leg is bothering you. The cramped quarters and constant jostling can have done it no good, sir, so I took the liberty of preparing this."

"Oh, Leo!" exclaimed Lady Alston. "With all the bustle of your arrival, I didn't even notice that your old injury was acting up—how frightful of me!"

"Please, Olivia. You know I don't care to have you make a fuss over it," growled the earl.

Allegra put the cup down on the table beside him. "I've left the recipe with the kitchen so that they may fix it in . . . the future, when you have need of it."

Wrexham looked acutely uncomfortable. "You need not have gone to such trouble. It's hardly a twinge." As he unconsciously stretched his leg out in front of him, a slight spasm of pain crossed his features, but he made no move to take up the tisane.

"Really, my lord, you are acting as childishly as Max did about taking his medicine." A note of exasperation crept into Allegra's voice. "It makes no sense to endure such discomfort if it can be helped, and you know that this helps. So I am going to stand here until you drink it." She couldn't help but turn to Lady Alston. "Is being stubborn as a mule also a trait of Sloane men?"

Casting a baleful glance at his sister, the earl picked up the cup and drained the contents.

Lady Alston struggled to maintain a straight face. "I'm afraid it is, Mrs. Proctor, though I must admit the females of our family are equally cursed—just ask Leo." Before Allegra could make any response, she went on. "Come, now that you are here, I insist that you take a glass of sherry with us."

"Oh, I couldn't—"

"Nonsense!" Her tone indicated she would brook no argument. "Leo, you will remain seated and rest that leg of yours," she added as the earl made to rise. "I am perfectly capable of pouring our guest a glass of spirits."

Wrexham sat down as ordered.

It was Allegra's turn to stifle a grin.

"Oh, dear," said Lady Alston with a guilty laugh. "I fear that the habit of ordering little Leo around is a hard one to break. I wonder he hasn't taken to boxing my ears now that he is no longer in leading strings."

"I just might, one of these days," he warned, but he couldn't refrain from smiling as well. "As it is, I find it no surprise that James has undertaken a long trip to St. Petersburg—and that the lads have chosen to go with him. No doubt the prospect of the discipline aboard a naval warship is a welcome respite from home."

"Wretch," she murmured as she handed Allegra a glass. "You might not believe it, Mrs. Proctor, but he can be quite charming when he chooses." Resuming her seat next to the earl, she motioned Allegra to take the chair facing them. "Actually, I am so glad you have joined us tonight. We have much to talk about if we are to implement our plans as soon as possible." With that, she launched into a detailed plan for introducing Allegra into Society that left even the earl mute with respect.

"You seem to have thought of everything," admitted

Wrexham when she inquired whether she had omitted anything of note.

"Good. Now, my modiste will be here first thing in the morning and has promised to have several gowns ready in time for making a number of morning calls before attending the Hightower's ball." She fixed Allegra with an appraising look. "I should think that a smoky shade of blue or perhaps a muted emerald would look marvelous with your coloring. Leo, you must give us your opinion. You have always had impeccable taste, and I know that even Suzanna sought your—"

The earl cut her off in mid-sentence. "I'm sure Mrs. Proctor has no interest in what I think."

Allegra seemed overwhelmed. "Lady Alston, I . . . I don't think it necessary . . . I mean, surely I don't need . . ."

The other lady waved away her protest. "You must trust me to know what you need in order to appear to be what you say you are. Oh, and if we are to present you as our relative, you really must call me Olivia." She paused for a moment. "And you must cease with the 'my lord' and 'sir' and call Wrexham by his Christian name as well."

Allegra felt the heat rise to her face as she recalled the only time she had ever uttered the earl's name.

"Oh . . . I couldn't—it really wouldn't be proper."

"I must insist. It would appear odd if you didn't."

"In that case, I . . . very well," she replied in a near whisper. She put aside her untouched glass of sherry and rose. "If you don't mind, I really do think I shall retire. It has been a long day, and we have much to do on the morrow."

"Good night then, Allegra," said Lady Alston.

"Good night . . . to you both."

When the door closed, there was a rather long silence as Lady Alston regarded her brother from under her lashes.

Wrexham shifted uncomfortably. "What?" he finally demanded.

"Oh, nothing." After a slight pause, she added, "Tell me about Mrs. Proctor."

"There is little to tell," he muttered. "Edmund has recounted the entire story to you."

"I mean as a person."

The earl appeared taken by surprise. His brows came together as he thought for a moment. "Ahem. Well, she possesses a keen intelligence as well as uncommon good sense—that is, most of the time. She has more spirit than most . . . and she is caring and compassionate. Why, when Max was injured, she exhibited more concern than Suz—" His jaw clamped shut. Reaching for his brandy, he took a long swallow before continuing. "It is a pity her brief marriage did not afford her a child. She would be an excellent mother." Then he shrugged. "There is nothing more to tell."

Lady Ashton refrained from any comment.

Wrexham drained his glass, then got stiffly to his feet. "I, too, have had a long day, Olivia, so I think I shall bid you good night." He bent down and pressed a light kiss on her cheek. "Despite your penchant for meddling, I am very glad to see you."

She squeezed his hand. "Good night, Leo, my dear. And try not to worry overly—I have a feeling that everything is going to work out for the best."

Chapter Eleven

Allegra shut the book with a sigh, then let her eyes fall closed as well, savoring a rare moment of solitude in the deserted morning room. The last few days had passed in a blur, with more fittings than she had imagined possible, excursions with Lady Alston to show Max the Tower and Astley's, on top of hours spent going over the nuances of behavior within Polite Society. And then there had been the first few morning calls to a select group of Lady Alston's friends. Since each one chosen could not resist a tempting piece of gossip, news of the arrival of the recently widowed—and extremely wealthy—cousin of the earl should have reached even the most reclusive member of the *ton* by now.

It appeared that she had contrived to get through the ordeal without making any egregious mistake. Why, she had even managed to chatter quite lengthily about absolutely nothing, a feat she would have normally considered quite beyond the powers of her patience. Indeed, Lady Alston had been well satisfied that all was going according to plan.

Another sigh escaped her lips. It was the thought of tonight that had caused the book to slip from her fingers. The prospect of facing a ballroom filled with bejeweled ladies and titled gentlemen—among them Lord Sandhill—was a daunting one. She found herself wondering whether Wrexham would put in an appearance. A familiar face, even a disapproving one, would be of some reassurance. But aside from a few brief glimpses at the breakfast table, she had hardly set eyes on him since their arrival in Town. He seemed to be going to great lengths to avoid being in her presence. Her mouth quirked in a rueful expression. Could there be any doubt why?

But she found herself wishing yet again that she had not sunk herself so irredeemably in the earl's eyes, that she could retrieve the comfortable friendship that had grown between them. She missed their spirited discussions, even though their opinions rarely matched. She missed sitting curled in one of the oversize wing chairs with a book while he worked at his desk.

"Allegra?" Lady Alston poked her head into the room and surveyed the growing shadows near the French doors. "Good heavens, my dear! It is way past time to begin preparing for the evening's festivities. Come along—Clotilde is waiting."

Allegra laid aside the small leather-bound volume with some reluctance and followed the other lady upstairs, feeling not a little unlike a lamb being led before a pack of wolves.

Some time later, Lady Alston's formidable French abigail stepped away from Allegra with a sniff of satisfaction.

"Pas mal," she announced under her breath as she surveyed the results of her labors.

"Clothilde, you are a true *artiste,*" murmured Lady Alston, causing her abigail's ample chest to swell out to even larger proportions.

Allegra stared into the gilt mirror, hardly believing what she saw. Her hair was twisted into a simple arrangement atop her head, but with an artful snip here and there, the abigail had created a tumble of soft curls to frame her face. The effect was amazing—she hardly recognized herself! The way the new gown revealed quite a lot more of herself than she was used to only heightened the feeling that she was looking at a stranger.

"Oh," she managed to whisper.

"You look absolutely stunning," said Lady Alston with a smile. "The color is perfect on you, just as I imagined it would be."

There was a knock on the half-opened door, then

Wrexham stepped into his sister's room. "Olivia, have you seen where the deuce they have put my—" He fell silent as he caught sight of Allegra.

"Doesn't Allegra look absolutely lovely?" asked Lady Alston.

The earl remained speechless.

"Be prepared, my dear, to find yourself attracting any number of offers," went on Lady Alston.

Allegra colored to her roots. "You are being absurd, Lady Alston. A female of my advanced years, not to speak of—"

"Olivia," corrected the earl's sister. A decided twinkle came to her eyes. "And we shall see just who is being absurd."

Wrexham finally found his voice. "Olivia, you don't mean to tell me you are going to let her appear like . . . like that in public?"

One of Lady Alston's brows shot up. "Whatever do you mean, Leo? She looks a veritable picture."

He couldn't tear his eyes away from Allegra's bare neck, exposed shoulders and creamy expanse of bosom. "Why, it's . . . hardly decent," he managed to growl.

"My dear brother, you have fallen sadly behind the times, hidden away up in the wilds of the north. This style is all the crack, I assure you, and certainly well within the bounds of propriety for even the highest stickler." She gestured to the front of her own gown. "As you can see," she added.

Wrexham hadn't noticed his sister's gown.

Allegra's color had only deepened. "Perhaps his lordship is right," she said in a near whisper. "It does seem rather—"

"Nonsense!" scoffed Lady Alston. "Put that absurd notion right out of your head. It is important that you appear as fashionable as all the other ladies." She turned back to her brother and fixed him with a glare. "And, Leo, do stop being such a stick in the mud. Can't you see Allegra is nervous enough without you carrying on like some crusty old curmudgeon."

The earl began to make some sort of retort, but the

look on his sister's face caused the sound to die in his throat.

Another attempt at protest by Allegra was just as ruthlessly squelched with a quelling glance. "The matter is settled," she announced as she continued to give Allegra's coiffure and dress one last appraisal. "Now, I shall fetch the figured India silk shawl from your room. It will bring out that unusual deep green of your eyes." As she made to leave the room, she took up a slim leather case from her dressing table and thrust it into the earl's hands. "And of course we must begin to bait the trap for Lord Sandhill. Leo, kindly help Allegra with this."

A scowl darkened Wrexham's features at his sister's blunt choice of words, but he took the box without argument. He opened it to reveal a finely worked necklace of matched emeralds, all nearly the size of a robin's egg.

Allegra gave a low gasp. "My lord, I cannot possibly wear that! Why, it must be worth a king's ransom."

The earl had already moved to stand behind her. "I'm afraid you have no choice," he murmured as his fingers lifted the heavy creation from the padded satin. "There is precious little anyone can do once Olivia has taken the bit between her teeth."

Their eyes met for an instant in the mirror as he brought the necklace around her neck. The simultaneous sensation of the smooth coolness from the jewels and vibrant heat from his touch sent a slight frisson down her spine.

His eyes fell away as he fumbled with the thick gold clasp. "I did not mean to imply that you . . . do not look well," he said haltingly. "I . . . I am simply unused to seeing you thus."

She essayed a game smile. "I assure you, sir, so am I. Indeed, I would not be at all surprised if everyone tonight sees me for what I am—a complete charlatan."

Wrexham didn't miss the note of self-doubt in her tone. His hand lingered to brush away a wisp of a curl at the nape of her neck. "You are less of a charlatan than most of the *ton*," he replied in a near whisper, with vehemence that took her by surprise. He took a step back from where she was seated, then spoke again.

"Now let's have no more talk like that. Where is the spirit I have come to expect from the female who thinks nothing of scaling manor walls? Surely, you are not going to allow yourself to be intimidated by an assortment of nodcocks and widgeons?"

Allegra gave a little laugh. "Well, if you put it that way—"

Further answer was forestalled by the arrival of Olivia with the silk shawl. She draped it over Allegra's shoulders, giving a nod of satisfaction at the fortune in jewels around her neck. "That should do nicely," she remarked. "Come along now, both of you. We are in danger of being more than fashionably late."

Allegra took a deep breath, both to steady her nerves and because the large crowd of guests and masses of cut flowers had already made the air feel warm and cloying. She had never seen such a crush. The ballroom was already packed, elegant ladies swathed in silk swirling by with gentlemen dressed in equal splendor. From the perimeters, groups of turbaned matrons sat gossiping, all the while keeping a basilisk eye on their various charges, while a number of gentlemen not given to dancing were sidling toward the card room. Her step faltered as she realized that somehow she had become separated from Lady Alston in the crowd. An elbow jostled her side as she searched in vain for a familiar face, knocking home the enormity of the task she had set herself. It was absurd, she thought grimly, to imagine she could bring this off.

A hand took her firmly by the elbow. "Try not to look as though you are about to mount the gibbet," counseled Wrexham in a low voice as he smiled and nodded an occasional greeting while guiding Allegra toward the far end of the room. "And try not to wander off by yourself. Olivia has a number of important people she must acquaint you with in order to smooth your entry into Society."

"Wander off!" she retorted in an equally low voice. "Why, one can hardly draw a breath, much less move of one's own accord."

His lips twitched. "A hostess considers her evening a sad disappointment if two or three ladies do not faint from lack of air."

He had her smiling as well. "Are they really so silly?"

"You must judge for yourself— Ah, there is Olivia. I shall leave you in her capable hands until she has finished her introductions." He reached down for her dance card and scribbled something on it. "Then I am commanded by my sister to lead you out for your first dance."

She couldn't disguise the surprise in her voice. "I am to dance with you?"

"I am afraid you must. Olivia assures me that for some reason or another, my presence as a partner will confer some sort of consequence to your debut."

She found it nice to be bantering with him again. "Ah, so you are rather like the dragons of Almack's—I need the stamp of your approval before any gentleman would dare approach."

He grinned, the first time he had done so in a long time. "Quite—though I hope my face is not quite so intimidating as that of Mrs. Drummond-Burrell."

Allegra laughed lightly, though she had not as yet met that august personage. "I will let you know, sir. Tell me, do you have the same power to ruin a female—" She stopped short, a tinge of color spreading over her cheeks.

The smile disappeared from Wrexham's face. In stony silence he guided her through a group of young bucks who were eyeing a plain, but very wealthy heiress on the dance floor to where Lady Alston was anxiously scanning the crowded room.

"Oh, there you are," she cried in relief. She took Allegra's arm from her brother. "My dear cousin, I must introduce you to Lord and Lady Westerville."

The earl bowed stiffly. "Until later . . . cousin."

Allegra bit her lip, but there was precious little she could do except paste on a smile and remember why she was here.

Somehow she got through what seemed to be an interminable series of introductions without disgracing her-

self. And though dreading her required set with the earl,
that, too, passed tolerably well. On leading her out, he
had confided that he was not a good dancer and would
try not to tread on her feet. Concern for his bad leg led
her to forget all thoughts of her own nervousness, and
by the time the set was finished, she realized that she
was indeed feeling more at ease. She flashed him a grateful smile, but had little chance to speak before she was
claimed for the next dance by a portly gentleman who,
Lady Alston had warned in a whispered aside, might try
to pinch her bottom.

The earl's words proved all too true. One gentleman
after another sought an introduction and a spot on her
card. Her head was whirling even faster than her feet,
trying to keep all the names and faces straight. With
great relief, she found her next partner was Lord Bingham, and he suggested that perhaps she would prefer to
sit out a set and enjoy a glass of ratafia punch instead.

His eyes swept over her with frank admiration after
he had fetched her a glass and led her over near an
arrangement of potted palms where they had a bit of
space to themselves. "You are looking very lovely,
Mrs. . . . Ransley," he said, remembering to use her
mother's maiden name, as had been agreed upon. "And
I see you have already made quite an impression on the
gentlemen present."

Allegra lowered her eyes. "You are most kind, sir, but
I cannot help feeling that everyone must know I'm not
really one of them."

"Oh, you may feel akin to us sooner than you think,"
he murmured enigmatically, then quickly went on before
she had a chance to wonder what he meant. "You are
doing splendidly." His eyes strayed across the dancing
couples. "Have you seen Leo?"

She shook her head. "Not since . . . our dance
together."

"Hmmm." He kept searching the crowd, then suddenly his shoulders stiffened slightly as his gaze came to
rest on a figure not far away. "Tell me," he said softly,
"do you feel ready to bell the cat, as it were, or would
you rather wait?"

Allegra forced her voice to sound more confident than she felt. "Not at all. There is no reason to put it off."

Bingham gave her arm a squeeze, then guided their steps back toward the refreshment table. Along the way, he feigned a stumble and brushed into the back of a thickset figure dressed in a foppish coat of loud puce.

"Your pardon—oh, is that you, Sandhill? Forgive my clumsiness. I must have been pushed by some young jackanape." He made a slight bow, then, as good manners dictated, he brought Allegra forward. "By the way, have you made the acquaintance of your neighbor's cousin, who has only just arrived in Town?"

Sandhill looked her over with interest, his eyes lingering on the glittering emeralds at her neck. "I have not had the pleasure," he replied with a smile. After the formal introductions had been made, he reached down to bring her hand to his lips.

It was all Allegra could to to repress a shudder at the man's touch. She forced an answering smile as the three of them began exchanging pleasantries.

Sandhill turned to regard her once more. "I don't recall meeting you in Town before?" He phrased it as a question.

Her reply was well rehearsed. "My husband did not care for the social whirl of London. He much preferred to stay at home and run his estate and shipping interests"—She gave a little sigh as one hand came up to play at her necklace—"though I have little cause for complaint. I'm afraid he rather spoiled me. Alas, now that he has left me bereaved of his presence, I can at least take solace in the little trinkets he has left me."

A predatory gleam came into Sandhill's eye. "My condolences, Mrs. Ransley. Let us hope that your stay in Town will help lighten your spirits."

Allegra brushed at an imaginary tear, hoping she wasn't doing it too brown. "Everyone has been so kind, especially my dear cousin Olivia, who has offered me the comforts of Wrexham House until I have engaged a suitable residence of my own, even though our mothers are only distant connections. I don't know what I would have done without her, seeing as I know hardly a soul in Town."

"You may certainly count me as a new friend, Mrs. Ransley. I would be happy to be of any assistance."

Allegra dropped a graceful curtsy.

"And now perhaps you will allow me the next set?"

Gritting her teeth, she placed her hand on his elbow and allowed him to lead her onto the dance floor.

It seemed like an age before the last notes faded into the trill of conversation and the clinking of crystal. Allegra gave thanks that the steps of the dance had made all but the most cursory conversation impossible. Still, every time his gloved hand touched hers, she had to fight off the urge to be violently sick. It took all of her considerable self-control to keep a smile pasted on her face and her eyes from betraying her disgust as he offered his arm to return her to where Lady Alston stood chatting with several other ladies of her acquaintance.

"I shall save you the trouble, Sandhill—I believe my cousin is engaged with me for the next dance."

Allegra felt a surge of relief as Wrexham appeared from among the milling couples.

Sandhill relinquished his place at her side. "Wrexham"—he nodded—"didn't know you were here as well. Thought you never came to Town."

"I have a pressing matter to attend to," replied the earl.

"Oh?" Sandhill flicked at a speck of dust on his cuff. "Nothing too serious, I hope."

"On the contrary, it is of the utmost seriousness, but I have no doubt that I shall resolve it to my satisfaction."

The other man shrugged his shoulders, making it clear he had little interest in the earl's affairs. He bowed politely to Allegra. "A pleasure making your acquaintance, Mrs. Ransley. I trust we will see more of each other in the days to come."

She nodded, not trusting her voice. Only when he had disappeared into the crowd did she whisper, "You may be sure of it."

Wrexham's hand came around her elbow as he took note of her pale features. "Are you all right?" he in-

quired in a low voice. "I have a mind to box Edmund's
ears for rushing you into Sandhill's acquaintance on your
first evening out."

Allegra was surprised at the earl's look of concern.
"Please don't ring a peal over his head—I urged that he
do so." She couldn't help but give a shudder. "I . . . I
just hadn't imagined it would be so repulsive." Her voice
caught in her throat. "It . . . it was worse than touching
a reptile."

It was funny, she thought, as she spoke the words—
the earl's touch didn't make her shudder in the least.

His grip tightened. "The damned bastard," he swore
under his breath. "I am sorry you had to endure that. I
would have liked to shove his teeth down his throat just
for the way he was staring at your . . . bodice."

"My bodice?" she repeated in some confusion. "Oh—
the emeralds. Yes, he did seem to take note of them.
But that is what we wished for."

"I was not speaking of the emeralds," growled Wrexham as the music struck up and his arm came around
her waist.

It was a waltz. Before Allegra had a chance to feel
nervous, he guided her into the first steps, and the hours
of recent instruction with the dancing master Lady Alston had engaged took over. She followed his lead effortlessly. Contrary to his earlier assertion, he had a natural
grace on the dance floor.

The earl abruptly changed the subject. "Are you enjoying your first ball?"

Allegra looked up into his eyes. "I would be less than
truthful if I said I was not," she replied. "It is all so very
overwhelming—and rather exciting. I've never seen so
many candles or flowers. And the people! The gentlemen in their finery and the ladies in their silks and jewels—they are breathtaking." She didn't add that the feel
of his body close to hers, the pressure of his hand at the
small of her back was rather affecting her breath as well.
It must be that, for she was feeling a little light-headed.

Wrexham smiled. "You are more than a match for
any of them," he said.

"That . . . that is . . . most kind of you," she stuttered,

her gaze falling away from his in embarrassment. "Especially since I am well aware that you don't approve . . . of my dress, of this plan, of . . . me."

His brows came together. "As to your dress, I admit to being sadly behind the fashions. It is clear that such a style is all the rage, and on reflection, I am all for it. As to the plan, no, I am not enthusiastic about it, but surely you cannot doubt that I wish to see Sandhill and son punished just as badly as you do. And as to you, I . . ."

Her eyes had come back up to meet his.

". . . I fear you have gotten some odd notion into your head. I do not disapprove of you. Though we disagree on any number of things, you have always had my . . . respect, Mrs.—Allegra."

Her insides gave a lurch at the sound of her name on his lips.

"Truly? I am very glad of it, sir."

His head bent close to her ear. "I have a name as well," he whispered. "I should like you to use it."

"I am very glad of it . . . Leo," she repeated.

As the last strains of the violin died away, Allegra was not unhappy that Lady Alston whisked her away from the earl's side and suggested they take their leave.

"My dear, I think it best not to exhaust you on your first night out. No doubt your head is near swimming with all the new sights and sounds and people."

Allegra nodded. Oh, yes, the evening had given her more than enough to occupy her thoughts.

Wrexham watched his sister usher Allegra from the ball-room as he took a glass of champagne from the tray of a passing footman and drained it in one gulp. *Not approve of her?* he repeated to himself. Why, it was all he could do to keep from pulling her close and covering that expressive—and opinionated—mouth with kisses every time he saw her. Tonight had been especially difficult. The sight of her in that stunning gown had nearly undone him.

His eyes closed for a moment. He had avoided her presence for the past few days, hoping to put her out of his mind. He had even visited an old mistress, but other than gratifying a physical need, it did little to draw his thoughts away from the way the candlelight looked on her hair, the fire in her eyes when she spoke of some radical new idea or the way she had just now whispered his name.

He looked desperately around for another glass of champagne. For one wild moment he considered asking her to return to Yorkshire when all this was done. After all, she was a widow, and if they were extremely discreet, Max need not know. . . . But he had dismissed the thought in an instant. He knew he could never face himself or his son if he used her in such a manner, no matter if she was willing to enter into such a liaison.

There was, of course, another option, but he refused to consider it either. He had long ago promised himself he would never be such a fool as to make *that* mistake again, no matter what.

Chapter Twelve

⟨⟨⟨⟩⟩

"It's hardly fair," groused Max as he jabbed a piece of broiled kidney. "I don't know why a mere accumulation of years should entitle one to have all the fun."

"I assure you, having to dance with that man was hardly what I would consider fun."

Max colored slightly. "I'm sorry. I didn't mean—"

"I know you didn't." Allegra smiled at him. "Actually, you would have enjoyed your father's verbal toying with Sandhill, though the man hadn't a clue he was being told of his imminent demise." She paused. "Of course, he didn't hear your father express the wish to plant him a facer."

"I should hope not—wouldn't that would ruin all our plans?" Max took another bite of his shirred eggs and chewed slowly. "Why did Father want to plant him a facer at a ball?"

"Because he was staring at Mrs. Proctor's dress." The earl came into the breakfast room and motioned for the footman to pour him a cup of tea.

Max eyed Allegra's figured muslin gown, with its long sleeves and prim neckline. "Whatever for?"

"There was considerably less dress last night," replied the earl dryly as he unfolded the ironed pages of the newspaper that lay by his plate.

His son turned back to Allegra with great interest. "Really?"

She found herself blushing furiously. "That's hardly fair of you, sir. You know I had little choice in the matter."

His face was hidden by the newsprint, but she thought she detected a chuckle.

"Leo, do stop teasing," ordered Lady Alston as she, too, took a seat at the table. "Allegra looked absolutely lovely last night." She regarded her nephew with a twinkle in her eye. "If you leave off sneaking into the billiards room with the boot boy and come give us a proper good night, you would see for yourself."

Max nodded thoughtfully.

Lady Alston's expression became more serious. "Things are moving at a more rapid pace than I imagined. I saw that Edmund brought you to Lord Sandhill's notice. Even at a distance, I could see he was eyeing the emeralds."

A sound something akin to a snort came from behind the paper.

Allegra nodded. "I think I managed to convey both my widowed state and the largess of my dear, departed husband. I also made it clear that I was seeking an establishment of my own, as we discussed."

Lady Alston nodded her approval. "I believe my husband's man of affairs has located just the thing for us. A charming little town house on Mount Street has become available as the family that had taken it for the Season was called back to East Anglia by the death of an aged aunt. As soon as he engages the requisite servants, we will see that you are moved in." Her brows came together in perfect imitation of her brother's expression. "However, we will need to offer Sandhill more enticement to ensure that he falls into our trap. I'm afraid I don't have much more to lend you that wouldn't be recognized as Alston's, and that would not do." She put down her cup. "Leo, perhaps we might borrow some of the Wrexham jewels—"

"Oh, no," interrupted Allegra with a shocked gasp.

The earl lay down his paper. "I don't see why not. I had planned to visit my banker this afternoon so I shall bring a few things back from the vault."

"I cannot allow you to risk—"

"As you have told me many times, there is no risk. The necklace we will leave in the empty house will be paste, but in the meantime, Olivia is right. You must look the part of the wealthy widow."

There was little Allegra could say in argument. With a reluctant sigh, she let the matter rest.

Max was not so willing to see the subject dropped. "I don't know why no one pays any attention to me in this affair," he said hotly, his hands balled in frustration beside his plate. "Mrs. Proctor, you cannot deny that at home I was of help. Yet here in Town, I am taken to Astley's and the Tower as if I am a mere schoolboy on holiday."

Wrexham let the paper drop. "Max . . ." he began, but then his brow furrowed in consternation as he seemed to be searching for the right words.

Allegra had been regarding the lad with sympathy and jumped in to fill the silence. "I am well aware of how unfair it feels to be told you cannot do something simply because of who you are." She studiously avoided looking at the earl as she spoke. "But in this case, it would be rather difficult to include you in the evening activities. We can hide the truth that I don't belong here with silks and jewels and a skilled lady's maid, but I'm afraid we can't disguise your age. If you came along, it would attract undue notice, which I'm sure you will agree must be avoided at all costs. So there is nothing for it, but to wait. You know you have a role to play later on. It is small but vitally important, and you must be satisfied with that."

Max swallowed hard and the resentment seemed to dissolve into grudging understanding. "I suppose I see what you mean," he said slowly.

The earl's face was inscrutable for a moment, then he pushed back his chair and rose. "Max, do you care to join me in a visit to Tattersall's? I think I may consider getting a pair for my curricle, if we are to be in Town for any length of time, and I should be interested in your opinion."

His son's eyes lit up at being included in such an important decision. "I should like that very much!" He scrambled to his feet as he bolted down one last bit of scone.

"Then perhaps we will stop at Gunther's for ices so you do not starve before we return home."

Max gave an embarrassed grin. "I'm growing. Cook says I need my sustenance."

Lady Alston watched fondly as the two of them left the room, still engaged in a playful bantering. "I miss the two of them dreadfully, you know," she said softly. "I do wish Leo would not keep himself quite so locked away. It does him less good than he imagines, and soon Max will be gone. . . ." Her voice trailed off into a sigh. "I wish there were something I could do to—but forgive me for burdening you with such thoughts. It is just that they are very dear to me."

Allegra nodded her understanding, not trusting her voice to hide her own feelings on the matter.

Lady Alston looked up from the letter she was writing. "Did you and Max have an enjoyable time?"

Wrexham stood in the doorway of his sister's sitting room. "Quite." He made a rueful grimace. "Though along with the intended pair, I found myself cajoled into acquiring a chestnut hunter that had better clear any fence known to man, given the price."

She laughed. "I'm sure you could well afford it."

"Well, it was worth every farthing, to see the expression Max's face, now that he can ride in Hyde Park with me on something other than—as he put it—a slug."

He strolled over to her escritoire and placed a large leather case in front of her. "I have stopped at my banker and chosen a few items I thought might suit. If there is anything else you wish to add, you may call on Hawkins at your convenience."

Curious as to what he had brought from the extensive collection of family jewels, she undid the heavy brass clasp and opened the lid. At the sight of what lay there, her breath drew in sharply.

"Is there something amiss?"

Her eyes came up to meet his. "No . . . that is, you . . . you have included the Wrexham diamonds!"

"I thought they would look well with the smoky fig- ured silk gown you mean for her to wear to the Wainwright affair." His eyebrow raised slightly at the look of surprise still evident on her face. "You did say that you trusted my taste, did you not?"

"Of course. But . . . but Leo, family tradition has always been that the diamonds are worn only when a countess is deemed worthy of . . ." She bite her lip. "Why, you never allowed Suz—" She cut off her words abruptly.

Wrexham's expression remained unchanged, though his jaw noticeably tightened. "You know I pay little attention to so-called tradition. None of these baubles are likely to be worn until Max takes a bride, so they may as well be of some use. Besides, as the diamonds have not been worn in ages, there is little chance of them being recognized," he pointed out. "Isn't that what you were worried about?"

Lady Alston's lips pressed together, but she didn't attempt to argue. Her gaze went back to the magnificent pieces of jewelry that lay inside the padded satin. "Well, it seems you have considered this all in a very practical manner." After a moment's hesitation, she went on. "Allegra will look quite stunning in these. And of course, I will see they are returned to Hawkins as soon as this is over, so that they are safe for the next Wrexham countess."

Wrexham regarded Allegra with a grudging admiration. He wouldn't have thought it possible, but on listening to her silly chatter and girlish giggles he had to admit she was managing to sound even more buffleheaded than most of the other ladies present.

Bingham approached and took up station beside him. "Amazing, isn't it," he murmured as he took a sip of his champagne. "Perhaps she should consider taking up a career on the boards when this is over."

The earl grunted.

The appearance of being dim-witted had not in the least discouraged a number of gentlemen from hanging on her sleeve. With each passing evening, the numbers seemed to swell. As one after another led her out to dance, Wrexham's ill humor increased.

"Some of the mamas have been heard grousing over you, bringing your lovely cousin to distract all the eligible men." Rich humor filled his friend's voice. "They can hardly be blamed, I suppose. The schoolroom misses certainly pale beside her."

Wrexham shot him a dark look.

Bingham cleared his throat and gave up any further attempts at conversation. After a moment, he excused himself to refill his glass and to seek more congenial company.

At last it was the earl's turn to lead her out. It was a waltz, which allowed them to exchange a few private words.

"Congratulations. You certainly have wasted no time in attracting a swarm of admirers," he said as his arm encircled her waist. Even to his own ears, his voice sounded peevish.

She looked at him strangely before replying. "Come, Leo, surely you know better than I that it is the lure of a fortune rather than any charms of mine that causes these . . . gentlemen to gather around me." Her mouth curved slightly in disdain. "Truly, they are even more ridiculous than I had imagined—hardly a halfway intelligent or original thought among the lot of them. Really, I don't know how you tolerate it."

Wrexham's grip on her hand relaxed slightly as he stifled a chuckle. "I don't," he admitted. "That is part of the reason I am quite content to stay in Yorkshire."

Allegra regarded him thoughtfully. "Only part? What are some of the other reasons? For surely you have more opportunity for socializing here in Town. I have seen the way any number of ladies follow your every move."

"Like predators," he said roughly. "They have only one thing in mind, and as I have told you, I have no interest in remarrying."

"Yes, you have made that very clear." She was silent for a moment. "Well, you will hear no argument from me on that score. It seems to me that the state of matrimony is highly overrated."

He should have been gratified by her words, but somehow, they only caused his mood to grow even darker.

They spoke very little for the rest of the dance, and after relinquishing his spot to a florid-looking young man with ginger side whiskers, he went in search of Bingham and suggested they leave the ball for the comforts of White's and a bottle of brandy.

It was quite late when the two of them repaired to the earl's library for one last libation. Bingham gave an amused chuckle as he strolled to the fire and stirred the logs to life.

"You know," he said, suddenly steering the conversation away from politics and the latest doings of the Prince Regent. "It appears that Allegra has won herself quite a bevy of suitors. Why, Blackthorn just hinted to me tonight that he was quite interested in the lovely young widow—and he's nearly as plump in the pocket as you are."

Wrexham picked up the nearest thing at hand, a small leather-bound volume of essays that lay half open on his desk, and hurled it against the wall. "Damnation, Edmund," he snarled. "Enough about Allegra!"

Bingham stared at the broken binding, then at his friend's rigid features. "I'm sorry, Leo," he said quietly.

Wrexham slumped into one of the comfortable leather wing chairs near the fire and raked his hand through his hair. "Forgive me. I . . . I fear I have not been myself lately. I don't usually give rein to my temper in such a childish manner."

Bingham poured them both a brandy. He handed a glass to the earl, then took a seat opposite him and remained silent for a time as he swirled the amber spirits in his own snifter. "That bad, is it?" he finally asked.

Wrexham made a wry grimace. "The devil take it, I've never met anyone quite like her. I can actually talk to her about things that interest me and get more than just a blank stare." He gave a harried chuckle. "Why, more than likely, she will know more about the subject than I, or at least think she does. Confound it, I even enjoy arguing with her." He let out his breath in a deep sigh and gazed moodily into the flickering flames before he went on. "And her intellect is matched by her kindness and compassion. When Max was hurt, she cared for him as if . . . he were her own child." There was a slight pause. "She is courageous as well, and resourceful—and so damnably attractive I can scarce keep my hands off her." Again his fingers tugged through his tumbled locks. "Good Lord," he said in a voice barely above a whisper. "If Max hadn't come downstairs to the library on the night before we left for London, I would have . . ." A look of self-loathing crept over his face.

Bingham regarded him with sympathy. "Don't rake yourself over the coals about it, Leo. I feel sure Allegra would be entirely capable of discouraging any unwanted advances—I take it she didn't swing a poker at your head."

"Not exactly," he mumbled, closing his eyes briefly at the memory of her torrid response to his kisses and the way her fingers had traced the line of his jaw.

Bingham allowed himself a slight smile. "So what the devil is stopping you? You have no need to seek a match for any reason but your own feelings, my friend. And you needn't worry on Max's account. He adores her."

Wrexham's head jerked up. "A match? You know I never mean to marry again."

Bingham took a long sip of his brandy before answering. "Don't be a bloody fool, Leo. She is nothing like Suzanna. Why, if I didn't have to replenish the family coffers, I might even try to cut you out myself." Ignoring the earl's astonished expression, he stood up and set his glass on the table. "She is a singular woman. Don't let one mistake cause you make an even bigger one. And now, I think it's time to take myself off. Good night."

He was out of the door before Wrexham could find his tongue.

It was easy to understand how one could become very used to this way of life, thought Allegra as she surveyed yet another ballroom filled with the glitter of lights, the rustle of silk, the heady perfume of fresh-cut flowers and the echoes of clinking crystal, gay laughter and a lilting Viennese waltz. It was . . . seductive. Yes, that was the word. It was tempting to become self-absorbed, to think only of pretty things and the evening's pleasure rather than real ideas and complex feelings.

Could it happen to her? she wondered as her hand smoothed the skirt of her expensive silk gown and then fingered the small fortune in gems encircling her throat? Of course, marriage would be her only entree into this world of privilege, once the charade was over, so it would mean she would have to trade her independence for such a life of pampered security, a life of never having to worry about a roof over her head or how to support herself, a life with . . . children, perhaps. It would be arrogant in the extreme to imagine she was above temptation—what person was? But when she considered whether she would rather read a book full of provocative ideas or sit down to breakfast with a man with whom she couldn't share her excitement, her fears, her outrage, her laughter, she gave a rueful smile and knew she was safe.

Yet it was not as if there were no admirable people among the wealthy and titled. She had to admit that her original beliefs had been as wrong as any other prejudice. The *ton* was no different than any other part of society—there was good and evil, intelligence and ignorance, kindness and cruelty. She had met more than a few gentlemen who not only held quite thoughtful views, but did not look horrified when she expressed an opinion of her own. And there were some ladies of recent acquaintance who had given hint of interests beyond embroidery and the pianoforte, and others whose sharp observations and keen sense of humor had made her wish to know them better. In short, it would not be impossible to have real friends here. . . .

"You appear rather thoughtful tonight."

Allegra was jerked out of her reverie by the sound of Lord Bingham's voice. He handed her a glass of ratafia punch. "Would you care to share what is bringing such an enigmatic expression to your lips?"

She took a sip from her glass. "I was merely thinking on how . . . quixotic life is."

He looked at her as if he expected her to go on. When she didn't, a ghost of a smile crept to his lips as well. "Ah, but that is what keeps it so interesting."

Allegra gave a little laugh. "That is one way of looking at it."

They stood together in a comfortable silence for a few moments before Bingham spoke again. "You are moved into your town house?"

"Yes, a few days ago." Her eyes filled with humor. "It is quite a novel experience, to be head of a household, with servants to order around at will—though of course poor Lord Wrexham has another drain on his coffers. I fear I had better not get used to it!"

"Hmmm." He gave her an odd look, then quickly went on. "So everything is in readiness?"

She nodded. "Sandhill is here, and I am engaged to stand up with him just before the supper dance. The trap shall be set then, and if all goes according to plan, it will snap shut tomorrow night."

Bingham raised his glass. "Well then . . . to everything turning out as it should."

A short while later, Sandhill bowed low over Allegra's hand. "Ah, Mrs. Ransley, you are looking particularly well tonight." His eyes were locked not on her face, but on the glittering sunburst pendant of sapphires and diamonds that hung from a thick choker of pearls around her throat.

She had steeled herself to accept his touch without flinching, but it was still an effort to force a smile. However she took some small satisfaction in having him pay his effusive compliments, unaware that she was the plain parson's daughter he had passed on many occasions with nary a second glance. As she had often noted, most people saw only what they chose.

"How kind of you, Lord Sandhill," she replied with a graceful incline of her head. "Quite a crush tonight, is it not?" she added, stating the obvious.

"Lady Kensington has a reputation as a splendid hostess." He gave a broad wink. "And his lordship's cellars are held in equally high regard."

She gave a little titter. "Oh, you gentlemen are so sly. So, is that the only reason you have made an appearance?"

"That, and of course the opportunity to dance with you."

Allegra forced herself to appear well pleased at his heavy-handed flattery. "Well, I am very glad that you are here, for I wish to ask a gentleman's advice on something, and my cousin has been too busy for me to seek him out."

"I am only too happy to be of assistance, Mrs. Ransley. Perhaps we should sit out this set and you may explain your problem to me."

Her eyelashes dropped demurely. "You are sure you don't mind?"

He offered her his arm and led her to a small settee next to a towering arrangement of tuber roses and lacy ferns. She made a show of smoothing her skirts, then folded her gloved hands in her lap before beginning. Out of the corner of her eye, she could see that she had his undivided attention.

"As you know, I am unused to the habits of London servants since my dear husband chose not to partake of the Season," she began, taking a moment to heave a lugubrious sigh. "And now that I am recently established in my own town house, I wish to convey exactly the right tone as an employer. That is, I wish to be seen as both generous and yet not weak, so that they may not be tempted to take advantage of me."

Sandhill's expression betrayed that he was fast losing interest in such a mundane problem, so she hurried on.

"My cousins have invited me to a picnic supper and fireworks in Covent Garden tomorrow evening. As it promises to be a very late night, I may simply stay with Olivia rather than return to my own abode. The question is, should I give my servants the evening off as a gesture of goodwill?"

His eyes narrowed very slightly as he appeared to give the matter considerable thought. "An excellent idea, Mrs. Ransley," he replied. "By all means, do as you say. I believe it would be just the right touch. One must be strict, but servants will work harder if they know they will receive an occasional unexpected reward."

Allegra let out a relieved sigh. "I am so glad you think

so." Her hand moved up to toy with her necklace. "I have been in a tizzy trying to make up my mind, and now you have made up my mind for me—oh, goodness!"

"Is something wrong?"

"The catch on my necklace—I hadn't realized it was so loose. I must have it sent off to be repaired." She leaned toward him and lowered her voice to a conspiratorial whisper. "You mustn't tattle on me, but I am such a peagoose when it comes to practical things. I'm afraid I am always putting off what should be done, or forgetting it altogether. Why, I know I am supposed to keep my trinkets in a bank vault, but just never get around to it. I know my late husband's man of affairs would be furious if he knew I simply kept them in my dressing table. But it seems like such a bother to be constantly running back and forth, and I do so like to wear them."

Sandhill patted her arm as a slow smile spread over his face. "Don't worry in the least, my dear Mrs. Ransley. Your little secret is safe with me."

All heads turned as Allegra entered the earl's library the next morning.

Unable to contain himself any longer, Bingham spoke first. "Well? Did everything go smoothly?

"For God's sake, Edmund, let her at least sit down before you ply her with questions," snapped Wrexham. He hadn't failed to notice the dark smudges under her eyes and the tightness around her mouth.

"Yes, I am quite sure he has fallen for it." She took a seat near the fire and gratefully accepted the cup of steaming tea that Lady Alston offered. "There is no doubt in my mind that he and his son will be there tonight."

"But you seem . . . nervous, Mrs. Proctor," said Max slowly, as he watched the cup shake slightly on its way to her lips.

"I suppose I am a bit on edge," she admitted. "Though it is not the sort of nervousness you mean. It's just that, well, I have thought of this moment for so long, and now, one way or another, it all will be over shortly. It seems . . . almost unreal."

"It will be very real when the Runners clap those two scoundrels in irons and drag them off to the jail," growled Wrexham. "Bingham and I shall see to that. You may rest easy that your role is done. You will be on your way to Covent Garden when we spring the trap."

Bingham began to pace the room. "Is everyone very clear on what the plan is tonight? We wouldn't want any last-minute mistakes to scare Sandhill and son off."

All heads nodded.

"Still, it cannot hurt to go over it once again. Max?"

"I am to impersonate Father and escort Aunt Olivia into our carriage at nine-thirty sharp. Then we will stop at Mrs. Proctor's town house, and I will escort her into the carriage as well, so that anyone observing us will see the evening proceeding exactly as Mrs. Proctor described. We are to drive off in the direction of Covent Garden, and travel for at least twenty minutes, in case anyone is observing our actions. Then we are to double back and go to Lord Bingham's rooms to await word from you."

"Very good. Leo, you will be stationed in the garden, for that is by far the most likely spot they will break in. I will be a street away with the Runners—"

"Why is Leo alone?" demanded Allegra. "It is too dangerous—"

"I'm afraid it can't be helped," said Bingham. "There is too great a risk they would notice more than one person trying to hide in that small space. And I have the friend at Bow Street, so I must stay with them."

"I shall be well armed, and at the arranged signal, Edmund and the Runners will be on the scene in a matter of minutes," said Wrexham in a low voice. "There is nothing to be concerned about."

Allegra bit her lip, but said nothing further.

"Any other questions?"

None of them spoke.

"Well then, there is nothing more to do than wait."

Lady Alston adjusted the silk shawl over her shoulders one last time. The clock on the mantel began to chime the half hour as she picked up her reticule from the tufted side chair and hurried into the entrance hall. She turned at the sound of footsteps behind her.

"Really, Max, you needn't go to quite that length to obscure your features—from a distance you look near enough like your father without having to disguise yourself like a highwayman."

A muffled sound came through the thick scarf wrapped nearly up to the eyes—eyes that were not at all the steely blue of her nephew's, but rather a deep hazel.

"Max?" She peered closer, then uttered a word that neither her brother nor her husband would have guessed she knew. "Is that you, Robert?"

The young underfootman's eyes grew even wider at the sound of the oath. "Y . . . es, Your Ladyship," he stammered, falling back a step or two. "Master Max said I was to assist you tonight—we have practiced, and I am sure I can do it without a mistake. He also said I was to tell you not to worry and . . ." The scarf had slipped down to reveal a slightly trembling lower lip. ". . . and you are not going to turn me out, are you?"

Lady's Alston's expression softened considerably. "No, Robert, of course I am not going to turn you out—though I should dearly love to get my hands on my nephew right now!" Her lips tightened as the clock fell silent. After a moment's hesitation, she placed her hand on the young man's arm. "Come, we must be on our way."

A short while later, the carriage rolled to a halt in Mount Street, and a tall, elegantly dressed gentleman emerged and mounted the stairs with slow, deliberate steps. The door opened at the first sound of the heavy brass knocker, and Allegra appeared silhouetted in the muted light of the entrance hall.

"Thank you, Knowles. I shall be staying with my cousins, so you and the rest of the staff may have the evening off," she said a trifle loudly.

The butler bowed low in thanks as she took the gentleman's proferred arm and descended to the waiting vehicle.

"Where is Max?" she demanded as soon as the door shut and horses began to move forward.

Lady Alston shook her head. She turned to regard the cringing young man on the opposite seat.

"I . . . I don't know, my lady. Truly, I don't."

Allegra look out an exasperated sigh. "I might have known something like this would happen. Max has been chafing for days at being excluded from taking an active part because of his age."

"Well, there is nothing to do for it now," said Lady Alston grimly. "Let us hope he does not do something foolish."

Allegra threw herself back against the squabs and stared at the curtained window. Suddenly, she turned to the underfootman. "Give me your walking stick."

The startled young man complied without hesitation.

"What do you—" began Lady Alston as Allegra rapped on the trap. "Allegra! I don't think—"

"Leo must be warned," she said as the carriage pulled to a halt near the corner of one of the quiet side streets. "You must continue on, as planned." Her mouth thinned into a tight smile. "Don't worry—I have a bit of practice in skulking around, remember? Everything will be fine."

Then she opened the door and slid out into the darkness.

Chapter Thirteen

~~~

She pressed up against the ivy-covered bricks and pulled her cloak tighter, grateful that she had thought to choose one of a dark hue. Her eyes searched the shadows, but there didn't appear to be any sign of movement. It had only been dark for a short while, and no doubt Sandhill and his son would wait to be sure the servants had all departed or were safely tucked away in their beds before attempting to enter the town house.

The faint sound of a boot scraping gravel caused Allegra's head to snap around to her right. The outline of a figure moving stealthily toward the narrow door set into the garden wall was barely evident against the gloom of the deserted alleyway. Though she could not make out a face, the set of the shoulders and the coltish gait were all too familiar. She was about to step out of her own hiding place when another shape materialized just behind the first one.

"Stop right there, else I'll slit you from ear to ear."

Allegra was close enough to hear the rough whisper, and to see the glint of the knife that was now pressed up against Max's throat. The speaker's other hand had him firmly by the collar of his jacket.

"You've picked the wrong house to case out tonight," continued the voice. "Now take your hands out of your pockets very slowly—you wouldn't want my hand to twitch now, would you?"

Max had enough sense to do exactly as he was told.

The blade stayed hard up against the jugular as the other man quickly searched the lad's clothing for any concealed weapon. Satisfied that there was none, he ordered Max to walk on to the gate, where he shoved him hard up against the weathered wood, then paused as if to consider his next move.

"You've just provided me with a rather ingenious way to throw off the authorities for this night's work, my unlucky friend. When they find your corpse inside the garden, they will think that a band of thieves quarreled over the loot and came to blows. I imagine they will spend months scouring the stews of Southwark and Seven Dials, but to no avail," he said with a nasty sneer. "The question is, do I cut your throat now or later? The chances are slim that anyone would stumble over your body. . . ."

Allegra didn't wait to hear any more. She couldn't be sure that Wrexham, hidden somewhere inside the garden, had any notion of what was taking place. Slowly, she began to inch her way around to come at Max's assailant from behind, careful that the soft kid of her slippers made no noise along the broken ground. Lord Sandhill's son, confident that he had things well in hand, had relaxed his guard slightly. The knife dropped an inch or two away from flesh as he continued to taunt Max with his coming fate. The blade then flashed up in the air to punctuate a point, and Allegra saw her chance. Grabbing the raised arm, she yanked it back with all her strength and knocked the young viscount off balance.

Max lost no time in reacting as the grip on his collar loosened. He spun around and drove a knee into the groin of the other man. With a grunt of pain, the viscount doubled over and collapsed to the ground as if shot.

Allegra eyed the writhing figure at their feet with great interest. "Where did you learn to do that?"

Max straightened his jacket. "Father taught me after my first meeting with this bastard." He couldn't restrain himself from delivering a kick for good measure into the ribs of the fallen man. "Not entirely gentlemanly, but effective. Ah, what are you doing here—"

"I might ask the same of you, but explanations had better wait. The viscount is not likely to be alone—"

The dull click of a pistol being cocked sounded from close by in the shadows. "How very astute of you, Mrs. Ransley. However, explanations *are* very much in order." Lord Sandhill stepped out from behind a small toolshed. "And pray, not a word of alarm, or the lad will get a bullet in his head. For your own sake, I hope my son has not been badly injured by your attack—he does not take lightly to opposition, especially from females."

"I am well aware of that," said Allegra evenly. "But at least he will not be attempting to rape anyone in the near future."

Sandhill's eyes narrowed, then he peered more closely at her face. "By God!" he exclaimed in a low voice. "You! I thought I had seen you somewhere before. You are no relation of Wrexham's. You are that mousy vicar's daughter." His expression became even harder as he mulled over his new knowledge. "Get up, Richard."

His son gave a low moan and pushed himself to his knees. Sandhill reached down and grabbed hold of his shoulder, hauling him to his feet.

"You hellbitch, you will pay for this," croaked the viscount, his form still slightly bent over. "When I finish with you, you will wish you were dead." He turned his malevolent gaze from Allegra to Max. "And you, you filthy little urchin, I'll—" His words stopped abruptly. "Why, this is the same bastard who was spying on me in Yorkshire! What the devil is going on here?"

Sandhill's expression became even more serious as he eyed Max. "Who are you?"

Max gave a faint smile and remained silent.

"Richard," snapped Sandhill. "Take up where you left off if the bloody fool won't speak up."

The knife pressed hard enough against Max's throat that a drop of blood appeared. The lad only clamped his jaw more firmly shut.

Allegra had no illusions about the seriousness of the threat. "I should think twice about murdering Lord Wrexham's son," she said quickly.

A low oath escaped Sandhill's lips. "Wrexham's son," he repeated. With a deep frown, he signaled his own son to hold up, then began to stroke his chin as he mulled over the new bit of disquieting information. After a few moments, however, his face became less grim.

"I have no notion of how you sussed things out, but bad luck for you that you did. Who else is involved in this crude little trap you have set?"

His words were directed at Allegra.

"Don't tell them a thing!" said Max.

"My dear Mrs. Ransley, surely you do not think me so dim-witted that I would believe only you and the boy are here tonight? If you do not wish to see young Master Sloane's throat slit this instant, you will tell me your plan."

Allegra bit her lip as she shot an anguished look at Max. "Lord Wrexham is armed and waiting in the garden. The plan was to allow you to take the necklace, then the earl would surprise you and keep you under guard while Max went to alert the constables. I was to be another witness to your misdeeds." She omitted mention of Lord Bingham and the Runners waiting nearby. Perhaps by some miracle . . .

Sandhill seemed to accept her account. He motioned toward the narrow entrance in the wall. "Call to him. Bring him out here. And remember, any misstep and the lad is dead."

"Don't—" began Max until the viscount's hand came roughly over his mouth.

Allegra took a deep breath and walked to where Sandhill had indicated. The marquess positioned himself right up against the stones to the right of the opening, then nodded at her to open the thick wooden gate.

"Lord Wrexham," she called urgently. "I must speak with you."

Sandhill then waved for her to step back several paces. There was what seemed a lengthy silence before the sound of someone moving through the bushes was apparent.

"What the devil—" began Wrexham as he slipped through the opening.

Sandhill's arm came down hard. The pistol caught the

earl a sickening blow to the head, dropping him to the ground.

Allegra let out a gasp, but the pistol was immediately in her face. "Shut up!" ordered Sandhill. He turned to his son. "Bring the boy and follow me! I have a plan that will see us through this unscathed, but we must act quickly."

With a rough shove, he propelled Allegra into the garden, then grasped the unconscious earl under both arms and dragged him inside as well.

"Into the back of the house," he called to his son, as he moved the pistol from Wrexham's pocket and tossed it into the bushes. "Hurry!"

Once all of them were inside the scullery door, Sandhill left Wrexham lying on the stone floor, lit a candle and moved quickly into the surrounding darkness. He returned in a matter of minutes, a smile of smug satisfaction on his face.

Maneuvering the earl's lifeless form down a short hallway, he came to a small, windowless room that served as a storage pantry.

"Bring the others in here," he said as he dumped Wrexham unceremoniously onto a pile of dusty holland covers.

His son pushed Max forward with enough force to send the lad stumbling, then took Allegra by the arm with a grip tight enough to make her wince. "Let me have just a few minutes with this one alone," he said to his father.

"Leave off, Richard," ordered Sandhill. "You'll have plenty of time to amuse yourself with females when we are well away from here. Besides," he added with a harsh laugh, "she will soon be ruing the day she ever sought to interfere with us."

The viscount reluctantly released his hold on her. "What do you have in mind?"

"Oh, I believe a raging fire is about to start, no doubt caused by the candle of a careless servant. As you can see, there is no window here, and the door is quite thick—and equipped with a stout lock. With all the woodwork and drapery, this place should go up like a tinderbox." His voice took on a dripping sarcasm. "How very unfortunate that the earl and his son were visiting with his cousin, but accidents happen."

Sandhill's son gave a low laugh. "You are brilliant, Father. Should we bind and gag them?"

"Whatever for? There is no one to hear their cries, and they will soon be overcome with smoke. Besides, on the off chance that more than just charred bones are found, we wouldn't want anything to look suspicious. Right now, it will merely look as if they took refuge in here hoping to escape the flames." Sandhill's lips curled upward. "Now go upstairs and find the damn necklace we came for while I fetch some lamp oil and enough rags and such to get things started."

The door slammed shut with an ominous bang, followed by the click of a key being turned.

Allegra immediately fell to her knees next to the earl. Sandhill hadn't bothered to take the candle from where he had set it down on one of the shelves, and in the faint circle of light she could make out that Wrexham was still breathing, however faintly.

Max was down beside her, his face pinched with guilt. "Is Father—"

"Yes, thank God, but I'm not sure how badly injured he is." She took hold of his wrist. "His pulse is weak, but regular. Is there a vial of salts or any type of spirits that you can see?"

Max jumped to his feet and began a hurried check of the jumble of crocks and bottles crammed along the shelves. Suddenly, he stopped and sniffed the air.

Allegra had noticed it, too. Already wisps of smoke were starting to curl up from underneath the door. There was the sound of splintering wood as more fuel was added to the growing fire outside.

"We haven't much time." She was on her feet as well. "Look for a thin piece of metal or stout wire—anything that might fit in the keyhole."

He managed a weak grin despite the gravity of the situation. "I suppose this is one lesson I will be especially grateful to have applied myself to."

*   *   *

"Hell's teeth, I wonder what is going on." Lord Bingham consulted his pocket watch yet again. "I would have thought they would be there by now."

"Perhaps they decided it was too risky after all," growled the tall, heavyset figure by his side. "Or perhaps you're mistaken about the whole thing." He glanced at the two other men hunkered down in the shadows. "I hope you haven't dragged us out here for naught, milord. I shall have a good deal of explaining to do to my superior if I've been made to look the fool."

"Have I ever led you astray before, Hawkins?"

"If you had, sir, I wouldn't be here taking such an unlikely story seriously." The big man shook his head. "Really, the notion of a high-and-mighty marquess as a common thief . . ."

"Hardly common, my friend, but a thief no less. You will see." Bingham turned back to look down the darkened street. There was no sign of disturbance, no untoward noises. Nothing.

"Wot's that?"

Bingham's head jerked around.

One of the men pointed to a wispy column of smoke rising wraithlike from among the gabled roofs. "I'd lief as swear that ain't from no chimney."

Bingham could tolerate the uncertainty no longer. He drew a pistol from the pocket of his coat and indicated for the Runners to follow him.

Their frantic search had still turned up nothing useful. The candle was burning perilously low, and Max was now on his hands and knees, looking behind a stack of crates for anything that might be of use.

"Help me check here," called Allegra as she struggled to open the doors of a narrow hutch used to store jams and preserves.

As he straightened, Max's eyes took on a strange expression. Uttering the same oath that his father was wont to use, he rushed straight at her, arms outstretched toward her head.

Allegra feared that perhaps he was becoming unhinged. "Max!" she cried, throwing up her hands to ward him off.

"Hairpins!" he said in way of explanation.

"Why, how very clever of you! That just might work."

She yanked several from the knot at the nape of her neck and hurried to the door. Max brought over the stump of the candle. Smoke was now beginning to cloud the air, and both of them couldn't keep from coughing as they bent over the iron latch.

"Take off your coat and try to block that crack," she said with rising urgency as she worked the thin piece of metal to and fro.

"Is it strong enough?" ventured Max after he had done as he was told.

Her jaw tightened. The wood of the door was already becoming warm to the touch. "See if you can rouse your father. We are going to have to make a run for it."

A low groan indicated that the earl was beginning to come around. As Max approached him, he had already lifted himself on one elbow.

"Hell's teeth—" he said thickly, then succumbed to a fit of coughing as he took in a lungful of smoke. His brows came together as he recovered his voice. "Max! What the devil are you doing here?"

His son helped him into a sitting position. "Ah, perhaps we had best wait until later for explanations. Right now we are in danger of being—"

"Got it!"

"Got what?" demanded the earl as he felt gingerly at the lump on his head. "And what are *you*—"

"The door," she explained. "Sandhill has locked us in a pantry and set fire to the town house. I've just now managed to get the lock open, but it's rather hellish out there. Can you walk?"

The last bit of information seemed to clear the cobwebs from Wrexham's head. In answer to her question, he scrambled to his feet and limped over to the door. Shouldering her aside, he opened it a crack, then slammed it shut.

"What is the quickest way out?"

"To the right."

He took a quick glance around the pantry. The guttering light of the candle showed a pile of damask napkins shoved in between two wooden crates. Snatching up a handful, he passed one to Max and one to Allegra.

"Keep this over your face." He grasped Allegra's right arm and ordered Max to take hold of the other. "Stay together. I'll go first—"

"Let me lead, Father. I know the way back to the scullery door and you do not."

Wrexham hesitated for only a moment, then yielded his place. "Very well."

Max placed his hand on the latch. At a nod from his father, he flung the door open and pulled the others into the burning hallway.

Fueled by several shattered bottles of lamp oil, the pile of smashed chairs and soiled linens thrown together by Sandhill was now engulfed by flames that licked up close to the ceiling. It had set the wainscoting on fire as well, and the smoke was so thick it was difficult to see more than a few feet ahead. Max picked his way toward the rear of the house as fast as he dared. Up ahead, after one more turn to the left, lay the scullery and safety.

Suddenly, the earl jerked Allegra nearly off her feet while reaching out to catch hold of Max's shirt and yank him back as well. A blackened beam came crashing down just steps in front of them, sending a shower of burning embers into the air.

"Is there another way out?" yelled the earl over the din of the roaring fire.

Allegra indicated the hallway to the right. "This leads to the front of the house. Perhaps the fire hasn't had time to spread."

"We shall have to chance it. The other way is far too dangerous. Follow me."

Sandhill, however, was leaving nothing to chance. The drapes and stuffed chairs of the small sitting room ahead on the right had been doused and set aflame. On the left, the drawing room had suffered the same fate. Acrid black smoke filled the air, its noxious fumes sending them all into paroxysms of coughing. Wrexham felt rather than saw a closed door in front of him and wrenched it open. It led into a small sitting room off the entrance foyer, where the situation seemed marginally better than what lay behind them.

"In here!" cried Wrexham, pushing first Allegra, then his son through the doorway before slamming the door on the flames licking at their heels.

Max caught Allegra as she stumbled against a delicate mahogany side table and dragged her across the way toward the other doorway, where the vague outline of a spindled staircase ghosted in and out of the swirling smoke. As the earl made to follow, the heavy velvet drapes burst into flame, sending him staggering back to avoid being badly burned.

"Richard!" The shout was barely audible above the crackle and roar of the fire. "Come away now, else you will trapped!"

The dim rectangle of light disappeared as the front door slammed shut.

Allegra didn't see the dark shape racing down the stairs until it collided full force with her, sending both of them sprawling to the parquet floor. A small object, its surface sparkling wildly in the light of the flames, slid across the polished wood and disappeared under an inlaid satinwood console.

A grunt of surprise turned into a roar of fury. "You again!" screamed the young viscount as he sprang to his feet. "You meddlesome bitch. This time you'll not escape to interfere in my plans anymore." The knife whipped out of his pocket, and he took a step closer to where she lay.

"Mrs. Proctor!" cried Max, trying to locate her in the thickening smoke.

She managed to elude the viscount's violent thrust with a roll to one side. By the time he had recovered his balance, she, too, was standing. He came at her again, this time more slowly, as if he meant to savor the experience.

"A pity I don't have time to finish what I began a year ago before I slit your ugly throat," he said with a sneer. "I believe it would give me greater pleasure than usual—"

A deep voice cut him off.

"Yes, well we know how you like to prey on females and boys. Let us see how you much you enjoy being matched against someone able to offer more than token resistance." The earl stepped from the swirling blackness and placed himself between Allegra and the viscount. He motioned with both hands. "Come on. Or are you as cowardly as most bullies?"

The viscount began to move uncertainly to his left, knife held at the ready. "Afraid of an old bookworm? Hah! Not likely." His bravado sounded rather forced, however, and the look in his eye betrayed something akin to fear.

"Mrs. Proctor!" called Max. "Father!"

"Stay clear, Max," ordered his father. "I'll handle this."

Wrexham matched the younger man's movements, his gaze never leaving the outstretched blade. The first feint only drew a grim smile from him.

"You will have to do better than that."

The blade flashed again, this time aimed straight for his ribs.

Again, he avoided it with ease, his fist landing a stinging blow to his assailant's jaw.

The viscount swallowed hard and began circling in the other direction. He tried a quick, oblique thrust, but met nothing but air. A growl of frustration escaped his lips. After another step to the side, he suddenly charged forward.

Wrexham spun away, but the movement caused his weak knee to buckle for a moment, leaving him vulnerable to another attack. The viscount turned and was about to slash at the earl's midsection when the tip of a parasol, its fabric a mass of flames, came hard across his shoulders. He gave a yelp of pain as he flailed with both arms to knock it away.

The earl slipped out of danger. "For God's sake, Allegra, get out of here!"

She picked up another parasol from the carved wooden stand next to her. "I'm not leaving you here alone."

Wrexham muttered something unintelligible, then his gaze shot back to the viscount. The younger man had recovered his equilibrium, but appeared confused on what to do next.

"For just once, I would appreciate it if you would heed my wishes without argument," said the earl very deliberately. As he spoke to her, his boot lashed out and caught the viscount flush on the knee. The blow knocked the younger man to the floor, and as he fell, the knife went skittering into the blackness.

"Max," called the earl. "Get Allegra and yourself out the front door *now*!"

His son finally managed to fight his way through the choking clouds to Allegra's side.

"I don't care what he says, I'm not leaving your father," warned Allegra in a low voice.

"Of course not," whispered Max. "You don't truly think I would abandon—"

The front door flung open. "Richard!" Sandhill was in a near panic. "The smoke is beginning to attract attention."

"I'm afraid your son is experiencing some difficulty in joining you, Sandhill."

"Wrexham?" cried the Marquess in disbelief. For a moment his silhouette was frozen against the night. Then he turned and fled without another word.

The viscount was back on his feet, his jaw slack with shock as he realized his father had abandoned him. He fell back a step as the earl advanced, then another and another. In another instant, he was in full flight, making for the open door.

"Family loyalty," muttered the earl in disgust.

A piece of burning debris fell from the ceiling, reminding Wrexham of his own priorities. Instead of pursuing the viscount, he turned back into the whirling smoke and quickly located Allegra and Max. With one hand firmly wrapped around each of their arms, he guided them—none too gently—out to safety.

The clear night air was a blessed relief, and they struggled to clear their lungs of the noxious smoke and fumes.

When he had finally ceased coughing and wheezing, Max was the first to speak.

"Father, I can explain—"

"My lord, it is *I* who should—" said Allegra at nearly the same time.

Wrexham held up his hand for silence.

Both of them stopped speaking.

"Both of you obeying, and at the same time—I must be dreaming," quipped the earl. He slowly reached out his hand and touched the cut on his son's neck. "Are you all right?"

Max nodded, not trusting himself to speak.

He turned to Allegra. "And you?"

"Yes," she answered in a near whisper.

He pulled them both toward his chest. "I am sure I will hear an earful of explanations, but they can wait for the morning, if you don't mind."

"Leo!" Lord Bingham came racing down the street at a dead run and clattered to a halt in front of them. "Good Lord, are you unharmed?"

Wrexham looked from his own singed clothing to the sooty faces of his companions, then back to his friend.

"Well, it's about bloody time you arrived."

Chapter Fourteen

~

It was still difficult to accept that the matter was finally over, thought Allegra as she sipped the last of her tea. Sandhill and his son had managed to elude the Bow Street Runners in the confusion set off by the fire. A small Dutch brig of dubious reputation had slipped its mooring near Isle of the Dog with the ebb tide, and it was assumed that the two of them were safely on the Continent by now.

Perhaps it was just as well how things had turned out, she mused. Though they had avoided imprisonment, the two villains had been publicly unmasked for the scoundrels they were—and Wrexham and his family had been spared the ordeal of a trial and the awkward questions that would surely have arisen. Lord Sandhill and Viscount Glenbury could never set foot in England again, and if the rumors on how badly dipped they were proved halfway true, she did not envy them their future life—it was all too probable that they would end up in some jail in Brussels or Vienna, or dead in an alleyway. So a certain justice had prevailed because she refused to accept defeat. Of that she could take a measure of satisfaction. It was true that none of the stolen items had been recovered, but if she were perfectly honest with herself, she knew she had never really expected that they would be.

She would find a way to manage without the money the book would have brought.

A log crackled on the fire, bringing her out of her reverie. She fingered the letter that lay in her lap and turned to where Lady Alston was engrossed in a game of chess with Max.

"My cousin Lucy will be returning to London the day after tomorrow. Are you sure you do not mind if I trespass on your hospitality until then?"

"My dear Allegra, I would have you stay much longer than that—"

She shook her head resolutely. "No, the matter has been settled for some time. It is time for me to return to my cousin's until I have found another . . . position."

Max's jaw set at her words while Lady Alston's face clouded with a look of concern.

"Perhaps I will speak—"

Her words broke off as Wrexham came into the room.

"I told you, Mrs. Proctor, that you need not concern yourself with that." They had both left off using each other's given name. It no longer seemed appropriate. "My man of affairs has taken charge of finding . . . something suitable."

Allegra looked for a moment as if she would reply, then merely turned to stare into the fire.

"Lockwood has also located an excellent young man to return to Stormaway with us, Max," continued the earl with a heartiness that sounded a trifle forced. "In fact, I have just come from meeting with the fellow. He has recently come down from Oxford with the only the highest praise for his intellect. His interests match yours, particularly in languages and the classics. And he is no dull dog either—he is a bruising rider and crack shot." Wrexham paused as he regarded his son's stony face. "Would you care to meet with him this afternoon so you can make a final decision? I . . . I think you will like him," finished the earl rather lamely.

An uneasy silence filled the room.

Allegra attempted to ease the tension. "Why, he sounds like . . . a great gun, Max," she said softly.

Max shot her an anguished look, then turned back to face his father. "I'm sure if *you* have decided he is suitable, it matters not a whit whether *I* like him or not," he said in a angry voice as he pushed his chair back from the card table. "Why pretend it does? You don't care at all about me or what I want! Hire whomever you damn well please—it makes no difference at all!"

"Max . . ." began Wrexham.

But his son had already stormed from the room, slamming the door shut with a thunderous bang.

"He's merely overset at the moment. I'll speak with him . . ." said Allegra.

"You will not—it's not your affair!" exploded the earl.

Two spots of color rose to her cheeks. "Forgive me. I didn't mean to interfere." Her hands clasped tightly together in her lap. "You are quite right, my lord. It's none of my business."

Wrexham took a deep breath. "What I meant was, Max must learn to deal with disappointment without always having you to turn to."

"Leo, perhaps you are being a bit harsh. After all—"

"I don't need your advice either, Olivia," he snapped. "Somehow I have managed to deal with my son up to now without interference, and I see no reason why I cannot continue to do so." He walked to the tea tray and made a show of selecting several cakes. "I will speak to him myself when—" His hand took up the silver teapot, then set it down again with a thump. "The devil take it, Olivia, is it impossible for me to get a hot cup of tea in my own house?" he said irritably.

Lady Alston rose without a word and rang for a fresh pot.

Abandoning his untouched plate, the earl stalked toward the closed door. "Have it sent to my study. I have a number of letters I wish to finish this afternoon."

Allegra finished penning her own note to her cousin. She lingered, however, at the graceful mahogany writing desk, her gaze taking in the rich colors of the Oriental rug, the opulent silk of the drapes and the elegant details of the sitting room for perhaps one last time. With a sudden lurch in her stomach, she realized how much she would miss it all—not the comfort and luxuries provided by the earl's fortune, but the Sloane family—Max, Lady Alston . . .

A brusque knock came at the door.

She turned, and a look of surprise crossed her features as Wrexham stepped into the room and closed the door behind him.

"May I have a word with you in private, Mrs. Proctor?"

"But of course, my lord. Is Max—"

"It has nothing to do with Max."

She waited for him to go on.

He walked over to one of the tall, mullioned windows and stared out into the walled garden for a moment before speaking again. "Your father's book," he said abruptly. "What was it worth?"

Allegra began to fiddle with the pen on the desk. "It hardly matters, sir. After all, we both know it will never be recovered."

"I have consulted with a dealer who is familiar with such things. It was French, a rare illuminated Book of Hours from the seventeenth century, I believe? He tells me such a book would fetch at least four thousand pounds." He cleared his throat. "I wish you to have the money. My banker has been instructed to deliver it to you at your convenience."

"It is a most generous offer, my lord, but I can on no account accept it."

"Why not?" he demanded.

"Because it is not right. A female does not accept money from a gentleman unless . . . unless he has a family obligation, which you, despite our charade, do not. You are in no way responsible for me."

"Consider it a bonus for your excellent work with Max. Surely an employer may reward a job well done."

Allegra shook her head doggedly. "It is beyond all bounds of generosity. Besides, we already agreed that the expenses incurred here in Town would serve as any bonus."

Wrexham let out an exasperated oath. "To the devil with propriety! Accept it as a gift from a friend."

She found it impossible to meet his gaze. "I shall always think of you as . . . a friend, Lord Wrexham, but I simply cannot take your money."

He swore again under his breath. "Must you always

be so obstinate? For someone with a modicum of intelligence, you are remarkably mule-headed. Cannot you understand that I am offering you the independence you so desire?"

Allegra sprang to her feet. "Must *you* always be so arrogant and high-handed?" she shot back. "Has it occurred to you that perhaps I do not wish to be beholden to you for my future? You think to order my life as you see fit, regardless of *my* feelings in the matter? Well, you may exercise an iron control over Max, but you have no such power over me."

She could see that her precipitous words had wounded him deeply.

His face paled perceptibly, and his shoulders went rigid. "I see," he said stiffly.

Allegra ached to reach out to him, to explain the jumble of emotions that had prompted her outburst. But her own mind seemed locked in a state of confusion, unable to give voice to her real feelings. It was hard enough to understood them herself! How could she begin to tell him the truth—that the thought of the future without his company frightened her more than she cared to admit. She had so carefully schooled herself to need no one, and now. . . . That he offered her money in such a cool, rational way had only made the pain even sharper.

Her gaze fell away to the folded note on the writing desk, a stark reminder that she would soon be gone from Wrexham's life. A sound caught in her throat, but she forced her features to remain impassive. It seemed nigh on impossible to express her fears or to undo the hurt she had caused. So she kept her eyes averted and said nothing.

When it became evident that Allegra was not going to break the pall of silence that had descended over them, Wrexham's jaw clenched even tighter. "Forgive me for my unwelcome intrusion," he said after a moment, his tone as icy as color of his eyes. "I—"

His words were interrupted by the sudden entrance of his sister, who was in a state of obvious agitation.

"Oh, Leo," she cried, seemingly oblivious to the tension in the room. "Thank goodness I have found you. I must leave for Alston Grange immediately!" She thrust a letter toward him. "I have just received news that Charles suffered an accident in Russia and has just arrived at Portsmouth. James could not leave his mission, but William has accompanied him and is taking him straight home. I must go to him!"

Wrexham took the letter and quickly scanned its contents. His face relaxed slightly. "It does not sound overly serious, Olivia. A broken leg is hardly a great source of concern with a lad like Chas. I'm sure you will find him chafing to to be up and about when you arrive. Your biggest worry will be to keep him quiet for as long as the doctor would like."

Lady Alston calmed down a bit at the earl's sensible words. "No doubt you are right," she said with a sigh. "Still, I feel I must leave immediately." She suddenly took notice of Allegra standing by the desk. "Oh, my dear, I hope you will forgive me for flying away so abruptly. I am sorry to—"

Allegra came forward and instinctively slipped her hands around Lady Alston's. "Do not trouble yourself over it for a second. Of course you must go to your sons! I am sure that as his lordship says, you will find Charles is well on the mend."

Lady Alston gave her a grateful smile. "You must promise to pay a visit to the Grange in the near future. I should like very much for you to meet the rest of my family."

Allegra murmured some noncommittal sound as Wrexham's sister turned back to her brother. "Leo, will you see to the carriage while I have Clothilde pack a light valise?"

"Of course, Olivia. I'll take care of everything." He took her by the arm and started for the door. Lady Alston turned and said a last good-bye.

The earl said nothing.

Max pushed his rook over two squares.

Allegra's brows rose slightly. "Max, you are putting your own king into check."

"Oh. Sorry." But rather than retrieve his errant move,

the lad propped his chin in his hand and heaved a sigh. "I'm afraid I haven't been paying much attention."

"No, neither have I," she admitted as she pushed the board away from them.

It was obvious that something was bothering him as he started to fidget in his chair. "I . . . I didn't mean to act as I did," he finally blurted out. "I was, well, I was angry."

She nodded sympathetically. "I know. We all sometimes say things we don't really mean when we are upset." .

He tried to put on a brave face, but his words betrayed his uncertainty. "Maybe he is fed up with having to deal with me. I know I have been a sore trial of late. Maybe he means to send me home with the new tutor and stay here in Town, like many other of his acquaintances. I . . . I should not wish for that at all."

"I am sure that is not so," she said quietly, though in truth, she was also concerned about the earl's strange behavior. He had left the town house shortly after the departure of his sister and had not returned that night. It was now late the following afternoon and still he had not put in an appearance.

Max blinked several times. "Then why has he not come home, if he does not mean to wash his hands of me?"

She could not give him an answer.

A knock came at the library door, and one of the footmen ushered in Lord Bingham.

"Good afternoon. I thought I might stop in and see you." His smile faded at the sight of their troubled expressions. "What is wrong?" He glanced around the room. "Where is Leo?"

Max's lip quivered slightly. "I had a terrible quarrel with him. I think he's gone away."

"Lord Wrexham left yesterday afternoon, and he has not returned since," explained Allegra.

Bingham's brows drew together. "That is not at all like Leo." He fixed her with a penetrating look.

"I'm afraid he and I also exchanged words," she

added in a low voice. "No doubt it is my presence he wishes to avoid, Max, not yours."

"You don't imagine anything has . . . happened to him?" asked Max hesitantly.

Bingham shook his head. "No, Max, I do not think you have any need to worry on that account." He made a slight grimace. "Let me see what I can do to, er, locate him. I imagine I may have a few notions as to where he might be." Under his breath he couldn't help but add, "And perhaps I will manage to knock some sense into him as well."

With that, he excused himself, wondering just how his friend was going to extract himself from this coil.

With a muttered oath, he left the smoky confines of the gaming hell and climbed back into his carriage. A visit to White's had directed him to one of the more reputable gambling establishments, which in turn had led him here. But it appeared he had missed the earl by a scant half hour. Bingham's lips tightened as he consulted his pocket watch. Then he rapped on the trap and gave his coachman a terse order.

There was one other establishment he could think of to try.

The heavy oak door opened slowly to the rap of the ornate brass knocker. A liveried doorman with the misshapen nose and flattened cheeks of a former pugilist regarded him for a moment through narrowed eyes, then stepped aside to admit him.

"Good evening, Lord Bingham," he said in a gravelly voice, holding out his meaty hand to relieve the gentleman of his topcoat.

"It is heartening to see that I still pass your scrutiny, Collins," replied Bingham rather dryly.

The answering grin revealed several missing teeth. "Madame Rochette would box my ears if I didn't keep my eyes peeled, sir. You know she is very particular as to who she admits."

"Why, Lord Bingham," came a sultry voice from behind him. "What a pleasant surprise. I don't believe we have been favored with your company for some time."

A tall woman dressed in an expensive gown of emerald silk came into the elegant entrance hall. Though well past her first youth, she was still strikingly attractive, even if the curves had become a bit more ample. She took his arm and led him toward a small drawing room done in rich shades of burgundy and gold.

"Actually, I am looking for a friend tonight—that is, I am looking for Lord Wrexham."

Madame Rochette's eyes twinkled. "Ah, Lord Wrexham. He is upstairs at the moment." Her eyes went to the ornate gilded clock on the mantel. "But I believe he will be down shortly. Are you sure you would not like to meet . . . another friend while you wait?"

His mouth twitched at the corners. "Your offer is quite tempting, but tonight I think I shall simply wait for Wrexham, if I might."

"But of course." She indicated an intimate seating arrangement near the crackling fire. "Let me ring for some champagne, and we shall have a comfortable coze—you must fill me in on all the latest *on dits*."

They were enjoying yet another laugh over the foibles of Prinny and Maria Fitzherbert when the scuffling of unsteady feet drew their attention. Bingham rose and approached the curved staircase in time to catch Wrexham as he stumbled down the last few steps. A dark stubble covered the earl's cheeks, and he reeked of brandy and the cloying scent of a strong perfume. His cravat hung in disarray over his wrinkled shirtfront, and the state of his tailored coat would have caused his valet to swoon.

"Come on, Leo. It's time to go home."

Wrexham ran a hand through his tangled locks as he tried to focus his bleary eyes. "Don't want to go home," he mumbled, his voice slurred with alcohol.

Bingham took hold of his friend's shoulder and guided him toward the door. "Yes, you do. Max and Allegra are quite concerned about you."

The earl dug in his heels. "Not bloody likely! They both wish me to the devil, so take yourself off and leave me be."

Bingham didn't loosen his grip. With the assistance of

Collins, he managed to get Wrexham into his greatcoat and down to the waiting carriage, despite a string of drunken protests.

Once settled against the squabs, the earl fell into a brooding sulk. Now that the effects of the brandy and carousing had begun to wear off, he felt only the same knifing doubt that had driven him to such desperate behavior. The spirits, the gambling, the willing partner in bed had only kept it at bay for a fleeting moment. How had he lost the regard of the two people who mattered most in his life? Was he really so pompous and selfish as his son and Allegra had implied?

He closed his eyes and tried not to imagine the bleakness of the days ahead. Instead, he let his fears be washed away by a new wave of anger. Anger at Allegra for being so . . . maddeningly attractive. Anger at himself for letting his carefully constructed life be turned on its ear. Anger at his sister and his friend for seeing how vulnerable he had become. Even a bit of anger at Max for simply growing up.

Bingham watched the warring emotions on Wrexham's face with sympathy, but knew there was little he could do to help, save remain tactfully silent.

The wheels of the carriage soon rolled to halt. "Come now, Leo, cry friends and let me see you to the door."

The earl brushed away his hand. "I can see to myself," he muttered, swaying slightly as he lurched toward the door.

There were limits to where even the closest of friends were allowed to trespass. With a resigned shrug, Bingham pulled back and let him go on alone. He signaled to the driver to take him home.

He had done all that he could.

Indeed, it was quite late. Wrexham didn't bother to knock for his butler, but after some fumbling managed to open the front door by himself. A single branch of candles illuminated the entrance hall. Dropping his overcoat in a heap, he took the candles and made his way to the library, rather than upstairs, feeling the sudden need for just one more glass of brandy.

Allegra looked up from the book she was reading as

he stumbled past the door, a grunt of pain on his lips as he clipped his bad knee on the polished oak. The beginning of an oath died away as the earl suddenly realized he was not alone.

"What are you doing here at this hour?" he demanded, trying to keep his words from slurring together.

"I was waiting for Lord Bingham to return with news of you. Max and I have been worried—" She took in Wrexham's disheveled state and drew in a sharp breath. "Are you all right, my lord? Where have you been?"

He steadied himself against the edge of a side table. "Where have I been?" he repeated slowly. The alcohol had fuzzed his reason. All he could dwell on was the painful realization that she found him odious in the extreme—well, he would give her ample reason. "Let me see," he continued. "First there was my club and quite a number of bottles of excellent brandy and port. Then there were two—or was it three—gaming hells. Can't remember, but as I seem to have quite a large amount of blunt in my pockets I must have won." He paused for a moment. "Yet I seem to have no trouble recalling the caresses of the lovely blonde in whose bed I have spent the last few hours. Ah, but I forget you have no knowledge of how pleasant the experience can—"

Allegra's face turned a deathly shade of pale. "No . . . no I do not. Nor does it seem likely that I ever shall." Her voice caught in her throat. "Believe me, sir, I hardly need you to remind me that no man would ever find the type of female I am the least bit attractive."

All the anger drained from Wrexham, replaced by an overwhelming sense of shame and remorse.

"Forgive my absurd notion that there might have been any cause for concern on your account. It is quite obvious you are capable of seeing to yourself. Good night, my lord—and good-bye. My cousin's carriage will come for me tomorrow morning, and then your life may finally return to normal."

As she rose and walked past him with a stiff dignity, he drew in a breath, but no words seemed adequate to express what he felt. The door closed quietly, and his eyes fell shut for a moment. Then he limped over to one of wing chairs and slumped against the rich brocade, burying his head in his hands.

Allegra threw over the covers and gave up any pretense of trying to sleep. She pulled on a wrapper over her nightrail and went to stand by the arched window. In the morning, she would be gone from here. Perhaps once she was away it would become easier to put the earl out of her thoughts.

She blinked back tears. All her carefully constructed plans seemed to have come askew. She had known there were risks involved when she had left for Yorkshire, but she hadn't realized that the biggest one was that she would lose her heart. She had thought herself safe from that ever happening.

Memories of the animated discussions, the heated arguments, the shared laughter came flooding back. She and Wrexham had come to a grudging respect of each other—and then, the unthinkable had happened. She wasn't sure quite how, but she had fallen deeply in love with him. It was clear he harbored no such tender feelings for her. Indeed, he had made it more than clear that nothing—save for Max—could touch his heart. He only offered her help in the same cool, detached manner as he would one of his tenants.

Yes, it was best to put all thoughts of him out of her mind. But Lord, she would miss the comfortable feeling of belonging to a family, of curling by the fire and reading aloud. . . . She realized with a start that she had left her book in the library. It was a slim leather-bound volume of Dante's poetry from the library at Stormaway that the earl had said she might keep.

It was the only reminder she would have of their time together.

She glanced out the window. It was not yet dawn. There was no reason she couldn't slip downstairs and retrieve it without causing any notice.

Wrexham hadn't moved. The candles had long since burned out, and the logs had turned to ashes, leaving the room with a decided chill. He hardly noticed as it couldn't come close to matching the clenching cold he felt in the pit of his stomach.

What a mull he had made of things.

His head jerked up at a slight rustling sound near the door. He could barely make out faint shape of a figure moving toward the desk. A flint was struck, and a single taper lit. To his amazement, it was Allegra who took up the candle and began to search the sofa until she located a small book among the plump cushions. Tucking it in the pocket of her wrapper, she turned to leave.

A soft cry of surprise escaped her lips as the light fell on Wrexham's haggard face.

"I . . . I hadn't realized you were here, my lord. Forgive me for intruding on you but . . . but my book. I did not want to lose my book."

Her hair was simply brushed back over her shoulders, but an errant curl or two fell over one cheek. As she pulled her wrapper more tightly around her slender form, she betrayed a trembling hand.

Wrexham rose and took a step toward her.

She fell back near the door.

"Allegra, wait," he said in a hoarse whisper. "Please."

She stopped.

"I know my conduct has been unforgivable but I wish to apologize—"

"There is no need, my lord," she interrupted.

Another few steps brought him close enough so that his hands could grasp her shoulders. "Yes, there is! I want you to know that I have behaved . . . like an ass because—"

He stopped to take a deep breath. It frightened him to go on. But it frightened him even more not to.

"—because it hurt that you don't care for me."

"Don't care for you?" she repeated in an incredulous voice.

"I know you find me arrogant, high-handed—"

Her fingers reached up to graze his stubbled cheek. "Not to speak of compassionate, kind, principled and intelligent. Why, Leo Sloane, you are the most wonderful man in the world. I shall *never* cease to . . . think of you."

He stood frozen in disbelief for a moment. "I am . . ." Then as she tried to slip by him, he crushed her to his chest. "I shall make sure you do not cease to think of me," he murmured huskily. "For I never intend to let you stray far from my side."

She looked at him in confusion. "But I am no longer Max's tutor. And even if I were, he does not need one for much longer."

Wrexham brushed his lips against her forehead. "Max may not need a tutor, my love, but I am in need of a wife. Are you by chance interested in the position?"

The look in his eyes made her feel rather warm all over. "But . . . you do not wish to remarry! You have made that more than clear."

"Have I?" he whispered as his lips traced a path along the line of her jaw. "I have said any number of idiotic things during the time you have been here, but that has to be the most foolish one." His expression then became very grave. "But perhaps it is *you* who does not wish to legshackled again. I can only promise you that the experience would be quite . . . different." He kissed the base of her throat. "And so would the chances of having a child. I should like that very much, you know."

His mouth took possession of hers, and it was some time before she could answer him.

"Leo." Her arms flew around his neck, her fingers threading through his long locks. "Oh, Leo." This time it was she who initiated the long, intimate embrace.

"Is that a yes, my love?" inquired Wrexham with a tender smile.

There was a decided twinkle in her eye. "Well, we have not yet negotiated the terms of the position, but I am sure we will come to mutually agreeable understanding. So, yes."

Without warning, the door suddenly flew open.

Max rushed in, then stopped short at the sight of them. "I heard strange noises and thought perhaps an intruder had . . ." The explanation faded into mute astonishment at the sight of Allegra and the earl wrapped in each other's arms. "Father!" he finally managed to exclaim. "What . . . what are you doing?"

"I am kissing Allegra."

"Well, yes, I can see that . . . but what I mean is . . ." His voice trailed off as a new concern seemed to pop into his head "I thought you told me it was wrong to . . . compromise a member of one's household."

"Ah, but Allegra is not in my employ any longer."

Max took a moment to digest that reasoning. "I also thought you said a gentleman could on no account be caught behind closed doors with an unattached female, else he should be forced—"

"That is quite right, but under the circumstances, I think we need not worry about the consequences of my actions."

The lad regarded his father's disheveled appearance and unshaven face with great interest. "Are you foxed?"

Wrexham laughed. "I am feeling quite intoxicated at the moment, but no, I am not foxed, Max. Oh, and by the way, in the future when I am behind a closed door with your future stepmother, you will kindly knock before entering." He paused. "On second thought, you will *not* knock. You will go away."

A delighted grin slowly spread over the lad's face as the import of his father's words dawned on him. "Mrs. Proctor is not going to be leaving us?"

Wrexham smiled. "No, she most definitely is not."

The lad's face suddenly sobered. "Are you going to send *me* away?"

The earl looked utterly dumbfounded. "Send *you* away? Why, whatever put such a maggoty notion in that head of yours?"

"Max was afraid that you had left because you were angry with him," said Allegra softly.

Max hung his head. "I know I have been a sore trial of late. Perhaps, like Mama, you don't wish to be bothered with me—"

"Come here, Max."

Max hesitated, his hands jammed in the pockets of his dressing gown.

His father released Allegra long enough to reach out and pull him close. "How could you ever think such a thing, you young jackanape? Surely, you know that nothing could ever change how much I love you," he murmured. "Mayhap it is you who wish yourself free of such a heavy-handed father. I know I make mistakes, but—"

"No!" cried Max. He took a deep breath, trying manfully to control his emotions. "I . . . I love you, too. All those terrible things I said—I didn't mean a word of it."

The earl only pulled him closer.

Allegra brushed away a tear of happiness. Her arm entwined itself with Max's. "I hope you shall not mind sharing your father with me."

Max gave her a big hug. "I shall not mind at all."

With one arm around each of them, Wrexham broke into a broad smile. "What a lucky old dog I am. Max, I think perhaps you should fetch a bottle of champagne and pour us all a glass. I propose a toast—a toast to the most wonderful family any man could wish for."

His son hesitated for a moment, then added his own postscript to the earl's words. "And to any future additions to the Sloanes—I have always wished I had a brother or sister."

Allegra's face turned a most becoming shade of pink as Wrexham grinned.

"Ah, for once there is something the three of us may agree on without argument."